DRAGON GOD

The First Dragon Rider Book One

AVA RICHARDSON

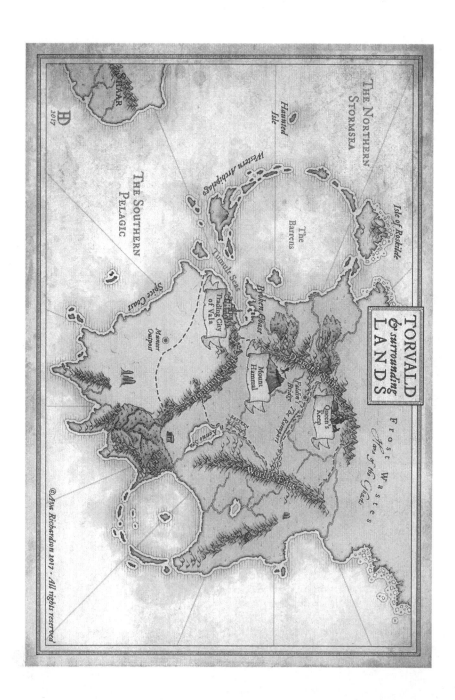

CONTENTS

THE FIRST DRAGON RIDER TRILOGY

Dragon God

Dragon Dreams

Dragon Mage

THE FIRST DRAGON RIDER

DRAGON GOD

AVA RICHARDSON

BLURB

The new world is calling...

Neill Torvald is desperate to prove himself—his father's warlord kingdom depends on him. When a vicious attack on the way to the Draconis Order monastery nearly kills him, it becomes clear that grave trials await him on this path. Jodreth, the wise monk who saves his life, advises caution upon entering the sacred halls. His mission is to learn arcane magic from the monks that will help to cement his father's power, but Neill will need more than magical arts alone to navigate the challenges before him.

Among the monks' students, Neill meets the lovely and mysterious Char, who senses evil deep within the ranks of the Draconis Order's members. She takes him to a dragon she has raised, Paxala, and the three of them become fast friends. Neill soon grows in strength as he and his fellow students gain ancient knowledge, and his closeness to Char blossoms into something more.

But when Neill 's brothers grow impatient and attack the monastery in a bid to seize power, he will have to decide where his loyalties lie: with his warlord father's domain, or the new friends he has made in the wider world.

MAILING LIST

Thank you for purchasing 'Dragon God'
(The First Dragon Rider Book One)

I would like to thank you for purchasing this book. If you would like to hear more about what I am up to, or continue to follow the stories set in this world with these characters—then please take a look at:

AvaRichardsonBooks.com

You can also find me on me on
www.facebook.com/AvaRichardsonBooks

Or sign up to my mailing list:
AvaRichardsonBooks.com/mailing-list/

PROLOGUE

MALOS & MALICE

*The **Personal Letters** of **Malos Torvald, Chosen Warden** of the **Eastern Marches**, as written in Autumn, the Year of the Fire-Ruby, Under the Rule of **Prince Vincent**, Heir Apparent to the Middle Kingdom.*

I do not know why I endeavor to keep such letters and accounts, but my Scribe Velini assures me that I must for the future of my people, and my sons Rubin, Rik, and Neill. That one day there might be those who will look back with interest on the history of Clan Torvald with fondness, nay, even pride. But not only that; one day we may need these notes about the Draconis Order – where their strength lies, and what doom or salvation they offer for us all. What does the Scribe know? Sometimes I wonder if even the name of Torvald will be remembered when I am dead and gone!

We live in troublesome, terrible times. There are bandits ever at our border, and the Southern Kingdom of our Three Kingdoms has made alliances with the murderous Raiders, if you would believe! Since old Queen Delia passed away, and her realm was divided into three, with each ruled over by one of her sons. What an idiotic idea from such an otherwise intelligent queen: to split the kingdoms, trusting that her sons wouldn't seek to poison, steal, seize, or overcome each other in their bloodthirsty struggle to the top.

So, this is why I write. I am one of the last Wardens of the Middle Kingdom, chosen, as my father and his father before him were chosen by the old queen along with the rest of Clan Torvald, to hold the border against the wilds to the East. But there are many warlords and petty generals who have sprung up in the murderous decades since the Old Queen's death. Each prince it seems, has enough trouble controlling his palaces and borders to worry about the common folk across his lands. So, the major families (like us in the Middle Kingdom - the Torvalds, the Flamma, the Lesser, and the Fenns) try to keep the realms together for our people, and our lands. But there are also hundreds of other bandits out there, each with a tin-pot helmet and a sword, each thinking a fort and a patch of land makes him a worthy rival to the throne. The Middle Kingdom, under Prince Vincent, will splinter and dissolve into nothing but ashes and bones if he continues to ally himself with whichever rebels he feels he must placate any given week. That is why us Wardens must stand firm against the rogues—it is up to us to hold fast to the rule of law and the idea of a just society.

THERE. It is done. I have spoken to Neill, my youngest son, and told him that he will answer the summons we have only just received, to go to the Draconis Monastery-- that nest of mystics and dragon-worshippers. I cannot spare my older sons Rik nor Rubin, and I fear that the people might never agree to follow a Far Southern-blooded half-Gypsy like Neill (despite how much I loved his mother).

Perhaps it will help the lad, in a way. I see the way Rik treats him, bullying and seeking to undermine him in my eyes. Were it not for these dangerous times, I would put an end to that – but I need Rik's strong battle arm at my side, and I cannot risk Rik having reason to leave my clan. It is a sad fact that when others look at Neill, they see just a young boy who cannot yet command an army. They see only the dark, curly hair and tanned skin of his mother's people, and not the real young man within. Perhaps sending Neill away to train as one of these dragon-worshippers will keep him safe from the taunts and the jibes of the others, although I doubt it.

If only he knew that he was my last hope – not just for Clan Torvald, but for the entire Middle Kingdom. I have told him he must discover the truth of the Order's strange magics. Can they really command dragons? Can they really reshape mountains and bare rock just by the power of their words and mind? If they can, then they would be a powerful ally, and they might be the key to turning this inevitable slide into the abyss for our fracturing king-doms. If the common people saw that we could command dragons, then surely they would take heart again in our future. They would not be so scared of the other kingdoms, or the bandits or Raiders. Think of what we could all achieve if we had dragons to carry our trade to the distant realms, to protect our borders, to dig our castles…

However, the opposite may also be true. The Order might in fact be our unbearable enemy, using their dragons to torment and enslave us all. That is also why I must send my most beloved son Neill to find out the source of the Draconis Order's power and if he cannot bring it to us, then at least he may be my eyes and ears and send back whatever intelligence he may observe to help us protect our people from such a terrible fate.

With Neill embedded deep in the heart of the monastery, Clan Torvald will be even stronger. Clan Torvald will stand against all enemies and threats – even if the princes and great men of this realm cannot.

Clan Torvald could even, one day, wear the Great Crown of the Old Queen…

SIGNED ~ *MALOS TORVALD, Chosen Warden.*

PART I
THE MONASTERY

CHAPTER 1
MIRED

The monastery hadn't *looked* that far away on the map, but now, my boots thick with mud and my pony refusing to take a step further, it felt like it might as well be half the world away.

"You'd need a blinking dragon just to get up there," I found myself muttering to the rangy, stubborn steed that my older brother Rik had sworn was the best of the bunch, and would take me all the way to the Draconis Monastery without slipping a shoe. This, like most of the other things that fell from out of my older brother's mouth, I knew to be a lie, but something in me had felt sympathy for the tough little pony.

You and me both are pretty unwanted, huh? I had thought at the time, and in return for my compassion, so far, the small mountain pony had kicked, bucked, bit, and balked at every boulder and hill and river on the week-long journey between the fortifications of the Torvald Clan and Mount Hammal. That was where the Draconis Monastery sat, and where I had been sent by my father, Clan Chief Malos Torvald.

But at least every movement I coaxed out of this pony got me nearer to my goal—not just the monastery itself, but to finding the information my father had supposedly sent me here to gather. That's what I kept telling myself, anyway, as I pulled at the pony's reins, and it took a halting step forward before stopping yet again. In all likelihood, my father had sent me here just to get me out of the way—the unlucky, unloved, illegitimate son that I was. The valley that I was laboring through was little more than a mountain ravine, tall rocky walls on either side, dripping with ferns and the constant rivulets of ice-melt from the mountain above. Why on earth had I ever decided to come this way? But I knew why. Ravines meant water, and I'd hoped to find a pleasant stream with low banks—an easy fjord to cross. Instead, on either side of the fast-flowing water was just heavy silt and mud. The light was green-tinged and shadowed by the overhanging vines and trees above, but through a gap in the undergrowth I could make out the slopes of Mount Hammal rising higher and higher, the trees thinning and being replaced with scattered patches of frost and snow – and there, sticking out from the top, the dark stone walls of the Draconis Monastery itself, impossibly small and toy-like.

Like the wooden forts and soldiers that my brothers were always playing with, I thought. It was hard to imagine that up there, on top of the world and so close to the cold and clear sky anyone could make a life, and certainly not monks in robes.

"And certainly not me, either!"

The Draconis Monastery was the last place I wanted to be. I should be at my father's side, like his other sons, learning how to be a warlord, learning how to lead our clan. But no. I was being sent to the middle of nowhere on a fool's errand, to be locked away and forgotten, most likely. I kicked at the mud in frustration, but with a sucking schloop all that I succeeded in achieving was removing my boot from my cotton leggings, and sending it sploshing across the gully.

"Great. Absolutely *great!*" I wanted to shout, but instead I kept my voice low. I'd already made enough noise and to be honest, I was slightly concerned about the fact that there were supposed to be dragons up on the mountain somewhere. Right now, I couldn't decide just what was worse: being eaten by a dragon in the middle of nowhere or spending the next few years of my life freezing my fingers off as a ward of the Draconis Monastery. At least a dragon might be more interested in my pony than in me?

Crack.

The sound that traveled over the watery glops and gloops all around me was sharp-edged and sudden.

It must just be a branch falling somewhere, I thought as I retrieved my dripping wet boot and bending to put it back on. It was freezing, and I knew that I would be lucky if I didn't end up getting a cold from this.

"We should never have come this way at all," I muttered to the pony, that had now stopped moving and was instead standing almost stock still but for a faint tremor running through his body.

"What have you seen, girl?" I whispered, turning my head to follow the direction of her pointing ears and flaring nostrils.

Thump-crack. This time, the sound was heavier as well as sharp, like something dragging itself across a rock, or claw or a scaled body…

"Easy now, easy there." The hairs on the back of my neck stood up as I slowly straightened. Dragons weren't supposed to eat people anymore. Not the dragons of the Middle Kingdom anyway, were they? The Old Queen negotiated with them to stop doing that, and my father had said it was rumored the Draconis Monks could control dragons. But so far, every market and cross-roads inn between here and the Torvald Clan lands had been filled with stories of people who had lost sheep, cows, or goats, of distant farmhouses seen burnt out on the edge of the wilds. What was to stop a hungry dragon from eating a solitary sixteen-year-old boy and his horse if it was hungry, no matter what some dead queen or some bookish monk had said? I bit my lip in worry (a habit that my dad said made me look weak), my hand moving to my belt for the sword that should be there.

Oh no. I'd left it still wrapped and tied beside my saddle, along with the shield, helmet, and anything else that I could possibly use to help defend myself.

"Pssst! Stamper, Stamper come here!" I hissed at the rangy pony using the name that I had optimistically given it when we had set out (aside from 'you mule' and 'no, please don't do that!').

Crack-thump!

Stamper's eyes rolled white and he leapt and spun, yanking the reins from my hand as he bolted away from the sound, clattering up the shallower side of the mountain gulley as if he hadn't been stuck at all. "Stamper, no!" I shouted, but it was no good. The pony was gone, carrying my saddle, blankets, warm clothes, food, and most important of all – all of my armaments. If whatever was making that noise was as terrifying as Stamper seemed to think it was, I was going to need my weapons. My heart was hammering in my chest as I crouched, bunching my hands in front of me as if to do…*what? What was I going to do to a dragon, or a bear, or whatever was up there?*

"Just keep it together, Torvald…" I tried to tell myself, breathing out through my nose. "You are a son of Torvald. You are strong." After not hearing anything for several long moments (including any sign of Stamper) my heart slowed, and I turned to splosh out of the mud, scraping and climbing up the bank behind the pony. *At least I'm only a little way away,* I grumbled to myself. *I might be able to make it up to the monastery above me without that stupid horse…* I had only just got my fingers to the top of the wooded incline when the source of the previous scraping, thumping, and snapping noise became abundantly clear.

Four men were creeping and climbing their way up the stony bank by the side of the river gulley, and from the look on their faces and the weapons in their fists they had clearly only one intention in mind, and it didn't look good for me.

Oh no… My heart hammered in my chest. I thought that I had managed to make it all the way to Mount Hammal without encountering any bandits or rogues on the road. It looked like I had been wrong.

Before I had time to recall the many contingency plans I'd brainstormed in the event I encountered trouble on my journey, the nearest man jumped at me, bringing his hatchet downwards in a terrible blow.

CHAPTER 2
JODRETH DRACONIS

"Agh!" I managed to roll out of the way just in time, as the man's hatchet hit the rocks that I had been holding onto. *Who are these people? Bandits?* My thoughts raced, everything around me was a blur, and my chest was burning as I tried to gulp for more air. My father had told me that bandits were everywhere in the Middle Kingdom – but on the steppes of Mount Hammal itself!? As I pushed myself up against the nearest tree, one of my attackers kicked my side with his thick boots. It felt like Stamper had kicked me as I reeled backwards barely managing to swing myself around the tree in the nick of time, as—

Thock! The man with the hatchet drove his blade deep into the trunk where my head would have been had I not put the tree between me and it.

I have no money—nothing to offer them, I thought desperately. All of my money had disappeared with Stamper, safely secured in his saddlebags. No time for complicated heroics, or trying to remember the martial lessons that my father and older brothers were always trying to beat into me. I turned and jumped further up the wooded bank of boulders, ferns, and tree trunks.

"Come 'ere!" One of the men growled, as the first was wrenching at his buried hatchet below. This man was larger, with a thick red beard and furs strapped to his calves and forearms. *A lot like one of the clan warriors,* I thought in panic, as fingers caught hold of my ankle and pulled with fierce strength. *But which clan? The Fenns? Igris?* If one of the other clans captured me then they could ransom me back to my father for more land or gold, or…. My mind slid away from the other possibility: that I was a bastard son, not even with full Middle Kingdom blood. Some clans wouldn't even think twice in killing me.

I couldn't stop from screaming as my body thudded against the boulders, but I thrashed and kicked out despite the pain, feeling my blows connect with some soft part of my attacker, and his grip loosen with an agonized grunt.

"Get off me!" Frustration mingled with anger in my heart. I wouldn't let my father down by being another casualty of war, or having to be rescued. What would he think of me then? My fingers tore at the roots between the boulders, before finding a stone that was almost head shaped, and I turned and swung it at the nearest bandit's leg. *Thunk.* It connected with a dull cracking noise, causing the man to scream and tumble backwards.

"Olof!" One of the bandits shouted, spittle dropping from his mouth as he abandoned his weapon and instead drew a cruel skinning knife from his belt. "Hold 'im down! I'll gut the little worm!" Hatchet-man sneered, as I felt someone's knees land on my side, sending pain rippling across my chest as the two other men wrestled me to the floor.

"Who are you! Get off! What do you want?" I was desperate. I had never been in battle before. I didn't know that it could all be over this quickly, and this soon. I had *seen* battle before, of course – you don't grow up being the son of Malos Torvald, one of the most famous and feared warlords of the Middle Kingdom without seeing the distant smokes and pyres of battle from your camp bed. But I was not my father, nor was I my older brothers Rik and Rubin. I was just Neill of Torvald, youngest son of a greater man…

"We got a message, little worm," the knife-wielding man said, ignoring his colleague Olof's pained cries behind him.

"A message for whom?" I managed to scrape out past the lump in my throat—the lump I strongly suspected was my entire stomach.

"For Warlord Malos and the rest of you Torvald upstarts. Stay away from the Dragon Mountain. The Middle Kingdom doesn't need you sniffing around here, and it doesn't want you here, got it?"

They recognize me! But surely these men were from another clan? I thought in panic. But I still didn't know which one. They must be jealous that the Torvalds were being summoned to train at the Order (that *I* was going to train at the Order).

"We can talk!" I tried desperately. My father was a fearsome warrior, but he wasn't an idiot. He knew how to parley, to make treaties with other clans…

"Talk? With you Torvalds? You still don't get it, do you?" The man was growling and panting from the recent chase. "Things have changed. There's a new power. The power of the dragons up there. And you Torvalds ain't having any of it—and you know what?" My attacker suddenly went very, very still. "I don't need you alive for your dad to get the message. This is gonna be written in your blood!" The man bellowed as if he hadn't heard me and lunged. At the exact same moment, there was a sizzling crack of thunder, or at least that's what it sounded like. I think I screamed, or shouted, I don't know because for some reason the whole world had gone suddenly incredibly quiet, and my eyes were filled with a searing white light.

All I knew was that the weight was gone from my body, arms and legs. I rolled to one side, blinking, willing my eyesight to return. Tears streamed down my cheeks, and with them my vision cleared. First it came back in dull greys and whites, and then more dark tones before finally color returned. It was like I had spent too long staring into the hottest part of a fire. My ears were still ringing as I turned to see what had happened.

Hatchet-man was lying slumped at the bottom of the nearest tree, a burn mark barely bigger than my fist discoloring the center of his leather jerkin. The other two men (three, if you count broken-footed Olof) had their own troubles. They were being attacked– by a man no bigger than me, I thought as he moved and whirled.

The man had short-cropped dark hair and a pale face. He wore the heavy canvas robes I recognized from the drawings my father had shown me of the monks of the Draconis Order, and yet he moved and spun like a fighter. I had no idea a monk could fight like this – he looked as though he could give Rik and Rubin a run for their money!

I watched as the monk who had apparently saved me turned on one heel once more, jabbing out with the staff that all of Draconis Order monks seemed to carry, striking at one of the men's face, before pulling it around to trip the other up. There was a brief, shocked shout as the man fell forward and disappeared into the gulley below, landing with a heavy thump and a splash.

The last remaining bandit tried to swing a short-sword past the monk's guard, but using his staff two-handed, like I had seen my father's spearmen do in training bouts, the monk rained blows upon the bandit until he fell into the gulley too.

"The other!" I pointed at the form of the man they called Olof crawling his way down to the edge of the rocks, and anger surged through me. How dare these bandits attack me! I stood up, hefting my rock.

"No, leave him," the monk panted. "He's only one man, and revenge is for the wicked." Even though his voice was raspy with excitement and exhaustion, he spoke in a cultured way, tinged with something of the north about him. I saw that his had a scrape across his knuckles that was running blood down his forearm, and I felt ashamed at not having helped him, ashamed that I had wanted revenge.

"Friend, please sit down. You have done me a great service," I said, ignoring the ache in every part of my body and trying to remember how the son of a chief *should* talk. Gratefully, the young man accepted my hand as I led him to a patch of moss and ferns that was slightly more comfortable and less blood spattered than the boulders around it. "Here," I said as I laid my cloak on the ground. "Sit."

"I'm fine, really. It's *you* who should be sitting down..." the monk said, and I realized then that the man was no older than me, sixteen or seventeen at most, perhaps. He still accepted my admonitions for him to sit down and at least catch his breath.

"Sir, you have surely saved my life from those brigands--" I kept my eyes averted from the spot where the men had been thrown from the cliff, but was suddenly struck by the image of the man falling, his arms flailing—arms wrapped in *fur secured with leather straps*, just as the clan warriors wore. But each of the Clans of the Middle Kingdom had their own habits. The Lessers didn't often wear furs. The Fenns didn't often venture this far from their marshes and rivers. The Igris were fierce all right, but didn't they usually use packs of hunting dogs in battle? And they were on the far side of Mount Hammal. We Torvalds wore the traditional fur and leather clan dress of course, but there was no way that those men had been Torvald men, had they? Surely I was mistaken. Probably they had just donned our costume to obscure their true identities. But still, the thought made my words falter until I gathered my wits. Could the men who had just tried to gut me have been defectors from my own father's army? Or some new bandit group I had never heard of? "And, uh—oh, right. Such a deed should not go unrewarded. I'm afraid I've lost my horse and have nothing to share with you, but…" my voice trailed off. I felt ridiculous and small. What sort of son of a chief was I?

"You don't need to thank me," the monk replied. As we talked, he stooped to take some moss from a rock and used it to stopper the bleeding on his knuckles. That done, he pulled a roll of bandages from his pack and began applying a bandage. "Stamper? That's a good name for him," the monk said with a half-smile on his face, and I wondered how he knew. "You'll find him not a little way up the path, where I tied him to a tree beside the road. I heard the horse first, and then the shouts." The monk laughed. "It looks like it's just not your day today, friend, was it?"

"It's not my year," I muttered. "But never mind my misfortunes, it seems that I have to thank you doubly now – once for saving my life from those bandits, and again for saving my horse and my pride!" The monk's easy-going laugh was infectious, as I found myself starting to smile, despite my apparent stupidity, and despite the terror that I had just gone through. "Come, I have a little coin in my saddlebags, and I will be able to offer you much more when we get to somewhere civilized!"

"You won't find anything civilized around here, I promise you that," the monk said darkly, "And I really don't need any payment. It is the job of a true monk of the Draconis Order to protect the mountain, the dragons, and its guests." The monk sounded serious, in what I could tell was a deeply-held conviction.

"Well, it seems that I know very little of the ways of monks." I nodded to the body of hatchet-man, who was still seated and clearly dead under the tree, and felt suddenly uncertain next to the young man. "I am Neill Torvald, of the Clan Torvald. I am in your debt," I said formally, bowing. *There.* That is what my father would expect of me.

"Hey, Neill Torvald, son of Chosen Warden Malos Torvald – try not to worry yourself too much. Whomever your father is, you are your own man and you seem to have a good heart." The monk accepted my hand as we both stood up. I took my sodden cloak from the floor, and he led the way through the trees to the nearby path.

"My name is Jodreth, lately Jodreth Draconis," the monk said with a shrug.

"Of the Draconis Order above?" I said, before instantly feeling stupid. *Of course he is.*

"How many other sacred orders of Dragons are there on this bleeding mountain?" Jodreth said with a laugh, slapping me on the back. "*Lately* of the Order anyway. I'm uh… I'm not really living up there anymore," Jodreth said, his eyes going far as it seemed to me that he was looking on other times.

I wanted to ask the monk about the Order, about what he meant that he wasn't living up there. Had he graduated? Was he an official Draconis Monk now? Sworn to keep the secrets of the ancient dragons and mediate between their species and ours? Is this what they did – just wandered around, bumping into teenagers and saving them from bandits? More than that, I wanted to ask him if he could help me find an easier path up to the mountain, but just then we came upon Stamper, who whinnied and stamped a foot impatiently from where Jodreth had tied him up to a tree. The horse eyed me imperiously, for all of the world as if he had been waiting for me to get that business with the murdering all over and done with, and come and feed him. "There now, Stamp's. Easy now." I reached out to rub the broad flat space between his eyes all the same. He might be a difficult beast, but Stamper was *my* difficult beast.

"You see? A good heart, Neill Torvald. Many chieftain's sons would have scolded or beaten their horse for running away," Jodreth said, turning to look at me with narrowed, speculative eyes.

"Well," I shrugged, "I'm quite sure Stamper was happier at home in his stable."

Just like I would be, I thought to myself as the image of the bandits with fur hides and leather wrappings flashed through my brain. My brain tugged again. I had only ever seen the clan warriors dress like that, to protect their arms and legs against the long marching and the cold and the rain when they were on tour. But surely no clan warrior would resort to attacking a lone traveler like me. And it wasn't as though clan warriors were the only ones who might think to wear such protection.

"Jodreth, can I ask you something?" I said. "Is Mount Hammal crawling with bandits? Is it a *very* dangerous place?"

"It is far more dangerous than you might think," Jodreth said and then seemed to shake himself. He gave that same laugh from before and went on. "The Mount Hammal, home to the dragons of the Middle Kingdom *is* dangerous. There are boar and bear and wildcat and, yes, bandits every now and again – and let us not forget our largest creature here."

"Dragons." I said, unable to keep the wistfulness from my voice.

Dragons. Ever since I had been young, I couldn't stop myself from looking up into the sky whenever the call of dragon-sign went up. They had always been far away and very small, little more than black specks on the rising winds, but I had craned my neck and peered at them all the same. Maybe not so unusual, as my father had ordered that there should be a constant alert for dragons should they ever cross into the Eastern Marches. Like most of the other warlords, he viewed them skeptically and, I think, with fear (not that the big bear of my father would have ever admitted to being scared of anything)—and yet he had sent me here. To learn the ways of the dragon-tamers. To learn their secrets. Supposedly.

"Ha, yeah. So, you have it too," Jodreth said. "Dragon fever. My family used to say the same about me, before I came here." The monk leaned on his staff and winced, and I wondered if he was more hurt than he was letting on.

"Are you all right? Was it those bandits?" I asked in concern.

"No, an old wound," he said, although I wondered how 'old' it could even be, given that he was only a couple of years older than me! "Dragon fever was the reason I was sent here myself, and I'd wager that it was the reason why Neill of Torvald was sent here too, huh?"

"Well…" I wasn't sure how to answer. In truth, it was complicated. Despite the fact that this Jodreth had saved my life, he was still a Draconis Monk, and that meant that there were still some things that I couldn't quite tell him. *Like the fact that my father didn't trust the prince of the realm, that he had sent me here to dig out the secrets of the Order's connection to dragons, to find out what its plans were.*

"In part, I think it's because my father thinks I'm a runt. My older brothers certainly do. They convinced him to send me here to answer the call of the Draconis Order, as someone had to from Torvald," I lied. In truth, I rather suspected that my father and my brothers wouldn't hesitate in going to war to *take* the secrets from the Order if they thought they had to.

"Did they now?" Jodreth's eyes narrowed, and I felt a blush rising to my cheeks. How could I lie to this man who had just risked his own life to save mine? I felt awful, but knew that my father would make me feel even worse if he learned that I ended up blabbing Torvald secrets to the first Draconis Monk I met on Mount Hammal, despite the circumstances of our meeting!

"Well... Your Order, they..." I started to stammer.

"I know. The Draconis Order have called for all of the younger sons and daughters and prominent peoples across the Three Kingdoms to come together to learn under them," Jodreth said. "As if knowledge will be enough to prevent the Three Kingdoms from falling into war and ruin." Jodreth frowned, seeming to consider his own words for a moment. "It is, indeed, a noble cause."

"But you don't believe it will work?" I asked, as we walked up the wooded path that led steeply up the mountain, over a small bridge and back towards the monastery itself. It was easy to talk to Jodreth, and I wondered if that was true of all of the monks. If that was the case, then I really had nothing to worry about after all, except who those bandits might have been and whether they were the sort who attacked indiscriminately, or if they had targeted me. I thought again of their fur hide wrappings with leather straps. Surely their attire was a coincidence.

"I believe that the Draconis Order can do anything they set their mind to," Jodreth said with a chuckle. "And if that is to unify the Three Kingdoms again, then all the better!"

"And yet you seem to think there's something wrong with that?" I said, feeling like I had missed a step somewhere here.

"Nothing," Jodreth said brightly. "Nothing at all. I only question whether it will *work*, that is all. Have you met the other princes? Or the other warlords yet? *Or a dragon?*" He added the last with a scandalized look of alarm.

"Well, no, I have older brothers, Rik and Rubin – they have gone to all of the council meetings and been a part of the delegations and what have you…" I murmured, feeling all of my young fifteen years old painfully. I had done none of those things. Only legitimate sons were allowed to take part in official business.

"Well, to say a dragon can be stubborn is like saying a bird likes to fly," Jodreth explained as the air grew a little colder. "Birds don't just *like* flying, they *are* flight itself. It is everything that they are. And princes?" Jodreth winked. "They seem worse. How will anyone be able to unite their wills?"

"Ha!" I laughed. That is what my father said about the three princes when he was deep in his cups. 'All they care about is what is looking out at them from a looking glass. No thought to the everyday people underneath the – and they hate each other. If Prince Griffith said he liked oysters, then Prince Lander would say he didn't just to spite him! If Prince Vincent won a riding contest, then Prince Griffith would buy every horse this side of the Western Isles, just so that he couldn't do it again!'

It made me smile to remember my father. He might be big and oafish and sometimes, yes, cruel (like sending his youngest child off to the middle of the Middle Kingdom with nothing but a horse and a sword) – but he could also be kind and funny when he wanted to be. *If only he wasn't always at war. And if only he could actually settle down and run that brewery that he wanted to.* I tried not to let myself think the very next thought that always followed on from that: *if only I actually had a father who cared about me, and not just a warlord and two angry older brothers.*

"Are you sad, Master Torvald? You look it," Jodreth said. Our steps had taken us further north and up the mountain, the trees beginning to grow smaller and thinner on either side of us as they clutched to the boulders with roots like fingers. The path switched across and back on itself, turning into interconnecting shelves of rock that led up to the bare and cold escarpment above.

"I, well…" I hadn't been expecting this question. "I didn't want to come here, you see, begging your pardon that is." I nodded to his robes. "I don't mean that it is not a nice place…"

"It *isn't* a nice place," Jodreth surprised me again by saying. "It's a monastery on top of the world. It's cold, and it's dedicated itself to learning and to living with some of the most fearsome creatures to ever walk the land." The monk went silent for a pause. "The Draconis Order studies strength, and power, the beings that have it, and how to use it," he said softly, before adding, "so, you're right to be wary, at least." Jodreth paused as we climbed, nodding up to where the stone walls and towers of the Draconis Monastery cut into the cold grey clouds above.

It was big this close, bigger and more impressive than even I had originally thought from the drawings and tapestries my father had kept. It stood like a stone crown on top of the mountain, its towers rimed with ice and frost instead of jewels.

"Just be careful when you're up there, and on the mountain, young Master Torvald," Jodreth said, and I knew that he wasn't going to accompany me any further up the path. "Already you have foiled one attempt on your life, and the sons of powerful warlords can probably expect more."

"You think someone was trying to kill *me*, on purpose?" I asked, the words of the dead Mr. Hatchet-man coming back to me. 'We got a message, little worm…a message written in your blood…'

"Bandits do come to Mount Hammal, but not often, and not likely," Jodreth said seriously, before his tone softened once more and he looked at me earnestly. "But even more important than that, Neill, is that you look after yourself. You are not just your father's son, a pawn sent here on the whim of powerful warlords and princes and monks. You are powerful yourself – and you have to decide what sort of man Neill of Torvald will become. What you will fight for. And what you will endure."

You're right, I almost said, despite the creeping feeling that either Jodreth the monk was a little cracked, or he knew something that he wasn't going to tell me. *Probably both.* Regardless,

I had little choice in my current situation. I did actually have to be here. I couldn't stay at home in the Eastern Marches. My father had commanded I come here. Rik had already made it quite clear what I could expect if I didn't obey. And this was my opportunity to prove to my father who I was, and that I could be a worthy Torvald heir when the time came, if he'd only just let me.

I looked up to say all of this to the monk only to find that, in my moment of musing, he had already taken his leave and was heading back down the way we had come.

"But Jodreth Draconis," I called back out to him, my voice carried on the wind that whipped over the mountain, "I still haven't paid you the debt for saving my life!"

"Pay me with your friendship, Neill Torvald," the young man called back, raising his staff once into the air in farewell, before turning and disappearing back under the crooked trees and stunted forest of the upper slopes. I raised my hand in farewell anyway.

Oh well, I sighed, the cold making me feel even more achy and tired. At least the path ahead was well marked with stone cairns that rose in spires on either side. As soon as I had stepped past the first set, there was a shout and rumble echoed from the clearly visible gates of the Draconis Monastery itself, the walls within which I would be living for next few years.

CHAPTER 3
WELCOME, TO THE ORDER OF DRAGONS

"Torvald, is it? You're late!" the man barked as he hurriedly limped out of the large gates of the Draconis Monastery moving just as fast as the retinue of servants that surrounded him. The others carried spears and staves, but none of them bore the same sorts of staffs that Jodreth had.

"I-I'm sorry, sir," I said though I was unable to find fault with my actions. As far as I'd been told, as long as I arrived by the start of the term, that was fine. "I was attacked on my journey. By four bandits," I added, feeling a little lame as I said it. I hadn't even fought them off myself, not really – and I was supposed to be one of the feared 'Sons of Torvald' – the best clan fighters in the Middle Kingdom. But there was nothing new there, was there? I might be okay with a sword or a staff compared to others of my age, but I was still the smallest and youngest son. Being a 'not-bad' fighter compared to any other teenaged boy wasn't good enough for a son of Malos Torvald.

The man was thin but not very tall, and wore the heavy black cloaks of the Draconis Order, cinched at the waist with a thick leather belt upon which many utility clips and pouches hung. From one of these he drew forth a stub writing chalk, and a small notebook. He grimaced at the pages he flicked through, his face sunken and lined with age.

"Hmm…" The man made marks in his little book, before nodding. "I'm Greer, the Quartermaster for this noble and fine institution you are about to enter." The man looked me up and down, as if I were a prime hunting dog, but clearly, he found something in me lacking. "Bandits you say? On the Mountain of Dragons?" He used the Middle Kingdom term for Mount Hammal.

"He's not lying, sir," said a woman with hair the color of dirty straw, and freckles scattering her cheeks. She wore the signature black cloak of the Order over a deep blue shift, and carried a basket from which she drew forth blankets, fruit, and bandages. "Here lad," she said (although, she could only be a hand-span of years older than me) and pressed a fresh apple into my hand. "I'm Nan Barrow, and I'm the House Mistress of the monastery. Don't you mind about old Greer," she whispered as she turned my arm over to look at the tears and mud splatters all up and down my tunic. "He's just sore that nothing's keeping to his schedule." The woman gave me a wink before turning to examine the bruises and scrapes on my forehead. "Yes, sir," she said in a louder voice, "he's got a nasty scrape on him there, and looks like he took a beating."

"Well, it wasn't a *total* beating," I said. "I did break one man's foot."

"Hmm. I'm sure you did, young master," Quartermaster Greer drawled, clearly uninterested in whatever I had to say. He was already turning to nod to the other servants. "Check the avenue, see that his horse is stabled, and prepare a room for him with the others." Greer squinted a look out into the horizon, before shaking his head sullenly. "No time, no time."

"Others?" I said.

"Oh, yes," Nan answered, as she finished wrapping the bandage around my forehead and laying a heavier cloak about my shoulders. "You're not the only one to be sent to us. Children from north, middle and south and all over have been turning up this moon." She tutted as she inspected my muddy clothes. "Well, I can do my best to fix them, but to be honest, I think they're done for, lad."

"Neill," I said with a smile. "Don't worry about it, I can fix them." My father may have been one of the most famous warlords of the Middle Kingdom, but that didn't mean that the Torvald fort was a palace. My father encouraged all of us to be able to mend our own gear, and look after ourselves. 'We're Wardens, little Neill,' I could hear his gruff voice telling me. 'Wardens first and foremost, here to fight for our people.'

"But thank you for your kindness," I added to Nan.

"Huh, a little lord who darns his own hose and has manners? Well, I never heard of such!" She laughed, an earthy cackle that drew a further scowl from Quartermaster Greer. Nan rolled her eyes and nudged me in the ribs, the pain of which made me wince. "Go on! You'd better follow the Quartermaster, he likes to get the measure of the new recruits before you meet Ansall."

Abbot Ansall, my brain supplied. I'd heard about him from father, but only as some sort of adviser to the old Queen Delia before she had died. "The head of the monastery?" I asked.

"The sacred link between dragon and humanity," Quartermaster Greer said as his bony, withered fingers clasped my shoulder, forcefully escorting me away from the House Mistress. "Yes, *that* Abbot Andros Ansall." With a none-too-gentle shove, he pushed me over the threshold and into the Monastery of Dragons itself.

NEVER WOULD I have thought a place so big and so well-defended was a monastery at all. Its main double-doors were made of triple-planked wood, with iron braces, and its walls were made of thick stone blocks studded with gate houses, towers, and ramparts.

"Stop gawking there, boy." The Quartermaster shoved behind me again, and there was a loud *clunk* from the doors as the servants came back in. "We haven't got all day, and you don't want to keep His Holiness waiting!"

His Holiness...? I thought with a rising sense of unease. That was not the way that father and my brothers referred to the Draconis Order. I had thought the members were like hobbyists, or like one of the smaller guilds we had in the Eastern Marches. Here, the monks of the Draconis Order appeared different. They were quiet and contained. Even Jodreth had been like that, in his own way, and they greeted each other with a nod or gestures with their hands, like it was a cult.

Greer pushed me away from the main stone pathway, past a large stone hall with many arched windows and separate 'wings' leading to join other buildings - what looked like storerooms, warehouses, and armories.

"Up the stairs, boy." Greer pushed, and in my amazement, I let him. We climbed a flight of external stone stairs to the high walls of the monastery, and the sharp winds whipped and tore around us. I had never seen stonework this finely wrought.

"Mind out!" Quartermaster Greer shouted, as, in my gawking at the monastery, I had not seen the dark, striding shape of a monk coming down the steps towards us. The taller man did not stop, and I was suddenly pulled back by the Quartermaster and soundly boxed on the side of the ears.

"Ow – Hey," I said, holding a hand to the ringing side of my head which was already sporting a bandage. I couldn't believe what this jumped up servant had done, as I turned to hiss at the much older man. "I am the son of Malos Torvald, Chosen Warden of the Eastern Marches," I reminded him.

"*Bastard* son," said the figure that I had almost bumped into, who had stopped a few steps above, and was looking down at me with a calculating glare.

My cheeks burned. It was true. It was the reason why my father had chosen me to come here and do his bidding, after all, and not his true-blooded sons like Rubin or Rik. I knew that I had been given a supposedly special mission from my father, but that was scant relief compared to the nagging doubts I had: that my brothers might have convinced my father to send me here for their benefit-- to get me out of their way, or that my own father had lost faith in me and believed my brothers would make better Chief Wardens than I could.

"Neill Torvald: bastard son of Warden Malos Torvald and Feeyah Shaar Anar, a Gypsy from the hot lands of distant Shaar of the Far South, and not the same Middle Kingdom noble-woman as your brothers," the monk above me intoned. Only one monk would have knowledge such as this man's. And then I realized who it must be. This was the man I must befriend, the man I must impress if I wanted to get the information my father sought.

His Holiness the Abbot Andros Ansall appeared to be of an age with my father, I guessed, in his later years but still spry. He had a long off-white beard through which he spoke in clipped, Middle-Kingdom tones. He was bald save for a small black skullcap but apart from the silver stylized dragon's head atop his staff, and the simple gold chain of office set with a black gemstone that he wore over black tunics and shirts – I would never have guessed he was the 'most sacred link between dragons and humanity' here or anywhere.

"I'm sorry, your Holiness," the Quartermaster Greer said, his voice instantly making my skin crawl as it dripped appeasement. "I will try to make sure the boy pays more attention in the future."

"That is *my* job, isn't it, Quartermaster?" The Abbot inflicted his precise judgement on the Quartermaster himself; a subtle punishment, I saw, for 'allowing' me to almost knock over the head and founder of the Draconis Order. To his credit, the Quartermaster didn't answer nor correct the Abbot, but merely hung his head.

"No matter, Quartermaster. I have the boy now," came a dry voice, followed by an equally dry chuckle from above. I had missed a step somewhere in the dark, and had landed in a foreign land – which was the truth. How could the son of the great Malos Torvald, Victor of the Longest-Day battle, destroyer of the Blood-Duke's rebellion, be treated like this? But I found that when I looked up at the Abbot above me, I couldn't bring myself to say anything. He was looking at me with the same sort of eyes that Jodreth had – like they could see right into my very soul and hear my innermost thoughts.

"Come, master Neill," the Abbot indicated that we would continue up the stairs. "Here at the Order we do not care who your parents are, or what were the circumstances of your birth," he said as Quartermaster Greer loped back down the stairs and we made our way up. "You may find this difficult to believe, but *I* myself was not born to any powerful family, or even a loving one, I have to admit." He made a chuckling sound as he continued. "I grew up amongst many older siblings who fought me for everything I had, which made me strong and self-reliant." The Abbot paused at the top of the wall as I joined him.

His harsh and strict words made me think of Rik's accusing laughter, the shoves and pinches he would give when he thought father wasn't looking. I didn't want to like this man, but I found that I could in part understand him. Maybe our similarities would prove useful.

We climbed up more stairs than I could keep count of, until we were climbing a tower which straddled the rocks underneath it, and stood higher than all the rest. To my right the mountain sloped down and away to the distant hills and plains below, dotted with small glints of light from the village huts.

"They are fearful of us, but good people," the Abbot said, following my gaze. "Many of our servants come from the village down there, and are glad for the work. But it is not peasant's hovels that I wanted to show you, Master Torvald. Did your father tell you much of what we do here?"

"Uh, not much, sir," I stammered. Actually, my father had told me that this monastery was where old monks sat around reading scrolls to each other and concocting ever more devious ways to wring money out of the palace purse, but I hardly thought that it was appropriate for me to say that to the Abbot himself.

"Yes," the bald man chuckled, and again I felt as though he could see right through into my very soul. "Few understand who we are, it is true." He drew out a large ring of iron keys, each one as long as my entire hand. He selected one key that had a small chip of obsidian set into it, and with a *click-thump* he unlocked the wooden door, and gestured for me to go inside.

I felt a moment of hesitation as I peered into the dark to see more stairs, and to smell the sharp tang of ozone.

"Come on, come on, Neill – no need to be afraid, up you go!" The Abbot laughed. I might be an illegitimate bastard, but I was still the son of a warlord after all, I knew that I shouldn't show fear.

"Flamos," the old man whispered behind me and I gasped as he summoned a small bright spark out of nowhere and it leapt from his hands to kindle the torch set into the wall sconce. I had of course heard of the magic that the Draconis Order had, but I had never seen it. I thought back to when Jodreth the monk had saved me, and I had heard a sound like breaking thunder and one of the bandits had been struck down. It was true – the dragon monks could control magic

"How… How did you do that?" I said, looking at the Abbot in the new light. He did not appear to be an aging scholar anymore to me, but strange, less human and more something *else.*

"There are many such powers and abilities that we learn here at the Order," Abbot Ansall said. "Which you too might learn if you have the proficiency."

"Oh." I wasn't the sort of person who could summon magic, as we passed first one window, and then another, before we finally reached the top.

It was cold, but the Abbot didn't even notice it. We stood in a room with a high, vaulted ceiling and open windows on all sides through which blew the icy mountain wind.

"Master Torvald, you may be asking yourself why I brought you up here, and the answer is through the western window over there," the Abbot intoned, and, knowing that it was also an order, I walked to the opening (almost as tall as my entire body), and peered down into a vast crater—all that was left of Mount Hammal's twin peak.

Dragons.

CHAPTER 4
ZAXX THE MIGHTY

D*ragons.*

The dragons of the Middle Kingdom were large and strong, with long necks, barrel chests, and stout legs, and they also came in many colors--green, blue, or orange. They were draped over the warm rocky outcroppings or sitting on the sandy banks of the steaming pools scattered here and there throughout the natural amphitheater the mountain-crater made. There wasn't much movement from the large forms, except perhaps a lazy tail flick or the shiver of a wing that from here looked no bigger than one of my father's banners, but I knew must be the size of a ship's sail.

"*Sssss,*" came a rumbling sound as one of the shapes walked out onto a ledge and sniffed at the darkening gloom of the setting sun. It was a White, one of the largest breeds of dragons, and as large as the Great House of the monastery. It moved slowly, sending its long, forked tongue to lick and taste at the air around it.

"Impressive, aren't they?" the Abbot said softly beside me, as if he might wake them even from where we stood.

"They're so big," I said in awe.

"Some of them," the Abbot informed me. "Some are small, Messenger dragons we call them, because they make excellent couriers if you can manage to raise one from an egg."

"But the larger dragons – you can't train them?" I asked, my heart hammering. My first day—my first hour, even—in the monastery, and already I was asking the exact questions my father longed to know the answers to.

"Ha, no, if only!" Another dry chuckle from the Abbot. "I see that you understand what it is we protect here, these are noble and ancient creatures – but there are precious few of them left, compared to the olden times." The Abbot's eyes flickered to the skies. "They are strong-willed, capricious beings, ones that do not easily make alliances, even to breed. And on the rare occasions they do mate, they are just as likely to destroy each other's broods– so you see why any living dragon who will ally with us is precious. But even more than that, some of the dragons are intelligent. They hold secrets in their hearts and lost lore that they may teach us, if they feel so inclined. But enough of that; I haven't even shown you the one that I wanted to, yet."

The one? I thought, unable to tear my eyes from the magnificent, immense, powerful creatures.

"Every student who manages to gain entrance to this monastery is brought up here, and I show them who we are, and why," the Abbot intoned as he joined me at the window, looking over my shoulder at the sight of the beasts below.

"The Draconis Order was set up over a hundred years ago, under the early days of Queen Delia. You know who she is, don't you, boy?" Abbot Ansall flicked an annoyed glance at me, and a shiver or paranoid fear ran through me. Maybe he *can* read thoughts as well!

"Queen Delia was the Mother of the Three Kingdoms, and her three sons have been left to rule one kingdom each. Prince Vincent is the ruler here in the Middle Kingdom," I said, repeating it almost by rote from the old scrolls that my father had made me read as soon as I could hold a sword.

"Good. Seeing as you are the son of Chief Warden Torvald, you know that there is risk of the unity of the Three Kingdoms falling apart. Forever," the Abbot said. "Luckily, however, Queen Delia had great foresight. She approached us, just a small band of simple dragon-mystics who sought to learn the ways of these noble creatures, to ask us to aid her in unifying the kingdoms." The Abbot smiled. "She knew that the Draconis Order, with the knowledge and power of dragons at our side were unstoppable. What petty bandit lord or war-chief could ever threaten the throne?"

The Abbot said all of this in a tone that was surprisingly bloodthirsty for a man of the cloth, but then again, there was nothing that he had said so far that wasn't true. *It just goes to show that everything that I think I know about monks and monasteries is upside down.*

"And that is why you summoned us here," I said. "The sons

39

and daughters of the warlords and war chiefs of the Three Kingdoms."

"Yes. Together, we will form an alliance that will protect each of the Three Kingdoms and last for generations. But it wasn't just the wish that you all would get over your differences, of course... It is my wish that you would come to see the majesty and power of the creatures that we ally with..."

The Abbot raised his hand, and seemingly at that very same moment there was a loud, shrill noise from beneath us somewhere in the monastery.

"What is that?" I said, as the very stones of the floor seemed to shake.

"That is the dragon pipes, look, Neill Torvald, look at the future!" The Abbot pointed out to a window beside us, and finally I saw what could make such a blaring sound. From one of the other towers there had been wheeled a man-sized brass contraption that looked like a series of flutes strapped together and connected to a single mouthpiece, through which a black-robed monk blew.

The pipes were answered by a rumbling sound, coming from the crater where the dragons lived.

"Here. Now, this is the one I show all of my students. Look, Neill Torvald, at the mastery of Zaxx!" Ansall said, his voice breathy with excitement.

Growling filled the air as a massive gold dragon emerged from the crater, the like of which I had never seen before. It was almost twice the size of the White dragon I'd seen earlier, and stocky, with sweeping horns like a buffalo and an outgrowth of broken and cracked horns along its jaw, spine, arms.

The dragon pipes blasted again, and I watched as smaller shapes dressed in black appeared on the edge of the crater. *Monks.* They looked impossibly tiny compared to any of the dragons, and next to Zaxx the gold, it appeared that one of them could easily walk right down the creature's gullet if he had wanted to open his mouth!

Zaxx lifted his head on a neck that was heavy with the folds of golden scales, some tarnished and old, forming a mighty ruff mounding on its shoulders. I watched as each of the encircling humans started hauling sacks that had been at their feet and throwing them down into the pit.

"What is that?" I whispered, watching objects, some large, some small, some that glittered wetly, some that smacked against the rocks with heavy thumps.

"Meat." The Abbot's voice was dry. "Zaxx is the mightiest dragon in the Three Kingdoms, and in return for his friendship we honor him with gifts."

I watched in awe, and horror, at what was happening below. Zaxx stepped forward on legs that looked as though they could smash tree trunks with ease, shoved the White out of the way, in order to be the first to seize the majority of the food spilling from above. His wings shivered with joy as he gulped and tore at the food between fangs that could have easily impaled me. Was winning the dragons' loyalty as simple as merely feeding them?

"So now you have seen their glory and their might, young Neill Torvald. You know what it is that we protect and champion.

You must put aside all previous loyalties and petty rivalries. The Draconis Order is the future!"

As I watched, I felt like I was on the crest of a wave about to crash into an unknown shore. Although the sight of great Zaxx was terrifying, there was something also awe-inspiring about the crater, about the dragons themselves. I felt the old stirrings of my childhood wonder and excitement of these ancient creatures. Maybe, in a way, I was the lucky one of all of my brothers to be sent here. But I did not know what the result would be or what would come next. My father and brothers, I knew, did not view the dragons with the same awe that I did. They feared them. Whatever the future would bring, all I knew was that it was unstoppable and it was happening, and that I was being swept up into it.

CHAPTER 5
NEW FRIENDS, OLD ENEMIES

I hadn't realized quite how hungry I was until the Abbot told me that I was on my way to eat, and then to bed, but my heart sank again as I saw the hunched shape of Quartermaster Greer standing in the courtyard with his little black book, already waiting for me.

The Quartermaster bowed his head as the Abbot swept past. His black boots and cane clipped smartly across the paving slabs to the tower with the strange brass circles and dishes hanging from every window. I would have asked what that tower was, but then my stomach rumbled and a yawn escaped me.

"Tired are we, Master Torvald?" Greer sneered, as his fingers pinched the back of my neck and thrust me forward to the Great House. I felt an instant burning of rage towards the man. *Just you wait until I get out of here, Quartermaster, I'll make you pay for treating me like this!*

But for the moment, there was little I could do. I had been

told by my father to go along with the rule of the Order, whatever they asked and whatever form it took. And that meant putting up with little men with big senses of self-importance like Quartermaster Greer. He shoved me past the open doors and through a drafty and cold stone corridor, to where the sounds of feasting, whooping, and shouting emerged. *Food!* When was the last time I had eaten – before being attacked by bandits and meeting Jodreth, was it? It seemed like an age ago, as it was now well and truly dark.

"Here. Get yourself a bowl and a seat," the Quartermaster Greer said as he turned the corner and pushed me into the swelter of noise, laughter and heat – all of which stopped the instant we appeared.

The banquet hall was full of students about my age, boys and girls. They all wore a black tabard over their clothes, giving the meeting a dour, somber appearance despite the now-silenced catcalls and the fading smiles. I wondered if the others here were wary of me, the new boy, or of Greer.

"Right, you lot!" the Quartermaster shouted. "Another little lordling for you," he said contemptuously. "Although this isn't quite true, is it, Neill?" he asked in his croaking and clear voice, and I felt my cheeks burn in shame.

Greer. The others were wary of Greer. At least we would all be unified in our hatred of him.

"Neill… Where do I know that name," said one of the boys from the hall, standing up as he reached to take a seeded roll from a basket on the table. He was heavyset with straight dark hair, and a gold earring in his ear.

44

"One of your Southern lot, by the looks of him!" shouted another student. It was true, I had inherited the southern curls and darker skin of my mother's Shaar heritage, even though my father was about as Middle Kingdom as they come!

"Lords and ladies, this is Neill Torvald, son of the Chief Warden Malos Torvald," crowed the Quartermaster.

"Oh, only a *warlord's* son," one of them said distastefully.

"Torvald! That's right – you're the illegitimate one, aren't you?" said the first, larger-set child who had been searching for my name. "Your mother is some Gypsy from the Far South…"

"Terrence, enough," said one of the other boys there. He was small with blond hair, and small reading spectacles perched over his nose. "Half of us here come from clan families anyway…"

"Oh, hark at Dorf Lesser, protector of the *lesser* families!" The larger boy rolled his eyes at the smaller boy as if the one who spoke up for me was almost as bad, but he sat down all the same.

"Boys! Girls!" The voice of the Quartermaster rang out, instantly silencing them. "I trust you will give *master* Torvald here a warm welcome. Now, get some food and go to bed!" he barked, slapping his thigh with the palm of one hand in a sharp *crack* before leaving the room, leaving me to my tormentors.

There was a moment's quiet, but the desire to eat overrode any growing caution as the hall descended once more into shouts and screams. I was glad of being invisible for a moment, as I took a bowl and started to help myself from the table of fruits, stews, cooked meats and cheeses.

"Don't worry about Terrence," said a voice at my side, and I turned to see that it was Dorf Lesser, alongside a girl who had come to formally 'greet' me (and get some of the spiced buns still available, I suspect). "He's Terrence Aldo, son of Prince Griffith," Dorf said.

"The Kind Prince?" I raised my eyebrows. Of the three princes that each ruled the different kingdoms, Prince Griffith of the warm south was supposed to have a heart as warm as his hot lands. "He doesn't seem very kind to me," I murmured, and Dorf laughed, before quickly covering up his smile and looking sheepish. Dorf Lesser was shy, I saw, and yet he had still stood up to my defense. I had known of the Lesser Clan of course, not as big as the Torvald Clan, and my brothers were always laughing about their gentle farming ways, but they did provide a lot of grain and food to Prince Vincent, our Middle Kingdom liege lord.

"Yeah, *one of a kind,* maybe!" said the girl at our side. "So, you're Neill Torvald, this is Dorf Lesser, and I'm Sigrid Fenn," the girl said. She was taller than me, but looked a little younger, with straw-brown hair and freckles

The Fenn Clan. I tried to remember what my father had told me about them. Odd bunch. Lived near the north of the Middle Kingdom, just as likely to turn and support Prince Lander of the north as they would Prince Vincent. *Father didn't trust them.*

Sigrid narrowed her eyes slightly as she looked at me, before sighing slightly and looking away. *What had I done wrong?* Was it because I didn't know who she was? It was Dorf Lesser who broke the awkward moment of silence.

"We three should stick together in this place," Dorf said earnestly, his hands folding over another spiced bun on the table.

I don't think that he knew that he was doing it. "We're all the same-- warlord's children."

Wardens, I thought, feeling my heart hammer as the words of my father echoed in my mind. *We're Wardens.* Father hated the term 'warlord' or 'war chief' – saying that it was a way for the noble families to talk down the many clans of the Three Kingdoms, and after that, we'd be known only as 'bandit lords.'

But I see what Dorf means, all the same, I thought, reaching out my hands.

"Nice to meet you," I said. "Nice to meet both of you." Dorf's larger fist folded over mine, and Sigrid tentatively clasped the other one. I felt as though we had sealed a pact of some kind.

CHAPTER 6
SCRIBE, PROTECTOR, MAGE

"*D*uck, roll shoulder, duck, roll shoulder…*" Dorf's constant litany beside me was beginning to get on my nerves to be honest.

"No, it's *duck shoulder,* then *roll,*" I said, convinced that we were going to get trounced again by the others.

It had been almost a week since arriving here at the monastery, and so far, we had done little more than exercise. Everything I had thought about monks being old and boring men with long beards and their noses in books was proving wrong. Quartermaster Greer had so far shown to be a devoted taskmaster, standing outside the dormitory block and banging a brass gong before the crack of dawn, to have us running around the main courtyard until breakfast. After that came general tasks, which could be anything from moving supplies to running errands, to helping out in the kitchens, mucking out stalls in the stable (and saying hello to Stamper as I did so; the little mountain pony seemed much happier now that he was amongst others of its kind, and didn't have a teenager coaxing her to travel every day), or hauling water from the well until lunch time, and then after that some more exercise and a few weapons drills. It was this last lesson; weapons and fighting skills that most of the other students looked forward to, as the general tasks were (according to Terrence and his cohort) 'beneath them,' though my father had always said that having intimate knowledge of such tasks was important for an effective leader of the people. Besides, I could see another reason for what Greer was attempting to do: toughen us all up (and especially the ones like Dorf, who did not perhaps come from such a martial Warden family as us Torvalds).

But I liked Dorf. Despite my father's pronouncement to be wary of everyone, and to keep my eyes open for clues, I found myself beginning to trust him, just a little. He was bookish, and shy—, the opposite of me in many ways – but he was honest. *But what of the bandits that attacked me on the road here – they could have been Lessers,* I reminded myself. However, comparing those rough and aggressive men to the sort of person I saw in Dorf made it clear that they couldn't be more different. *If it was the Lessers who attacked me – then I don't think Dorf here knew about it at all.*

"Really? Duck shoulder and then roll forward – how on earth are you supposed to do that!?" Dorf said as the morning gong sounded again. We were going to be late, and the Quartermaster hated it if you were tardy for the morning session.

"Just like this, Dorf!" I said, taking a half skip to show him the simple maneuver that Greer was teaching us. I turned to one side, ducked my shoulder and rolled my body forward as I leapt, the result would put me beneath any opponent's swinging fist, and hopefully ensure they were left unprotected for me to-

"*Oof! Hey!*" I collided bodily with someone. We landed in a heap against the far wall, and the papers that my victim had been carrying were sent everywhere.

"Hey, why didn't you look where you were going?" the girl said angrily.

"Oh, by the rocks and stones, are you okay?" I said, rubbing my shoulder where it had hit a wall. "I didn't hurt you, did I?" I was mortified, feeling suddenly oafish, embarrassed, and stupid in front of the girl.

"No, you're not *that* good." The girl brushed down her tunic, before looking at the mess of papers. Twin spots of high color were on her pale cheeks, and her silver hair was a mess, but she didn't look completely furious. "It'll take me ages to get this together," she huffed. She was a little older than me by a year or two, and clearly wasn't too flustered by what had happened. I was surprised that I hadn't seen her before.

"I'll help you!" I said, instantly feeling bad. Father had always told me to try and rectify my mistakes – it was the only thing that separated us from bandits and Raiders, after all…

"Uh, Neill? The training?" Dorf said uneasily, looking down the hall to the open doorway and the freezing, pre-dawn light outside.

"Go, go, Dorf, I'll be okay – this won't take but a moment," I said. It wasn't really his fault anyway. "And no sense you getting in trouble with Greer for my mistake…"

Dorf gave me a grin and hurried off and out of sight.

"Well, in that case, maybe I should just leave you to pick all this up so *I* don't get into trouble either," the girl said at my side, making me wince. *Fair point.*

"Yeah, sure – I'll catch up…" I said, picking up one of the sheets of paper to see an array of arrows, circles and lines, filled with what looked like instructions. I had no idea what order they were supposed to go in.

"Yeah right, as if I'm going to leave you to that, huh?" The girl pointed to a sheet I was holding, and then to a pile at her side. "Let's make two piles-- group strategies," she pointed to the paper I was holding, "over here," she indicated a pile of papers near her. "And individual movements, like this one"—she offered up a piece of paper with *vaguely* different circles and arrows, "over here. All right?" Even squinting at the diagrams, I couldn't see the difference.

"Uh, I think so…" I said uncertainly.

"Oh, don't worry about it," the girl shook her head, chuckling as she sorted through the papers. "Greer will no doubt find something wrong with it, whatever I present to him."

"Sounds like him," I said under my breath, still smarting from the many small shoves and pinches that he managed to inflict on me almost daily.

"I'm Char Nefrette, and you must be the infamous Neill Torvald." The girl stuck out a hand. I must've made a strange expression because she added, "My dormmate Sigrid told me about you." I shook it, once, wondering what making friends with this new girl would mean in this world of shifting alliances.

Nefrette? I hadn't heard of that clan before, and it wasn't one that father had told me to be wary of. Did that mean that she was unimportant to my fathers' cause, or that she was something entirely new?

"I can see you trying to work out who I am, but you won't get there," Char finished, piling the papers and gestured to her long, silver hair. "I have my mother's looks, just as I presume that you have yours. You don't look much like the rest of the Torvald Clan, that's for sure."

"Oh." I felt suddenly stupid. "So, you're a…?" I blushed.

"A bastard?" Char said stubbornly. "Yes. That is what Prince Vincent calls me, but not my father, Prince Lander."

Prince Lander of the North, the worthiest successor to Queen Delia's throne. The words of my father almost sprang unbidden from my mouth, before I stopped them. My father had a lot of respect for the rangy, hard-edged ruler of the Northern Kingdom, even though he was 'officially' our enemy (as we were beholden to Prince Vincent and the Middle Kingdom, our clan's home). *My father likes him because he's the only one keeping the Wildman out of Three Kingdom lands,* I reminded myself, wondering if I could see a trace of that hard-edged determination here in Char, too.

"So, your mother was a… Wildwoman?" I said awkwardly.

In response, Char just raised an eyebrow over her lake-blue eyes. "Just as your mother was a traveling Gypsy?"

Ouch. I nodded. "The Gypsies of the Far South are an ancient and noble people. We traveled out of the hot lands far, far to the south of here and have spent many generations traveling the world. My uncle is a Headman, like a prince I guess, of his group and his sister, my mother, was a Matriarch."

Char nodded, accepting the challenge. "As are mine, but the Wild families don't have titles. As you know, my father's official wife and princess has never given him any heirs, and so, in the tradition of the Wild North he took a mistress because— well, I don't suppose I need to explain all the benefits he might've seen to the arrangement. His mistress was my mother, a proud shield-maiden of the wilds, who agreed to form a truce between her family and the Northern Kingdom." She shrugged, picking up her papers. "If there is one thing that we have in common, Neill Torvald, is that we understand, of everyone here, that power and respect is not all about where you come from or how noble your family is!"

I found myself grinning in response.

"Torvald! Nefrette!" A sudden shout from the doorway, and we turned in horror to see the form of the Quartermaster Greer striding towards us both. "What are you doing, dawdling in the corridors while the rest of your brothers and sisters freeze in the morning dew outside? Are you both *that* selfish?"

He seized me painfully by the ear, but I noticed he didn't do the same for Char. Was it because her father was a prince with his own kingdom and generals, whereas mine was a lowly Warden?

"I'm sorry, sir, it was my fault." Char said. "I dropped the papers I was preparing for you." She offered the stacks to Greer, so that he had to relinquish his hold on my ear to take them.

"Hmm. Well, I see that your skills as a Scribe are apparently getting worse!" Greer leafed through the pages. "I told you to translate and collect them together, but there are mistakes littered through them! Outside, the pair of you!" he barked.

"Scribe?" I whispered to Nefrette, as she shook her head and held a finger to her lips – and then we were out in the freezing cold where all of the students were standing in rows, arm's length apart, and shivering. Their baleful stares were on us as we joined the back of the collection, and marched out, where Abbot Andros himself stood, atop the wall.

"BROTHERS AND SISTERS! STUDENTS!" the Abbot bellowed. It was still grey in the dawn light, and the air was freezing, but we all stood unconsciously to attention.

"Thank you all, for joining us – even those of you who have been through this process before!" the Abbot said and I realized there were other students here like Char, whom I had never seen before. Like the silver haired northerner, they were all older by a year or so, but still wore the customary black robes.

"You are here to be trained, and to create unity for the much-troubled land of the Three Kingdoms – today is the first part of that process!" the Abbot intoned. "The Quartermaster has informed me that the time is right and that all of the new recruits are sufficiently sound of body and mind for the next stage, which will be this: you will be chosen for one of three roles, suited to your abilities and character. Through these roles you will learn your place in the world." He paused, and looked around the crowd of youngsters. For an electric moment, his eyes connected with mine as they swept past and my stomach felt suddenly unsettled. How would being chosen for a particular role for the year or two that I'd live here help father, and my brothers, and the people of the Eastern Marches? I already knew my place in the world, as the bastard son of a Chosen Warden. I would be forever overlooked and discounted. No role I took here at the monastery would change that, once I returned home.

I don't know what is going to happen to me once I return home, I reminded myself, once again feeling the heavy lump of worry and loneliness in my throat. My brothers didn't look like me. They would be generals and wardens and warlords and whatever else. But for me? Father had always said that I would have a place at his side, at the side of my brothers, that I was a true-born Son of Torvald – but what would his word mean after he, the unstoppable old bear, had passed away? I imagined becoming some lesser clerk or captain in my brother's employ – if they even suffered to keep me around at all. *I don't know how my brothers will view a trained dragon monk hanging around in their halls,* I thought. It's not as if they have showed any particular love for them before now – so why would it be different when I was the one?

"The Draconis Order are monks, but we each have a purpose. Scribe. Protector. Mage. If you are chosen as a Scribe, it will be your sacred duty to preserve the lore of the Three Kingdoms. As a Protector, it will be to defend the Order, the dragons, and the throne. If you are lucky enough to have the aptitude, to be a Mage, the rarest of all of us, your duty will be to carry the powers and the teachings of the Order itself. You will be tested, recruits, and assessed over the weeks that follow to determine your calling." His voice rose, as he brought his speech to a glorifying close. "But know this, sons and daughters of the Three Kingdoms – together, we will be creating a new age!"

CHAPTER 7
CHAR NEFRETTE

T*he new boy was weird,* I thought as I got my things ready for yet another day at the grueling Dragon Monastery. I had been idly thinking about that new Torvald boy as I crept down the stone stairs. Sigrid had told me that she had met him, and that he was 'that bastard son of Torvald, sent here as a punishment' and that had made me all the more curious about him. He was different from the others. After all, most of the instructors and monks here thought *I* was some 'bastard child' and not worthy of learning about dragons.

Maybe I'm just feeling lonely, I thought to myself with a sigh. Which was crazy, really –I spent most of every waking moment surrounded by people, and for the most part, the other students treated me fairly well. Sigrid could be funny, and I was starting to think of her as a real friend. Why would I be lonely?

Because I want to meet other people like me. My rebellious thoughts answered me on the cold steps in the greying light of pre-dawn, my bag heavy with meat and cheeses.

"Char? You're up early, where are you going?" Sigrid said. *Drat!* I'd been trying to be quiet enough that Sigrid wouldn't wake and notice me gone. Sharing a room was terribly trying. Back home I was used to coming and going whenever I pleased without disturbing anyone.

"I could ask the same of you!" I nodded, seeing that she, too, was dressed (just not in all of the heavy cloaks and furs that I was). The air was cold, but it wasn't as freezing as the real deep mountains, where my mother's family came from. Sigrid, however, was shivering.

"Yeah, just getting some more wood for the fire," she said, rubbing her hands together. Each of our dormitory rooms were shared between at least two students, and we each had a small hearth which we were expected to tend ourselves.

"Oh, I'm sorry, Sigrid, I should have brought some more logs up," I said. "I was the first up, after all."

"Don't worry about it. You mountain folk have ice in your veins." Sigrid laughed. "Not like us southerners. You probably think this is just another balmy sunny morning!"

Not quite, I thought, but I laughed all the same.

"You still haven't answered my question, though." The girl fixed me with a sharp stare. "Where are you going so early?"

But I had to go *now*, before true dawn, and why I couldn't afford to wait around to explain myself to Sigrid. "Oh, it's a mountain thing," I said quickly. "An old custom. We go to honor the snow fall."

"But it's not snowing out there," Sigrid wondered, stepping on tiptoes to look out through the bare window into the courtyard of the monastery beyond.

Damn! "No, precisely," I said a little haughtily, trying to pretend to be the 'mysterious wise wild woman' image that my father had teased my mother with. "I go to celebrate the snow fall that *might* come, and to avert any more snowstorms."

"You can do that? Stop the snow from falling?" Sigrid looked doubtful.

Of course not, I thought. These lowland people were really gullible when it came to what we did up there in the mountains! "I don't know, but it is our way," I said. "Now, if you will excuse me, I must go."

"Of course, Char, of course," Sigrid said. "But remember what the Abbot said – we're going to be tested and sorted into what monk we're going to be. I hope that I get to be a Protector."

"I hope you get the opportunity," I said, a bad mood beginning to settle on my shoulders. I had already been tested of course, as I had been here longer than Sigrid, and it had been the Quartermaster who suggested I would make an excellent Scribe despite my not having any particular proficiency with ink and quill. He must have known that all of this difficult symbols and complicated words of the monastery were nothing like the mountain runes and markings. I think he just had something against me and wanted to keep me from the other more prestigious roles. *Anyway.* I was going to be late, and Sigrid, although no fault of her own, had reminded me what Greer had told me not so long ago. That he was certain *a delicate girl like me* was perfect

Scribing material because I knew the true impact of impurity and imperfection. It was a nightmare trying to learn how the Abbot wanted things to be said in my hours of transcribing the old scrolls – I would much rather be out there on the mountain with Paxala, or learning to fight with the others.

Paxala. I remembered how late I was already, and my anxiety added speed to my steps as I swept down to the ground floor, pausing as I slipped out of the tower door and into the cold beyond.

SIGRID HAD BEEN RIGHT. It was cold out here before true dawn. I had just a little time to cross the mountain and get down to the cave. My steps took me out, across the courtyard (traveling quickly and quietly, as my mother had taught me well) and out through the Kitchen Gardens. The leather knapsack was heavy on my shoulder as I half-jogged, feeling my tired muscles beginning to wake up.

At least the monastery keeps us fit, I thought, as I jogged up the path through the incline of rock and gorse bushes, seeing the ridge and the dragon crater beyond. There was a lark beginning to trill over the mountain heaths below us, and the grey was giving away to softer, muted colors. I didn't have much time at all if I was going to get out to Paxala without being seen and back again before lessons started.

The Dragon Monastery was not like anything that I had ever

experienced before. When my father, Prince Lander of the North, had suggested to me that he would have to send me away, I had thought that it was a punishment. I had kicked and screamed and would have shouted his little stony fortress down were it not for my older brother, Wurgan. He, too, was an illegitimate princeling just as I was an *almost* princess. But he had been accepted by my father's lowland advisers and captains much more than they accepted me. It was because he was a general of our father's armies, while I was but an illegitimate brat. At least as far as they were concerned.

"Little sister, stop with this. It is unseemly," I remembered Wurgan had counseled me over his first silver-gold mustache. "You are a prince's daughter, after all – a princess!"

But I am not, am I? I repeated in my mind what I had said so long ago. I and Wurgan himself were all just more scions in the way of the throne. It was a wonder that Lady Odette, our father's *real* wife, hadn't had us poisoned years ago – but she knew as much as we did that we were Prince Lander of the North's only offspring.

But still, I had always been made to feel second-class somehow by the suspicious looks and glances of the lowland captains and soldiers. It was my silver hair, wasn't it? It marked me out, just like my mother and the wild people of our heritage.

Wurgan had explained to me that I was being sent to this Dragon Monastery not because father didn't love me, or that because I had been bad (although I probably had, I was forever running around the fortress playing, or else bringing in wild creatures I had found from the mountains and trying to tend them there).

"Our father is in trouble; don't you see, little sister? And all of our fighters are busy, and no matter how good my sword arm is – there is nothing that I can do to avoid the trouble coming. Only *you* can," he had said seriously, going down on one knee to straighten my jerkin. Even though the event had been two years ago, I remembered it as clearly as if it had been yesterday.

"*You're good at this,*" Wurgan had said seriously. "You've always been better at listening to people, and to speaking what needs to be said without starting a fight. As for me?" My brother had grinned and flexed his arm muscles. "All I know how to do is to use my sword to end arguments. But we need allies. The north needs allies. Uncle Vincent is allowing the bandits from the Middle Kingdom to harry and attack our borders, but if we say anything then the Three Kingdoms, and the mountain realms and the wild people will all be plunged into war. Our father thinks that *you* can help make peace with these strange lowland lords, by going to this dragon-place and making friends."

But I never wanted to come here.

But I had come to the monastery, and now, after all of that time, I had finally made a friend. No, it wasn't Neill Torvald, though of everyone I'd ever met here, he seemed like he might actually understand me.

No, my friend was a dragon.

THE FIRST RAYS of the sun were coming over the ridgeline behind me and crossing the horizon, which meant that it wouldn't be long until the monastery started waking up. *I'm late,* I chided myself. Did Sigrid suspect anything? Of course, everyone suspects everything in the monastery, I thought a little glumly. *But no one will miss me for breakfast,* now that I had told Sigrid about my 'welcoming the snow' ritual. Poor Sigrid. She was nice enough, really, but she had a habit of being in the exact wrong place and being terribly gullible.

If I skipped breakfast that would give me about an hour with Paxala. I'd been visiting her for a year now, but still, I worried constantly that I might offend her or somehow cause a breech in our friendship. Even more, I worried about what would happen if anyone realized what I was doing—or caught me smuggling such large quantities of cheese and bread.

I scoured the fog hanging low over Hammal Lake and the hazy green tops of the trees, but I couldn't see her anywhere. I was too late. I'd finally ruined everything.

"SKREAYAR!" The ground rumbled with a sound that I could feel in the very pit of my stomach as one dragon, and then another, and then *another* in the crater a way behind me started to greet the dawn. The loudest, deepest, and scariest shriek (one that reminded me of avalanches in the deep mountains) was from Zaxx the Mighty himself. I felt suddenly afraid, as if even merely thinking about the monstrous gold dragon was enough to summon him. To the monks and the other students, Zaxx was a thing of reverence: like a god – he was just so clearly powerful. None of us had ever seen *anything* as impressive as Zaxx.

But if Zaxx was a sort of dragon-god, then he wasn't the sort that I wanted to pray too. I couldn't say for sure, but there was something terrifying in the lidless way that he regarded the other dragons, and the humans both. Calculating. Judging. There was nothing like Paxala in those flaring gold eyes. Nothing that I could relate to.

Maybe what Abbot Ansall says is true, and Zaxx is one of the First Dragons, the father of every dragon that came after...

It made me shudder.

"Zaxx - is no father," a voice said, but it wasn't one that spoke with words, but with thoughts. I could feel the voice as close as my own, and pressing into my mind. I stopped in my tracks, as a feeling like ice water cascaded over me. I didn't know how to say this, but I thought, I thought...

Paxala. The voice I had just heard sounded like what I felt Paxala would sound like, if only she could talk.

But that is impossible. I shook my head. It must have been a trick of my mind.

"Skreayaar!" The shrieks and calls died down, and I heard then – for real this time – a whistling noise coming from the lake.

"Oh, Paxala no, shhh!" I muttered as I picked up my steps – not talking to the dragon but talking to myself, really, as I hurried down the last of the incline and then on the gravely beach around the lake, as the fog started to lift.

"Paxala?" I whispered into the tree line. "Pax? There's a good girl..." I called again, taking the bag of food that I had brought from my shoulder. There, below where a mountain stream emptied into the lake via a waterfall, was a cave obscured by the water. It was damp near the front, but farther in it was dry and, given the number of branches and blankets I had snuck in over the last year – it was even warm. That was where I had left the dragon. My dragon. The one I called Pax, short for Paxala. From somewhere in the murk, there was a snarl and the sound of a heavy beast moving around.

"Come now, Pax," I tried. "You just have to be quiet, don't you? Otherwise Zaxx will hear you, and the monks have said that he's already rejected two broods before…" I tried to reason with her – not sure that the dragon could even understand me. *And if Zaxx heard her, then he might come and finish the task he started with her parents. For some reason, Zaxx had taken a dislike to the Crimson Reds, and tried to crush their eggs after he had killed them.*

There was a snarl, as a large red snout pushed its way through the waterfall, and took a deep, flaring sniff of the air.

"You can smell the food, can't you," I whispered. Pax seemed to like being talked at, so I kept it up as I opened my backpack and allowed the smell of the old joint of ham to waft into the cold morning air. By now the dragons of the crater had stopped their distant dawn anthem – but that did not mean that they were silent. There was still the odd haunting shriek, jabber, or roar. I took a deep breath, feeling a little calmer. Maybe Zaxx wouldn't notice the grunts and whistling chirrups of this red dragon amongst all of the others that were nearer to him in the dragon crater.

The snout withdrew, back into the cave before suddenly Pax burst out of the waterfall in one smooth glide. Her leathery wings were almost as long as the entire Monastery Main Hall, I realized as she flew above me, scaled legs tucked under her, each talon as long as my arm passing just a few feet from my head.

"Yeah!" I cheered. Every time I saw her it made my heart soar. She was a Crimson Red dragon, and, if she survived into adulthood she would be large as well. I felt a fierce pride of her as she alighted on the gravel beach, snuffing the air towards the ridgeway (and the other dragons beyond) before ducking her head to lap at the water of the lake.

"Here Pax, here." I started with the joints of ham, throwing them ahead of us for the young dragon to bound after, and then the wedges of cheese, the bread, and cured fish – anything that I could find, barter for, or steal from the kitchens. "We'll have to get you fishing, soon, and hunting properly," I said absently, looking at the way her scales sat close to her ribs. Too close for my liking. "But only when I know that you can be silent, at least as we hunt this close to Zaxx and the others." I threw the bits of food over the beach, and watching as the Crimson Red cocked her head to whistle at me. I had in mind that we would hunt the way that my mother's people hunted falcons. I would have to whistle and call to scare out game, and she would fly to catch it. Or maybe I would have to shoot the game with my bow and arrow, for her to fly to catch...? It frustrated me how young Paxala really was, despite how large and capable she seemed to be. Dragons must mature slowly, I think – because Paxala had only just learnt how to fish. She had never been hunting for land game, and I did not even know how to start teaching her.

"Why be silent? It is morning, and dragons sing in the morning. " Again, the voice pressed itself into my mind, and I coughed with the shock of it. I ducked, looked around behind me, to either side of me.

There was a whistling set of chirrups in front of me, and I turned to see that the Crimson Red had bounded forward a few steps, and was regarding me like I was playing a game.

"No, no, it's not a game, Paxie..." I whispered, my heart hammering in my chest. *Had that really just happened? Was there something wrong with my ears? Had someone followed me here?* I looked around, suddenly scared.

"Paxala, " the invisible voice said, and I had the uncomfortable feeling that the strange voice was reprimanding me. *Had I gone mad?* I searched first back at the waterfall and the cave the tree line, the ridgeway (now crested with bright sunlight) the beach...

And there stood the Crimson Red, directly in front of me, and lowering her head to my level. Warm, sooty breath breathed over me as she ignored the food on the ground, and ever so gently, bumped her snout onto my head.

"Hey!" I said, feeling my fear subside just a little. I had heard the ancient stories of course- who hadn't? About the counsels that the Abbot had with the dragons when he first came up here to build his monastery, and that the dragons had listened to him, and talked back to him in human tongue. But my father and

67

brothers had thought that they were just stories used to scare or inspire people. Not, you know, *real.*

"You… You can talk?" I said to the dragon, who chirruped at me.

Maybe I was going mad. I started to think. Maybe this was one of the reasons why the Abbot forbid any human contact with the dragons that wasn't under the strictest of monk supervision. Maybe they sent you mad, like they had an illness or something. My brother Wurgan had once eaten a bunch of wild mushrooms that had made him see things and speak to people who weren't there for two solid days. What if I had caught an illness like that?

"Char is babbling." Again, the voice that *sounded* like what I had always *thought* that Paxala would sound like, reptilian, female, warm, and humorous. And once again, the Crimson Red bumped her snout on the top of my head, a little harder this time as if in rebuke.

"So, you can talk." I looked at her, and knew that it was the truth as she regarded me with her flashing golden eyes. She blinked.

"When I want to. Not many dragons share minds."

"Sharing minds? Is that what we are doing?" I said in awe. *Can you hear all of my thoughts?* I thought, looking at the dragon's great golden eyes, but there was no flicker of response from her, no return of that warm, feminine, lizard intelligence to my own. *So, my thoughts were still my own. Or some of them are, at least.* I wondered if it was like opening a door, when Paxala chose to open it she could wander in and speak to me, but most of the time it was closed? *A window,* I corrected myself, because that felt better, more *right* somehow inside my own head. I put my hand out to touch her scales. They felt warm, and as strong as steel. It was like seeing her all again for the first time.

Paxala had just been a mewling cub – or newt, as some of the older monks called that state – when I had seen her. I had traipsed out onto the wilds behind the ridge--angry at Quartermaster Greer for treating me with such disdain and casual nonchalance just for being 'a girl'-- when I had seen something. A patch of splintered trees on the slopes below, a glitter of pale blue that shone as strong as the sky above. When I had gone to investigate, I had found the broken fragments of sky-blue egg (as large as my torso) and a baby dragon tottering on its four legs like it was walking on stilts. Already larger than a dog, and almost the size of the little ponies the monks kept. The red hatchling newt had looked at me, and bleated in a pathetic way, its legs wobbling and its eyes barely open. What could I do? I had brought it here, somewhere warm and out of the way while I sought some of the monks for help.

It was lucky I ran into Nan Barrow first, I thought with a shiver of dread at how close we had come to throwing all of this way, unknowing at the time. I had run through my usual secret path into the back of the Kitchen Gardens, and collided straight with a worried Nan Barrow, telling me I had to stay inside monastery grounds, as the monks had issued a curfew after some large dragon fight the night before.

I had told her about finding the newt, and that I needed help caring for it, and that I had to tell the monks – and she had told me not to. *"Zaxx is trying to assert his dominance in the crater, and that young hatchling isn't his,"* Nan Barrow told me. *"It's up to you to keep the creature safe for the moment, Char, at least until we know where to take it."*

Instead of going to the monks, she had said that I should go back to my studies and come back after dinner. In my absence, Nan had managed to arrange blankets and fish to be delivered to the cave behind the waterfall – and ever since then it had been our secret. That had been almost two years ago, and in that time Paxala had become a strong, young dragon, and somehow miraculously, still a secret.

"But how, Pax...?" I tried asking my friend for answers directly of this strange ability, but it seemed that dragons didn't feel the need to answer every question asked of them. She then slowly bent her head to eat the nearest hunk of ham delicately.

"But, but Paxie..."

A snort from the young dragon, and a lash of her tail that sprayed beach stone everywhere. *"Paxala, or Pax."*

"Of course, I'm so sorry," I said, feeling oddly out of my depth. I was being tutored on etiquette by a creature that I had raised from hatchling to young dragon. "But why now? Why never before? Why don't all the dragons speak?" I had so many questions to ask her, now I knew that we could talk together. Before, it had been a matter of observing her behavior, trying to gauge the best way to look after the hatching egg that I had found...

"Char saved me," the dragon said. *"And I told you my true name."*

Was that what had happened? I thought. I didn't remember

any reptilian voice suddenly popping into my head a year ago, but then again all I did remember was that one day I was looking after a baby dragon, and the next the name 'Paxala' was there and shining inside my mind. Maybe she *had* reached in and planted the name there, and I just thought that *I* had come up with it?

"Char couldn't listen. At first. And Paxala didn't know how to talk," the dragon said very pragmatically, sitting down on her haunches with a heavy, contented *whumpf* as she tore into the cured fish. *"Mhm. Fish!"* She made her rattling, contented-purr noise.

"All this time…" I shook my head in wonder. I had found the hatchling egg one day early on in my time here at the monastery. Just a few weeks after being sent here, and sick to the teeth of Quartermaster Greer's attitude towards women and the wild folk, I had stormed onto the mountainside, to be amongst the elements, and, as my mother always advised me to do - 'walk it out.' I had grown tired, and my white-hot fury diminished, but the anger remained. I reminded myself that I was here to make peace on behalf of my father, but that didn't mean that I had to take insults. I had just decided to calmly tell Quartermaster Greer of this new dedication, when I had heard a high-pitched screech, like a baby – but not a human one.

I had followed the noise to a flattened bit of forest with broken and splintered trees, where it seems that there must have been some sort of dragon skirmish. They did that occasionally, when one of the younger dragons decided that it wanted the best sunbathing spot, and Zaxx had to reassert his dominance.

But here, something different had happened. There had been blood, and broken trees – like there had been a massive fight between the creatures, and there in the center was a cracked egg, already hatched, and with Paxala tottering from it on unsteady scaled legs. She had been just a little smaller than one of the small mountain ponies that the shepherd brings up here occasionally.

So, what could I do? I did the only thing that I could–I cared for her by bringing her here, and every day bringing food, provisions, toys, what I could to try and keep the baby dragon alive.

"You did, Char. You saved me." Paxala looked at me once again with those gold and green eyes, and I felt a wave of fierce, loyal affection wash over me. Tears came to my eyes.

"So, now what?" I asked of her, but she returned back to the food that I had brought. Life was simpler for a dragon, it seemed. Even one that could share minds with a human.

A loud noise blared three times.

"The dragon pipes," I said in alarm, as Paxala sniffed at the air in the direction of the monastery. "That means that I am going to be *very* late for the first lesson of the day. Drat! I guess I know what is next for me…" I turned to look at the young Crimson Red, happily eating her stash of food that I had brought.

"I, uh, I will try to get back later, if I can."

She chirruped in answer, and continued to eat. With an astonished look, I turned and ran back the way that I had come, not stopping until I got back to the monastery itself. I was elated and I was overjoyed, but I was also a little scared, to tell the truth.

Why was I the one to hear dragons in my head? How come I

had never learned of anyone else having this ability? Why hadn't the monks ever taught us about this skill? Certainly, no monk I had seen seemed to have the kind of relationship with any of their charges that I had with Paxala. Could it be they didn't even know it was possible?

CHAPTER 8
TESTING

Our testing was to start the very next day, and it was a day that I had awoken to find a rime of frost up the green-glass windows of our dormitory room that I shared with Dorf.

"Huh!" The larger boy was shivering where he sat in his bed, unwilling to get up. "If I manage to live out the winter, it'll be a miracle!" he said through gritted teeth, and I could only agree with him, although it was clear that I was much more equipped to deal with it than he was. I crawled out of bed and set the fire, blowing on the coals and the dried wool to get the kindling to catch.

Whoosh! In just a moment the fire had roared into life, and I felt the welcome warmth wash over me as I rubbed my face and got dressed. Feeling a little better, I wandered over to crack the ice on the window and peer out at the day.

"We Lessers are supposed to live in rich grain fields on the river plains, not on the tops of mountains," Dorf grumbled, still wrapped in his blankets as he took my place at the hearth. "I don't know how you put up with it."

Another reason why those bandits that attacked me probably weren't Lessers, I thought. I had never heard of the Lessers going out raiding at all, preferring to protect their fields and flocks. "Me?" I said over my shoulder. "Never mind me – what about *her!*" I rubbed at the window so that I could see a little clearer. The lock of her platinum-white hair that had escaped from under the heavy black cloak and cowl gave Char Nefrette away immediately, as she crossed the courtyard outside, heading for one of the side doors that led out onto the mountain.

Where is she going, I wonder?

"Oh, Prince Lander's girl?" Dorf peered over my shoulder. "Oh, she's half Wildman, isn't she? She can probably dance through the snow and not care. Probably out to do weird Wildman things on the mountain," he said, causing me to frown.

That was a little unfair. People said the same kind of things about me, too. 'Off to do weird Gypsy things' and such. Dorf Lesser wasn't being mean, he just didn't know any better. *But saying something stupid doesn't mean you didn't say it* – as my father Malos would say. "Back in the Eastern Marches, I would hear my brother's saying almost the same thing about me," I said with a frown and a shrug. "That I'm half-Gypsy, so I must be able to read palms and curse people and do weird things…"

"Oh! I didn't mean…" Dorf flushed an embarrassed scarlet. "I'm sorry, Neill – I was being stupid."

"It's nothing. Already forgotten," I said with a half-smile. It was easier to forgive and forget Dorf's clumsy jokes than it was the demeaning looks and sniggers from people like my brothers, who really ought to know better.

I looked back to the courtyard, to catch a glimpse of the small door closing in the outer wall, and a flash of white and black. *Curious,* I thought.

"Hey – you like the Nefrette girl, don't you? Is that why you're mooning over her?" Dorf punched me teasingly in the shoulder.

I blushed. "No! Of course not, I'm just intrigued that's all," I said, feeling suddenly annoyed and angry with Lesser.

"Char and Neill…" He tried the words out in funny voice, pulling faces at me.

"Oh, shut up, you big oaf," I said, punching him back playfully. "Come on. Today is the first tryouts."

"Ugh. Well, I think we all already know what *you're* going to be," Dorf moaned. "Protector."

"I hope so." I was coming to the slow realization that, apart from a few people here, I was actually one of the better fighters of the students. It was something which I had never dreamed of being, given that I wasn't the biggest or quickest. *But I guess that a childhood of getting picked on by my older brothers made me learn how to fight.*

"Don't worry, Dorf, you're sure-fire Scribe material." I congratulated him, knowing that from the stack of scrolls and books that he kept by his bedside it was what he would have wanted to become. Dorf just looked at me in near alarm as we left the dormitory room.

"Scribe? Yeah, that would be great I guess – but I'm holding out for becoming a Mage!" he said, and I shrugged.

"You never know, Dorf, you could be," I said, my mind starting to churn with the orders from my father. *Find out where their magic comes from. How did the Draconis Order get so powerful? How did the dragons 'teach' them, as the Abbot had implied? Was there some other source of their power here on the mountain?* And could I get Dorf to tell me the secrets of the Order magic if he learnt it?

DAMMIT! I bit my lip to stop from cursing as I heard another set of footsteps approaching. We had the morning free to 'mentally prepare ourselves' for the rigorous testing the Quartermaster had promised would come later that day.

I had taken the opportunity to slip away from the others, and try to find out where the Library of the monastery was. Maybe it was down there that there would be heaps of scrolls detailing how the Draconis Monks summoned their magic, or teaching how to do it. I mean, they were monks, right? They *had* to have a big library....

The other students were variously either practicing their physical skills, martial training, or letters in the Great Hall, but there were more that were spread out around the monastery. Some in the stables, some finding solace in the Kitchen Gardens for their studies. It wasn't *so* unusual for me to wander the corridors of the main building, looking through doorways and down corridors.

This corridor led away from the Great Hall and was lined with wooden doors, all closed. The first few I had stood by, waiting with bated breath until I was sure that no one was coming, before taking out my small knife and trying to lift the hinge mechanism or pick the lock. So far, I had managed to open *two* – and both leading to stores of incense, barrels of wine, and musty tapestries. *Who knows what information father can use?* I thought as I pocketed a small cloth packet of incense, in case it had some special properties essential for magic, though after the second corridor of storerooms, I started to regret my decision to take the incense. I was beginning to smell distinctly floral.

I stopped at a T junction in the hallways, with steps leading up on my left, or down on my right. *Where do you keep secrets?* I thought. *Down.* That was when I heard the first set of steps as the first shape was hurrying towards me from the gloom below.

It had been one of the Draconis Monks, a smaller fellow with dark, quick eyes who had looked up at me in alarm, but had then said nothing, and walked past. After that close call, I carried on, but the next set of footsteps was following down from *behind* and above me, and I froze.

"You there. Student?" said an imperious voice, and I turned around to see a very round, very large monk with a red beard glowering down on me.

"Yuh-yes, sir?" I said. *Dammit!*

"Students aren't normally allowed down here. Have you got written permission?" he said.

I opened my mouth about to lie that I had but I might have lost it – but the monk was too wily for me. He could see that whatever I was up to, I had no bit of paper as he clicked his fingers and shook his head.

"No, no, no. This won't do at all. The Galleries are restricted, and I don't care where you left the permission or forgotten it, or it got eaten by a dragon or something. Off you go, student, and don't be so nosy next time – or I'll report you myself to Quartermaster Greer!" the red-bearded monk huffed, jerking a thumb over his shoulder and leaving me in no uncertainty as to what I had to do.

Drat. I tried to smile, but my gritted teeth wouldn't let me, as I returned the way I had come.

*Well, I know a little bit more about where the Library **isn't**,* I thought glumly, as I made my way back up to the main area of the monastery.

"YOU MIGHT HAVE HAD the morning off, little masters, but that doesn't mean for a second that I'm going to go easy on you!" Quartermaster Greer yelled, in what was becoming quite a predictable routine. He had us standing in the cavernous and frigid Great Hall, where, inexplicably, the many hearths were never lit. At one end of the hall beneath a large stone dragon's head were carved statues of people I had never heard of. The sculptures looked so life-like that they appeared almost to move if I looked at them from the corner of my eye. The Quartermaster stood at the end of the hall in his traditional black robes and with his little black book, as he organized us all according to gender.

"Now, girls can go sit down at the back of the room," Greer announced, which made me feel all the more uneasy. Although my elder brothers Rik and Rubin were cruel, arrogant and oafish in their own way – even they never thought of jobs as belonging to men or women. A job was for whomever was capable of completing the task. *'It's not about whether you wear skirts or trousers,'* my father had always said. *'It's about skills and wits.'* He had been talking about fighting and soldiering of course, but he had also applied the same logic to the advisers he listened to, or to ruling a kingdom. I had grown up learning to look at the whole population as possible allies or possible enemies, and learning not to base my assumptions on the gender someone was. My trepidation only increased when, Greer finished his thought —"because we know that it's the boys who will be protectors."

What? I couldn't believe that Greer had said that. I looked around in confusion at those around me, to see Char, Sigrid, and the other girls grumbling and shaking their heads at the slight. There were a few muffled giggles from some of the boys, and I glared in their direction to see that it was Terrence (of course) and his cohort.

"This is crazy," muttered one of the girls as she barged past me. She was older and taller than me, and had skin as dark as onyx, and I recognized her as from one of the Raider families of the southern lands, infamous for those among them who had taken to a life of pirating on fast-traveling boats along the coasts of Prince Griffith's lands. To me, the girl looked lean and toned, with hair that was braided and pulled back into a tight topknot. *I wouldn't want to fight her,* I thought, as there was a clatter at the front of the room, as the Quartermaster brought forth woven crates full of what looked like leather clothes.

"These will stop you from killing yourselves," Greer said sadly (I reckon that he would have rather that we did hurt ourselves and be forced to go home). "A hat and gloves." He displayed the items disinterestedly, before throwing them to the nearest boy. "Put them on, and we will spar in pairs. Two pairs at a time, and the rest of you go sit down at the other side of the hall."

I was glad when Terrence Aldo was chosen, along with two of his fellow second-sons and distant cousins, to be one of the first pairs of fighters. They took a moment to congratulate each other ahead of the fight as they put their leather caps and mitts on, all apart from one boy with hair that was shorn short so that he looked near bald, or ill. His bare head made him look vulnerable and his eyes even bigger and grey than they really were.

"Who's that?" I whispered to Dorf beside me. He had been here a few days more than me, and so already had the chance to get to know who most of the other students were.

"That's Maxal Ganna," Dorf whispered with a meaningful stare.

"What does that mean?" I shrugged, watching as the smaller boy was the last to collect his things.

"Son of Ganna Draconis? One of the greatest Draconis Monks of our age?" Dorf shook his head as he tried not to laugh.

"Really, Neill – what do they do out there in the Eastern Marches all day? Didn't your father teach you anything?"

I wanted to say that my father had taught his sons how to ride a horse and to swim and to plan a war, but before I could point this out, Greer slapped his short wooden cane against a stone table, signaling the bouts to begin.

Terrence Aldo was matched against Faris, one of the other southern kids. Even though Faris was clearly the larger, he went down in the first few seconds, clutching at his shins as if Terrence had broken them. We watched several more battles in which Terrence came out ahead every time, yelling "Submit! Submit!" and earning snorts of derision from the dark-skinned Raider's girl opposite us.

"Next pairs! Come on, get moving Lesser – or are you too afraid?" Greer shouted at our bench. Even the words that fell on Dorf's shoulders made him hunch, and I promised myself to try and go at least a little easier on him as we collected our leather caps and gloves.

"Okay, Torvald, prepare to face Lesser wrath," Dorf said jokingly, although I could see the whites of his eyes as he eyed my fists warily.

"*Just concentrate. Try to hit me,*" I whispered at him, even lowering my guard as Greer slapped his little cane.

Dorf swung wide, his fist nowhere near enough to connect with me. It was too ridiculously easy to dodge his wild attacks after I had brawled with my own brothers and the soldiers of their guard for years. *Guards with fur wrappings and leather straps, my* brain supplied, triggered off by the similarity of what I was doing now.

Those bandits that had attacked me. They had worn the clothes of Torvald soldiers, I thought, as Dorf managed to shove me backwards in my distraction. Seeing Dorf in action though, it seemed clear to me that there was no chance that either he or the Lessers had been the ones responsible. Dorf couldn't lie if his life depended on it, and, if the rest of the Lessers were anything like Dorf – then they couldn't fight at all!

My instincts kicked in, as I sidestepped and allowed his weight to carry him past me, as I lashed out with a foot, sending him tripping over to a loud thump on the floor. This was too easy. Too embarrassingly easy, really. *There's no honor in winning a fight against a weakling* (another of my father's great battle mottos; not that my brothers seemed to care about how much smaller I was than they as they had kicked me around the practice fields). This time Greer did not clap me, but merely gestured for me to join the victors' table and take up a cup of the honey mead, saying, "Well, if you can't even bring yourself to hit him when he was standing there as gormless as a statue, Lesser, then you are clearly no Protector."

"Sorry." I tried to whisper to Dorf, who was pushing himself up and shrugging like it was no big deal. I felt bad about beating him, even though it was in both our best interests if he ended up a Mage. And, unlike Terrence, I didn't have to mop the floor with my opponent just to prove my own skill as a warrior. Still, when I got to the table, I couldn't help but be pleased Terrence and

Archibald were eyeing me up warily. *Good*, I thought as I leveled my gaze at them. Now they know I can't be bullied. After a long moment, they both nodded, and a surge of pride went through me, mixed with something like relief. We were all a part of something now, whether I wanted to be included in his group or not.

A few more joined our ranks from the other students, but of the last bout, there was no clear winner as the boys ended up rolling around on the floor, panting in exertion as they tried to overpower each other. The bout was only stopped by Greer with a sigh.

"I've seen enough. If neither of you can clearly win a fist-fight, then I doubt that you can defend the walls of this sacred place!" he said, turning to us 'victors.' "So, five of you altogether, is there? Well, I think that is probably as good as we can expect. You will all be put forward to train as Protectors, unless any of you test exceptionally well in the other tests..." Greer spoke to us, and I could see that he had little interest in what was happening behind him, as the dark-skinned Lila Lanna stood up and calmly walked across the floor towards us.

"Quartermaster?" she said, her voice solid and unafraid. "I've been fighting since I was eleven years old, on the decks of my father's ships. I want the chance to become a Protector." She stuck her chin out defiantly.

Greer turned on his heel. "What do you think you're doing, Lanna? Who told you to get out of your seat? How dare you go against my orders?" The Quartermaster took a step forward and raised his short cane and I thought for a terrible moment that he was going to strike her. I stepped forward.

"I'll fight you, Lila," I offered. "I'm no great warrior, but if you can match me then it'll show you're just as good as any of us would-be Protectors, right?" *It was what my father would do,* I thought, before instantly realizing that wasn't why I was putting myself forward. It wasn't because of my father it was because this was the right thing to do. There was no reason that Lila didn't deserve to at least test to be a Protector – no reason at all save blind prejudice-- and if the Draconis Order was serious about protecting the dragons, then they would do better by having the best warriors—male and female--out there on watch. From what I'd seen of Lila practicing, I knew she was far more skilled than many others I saw around me.

Greer scowled at me and Lila both. "I should have known you two would be insubordinate. The Raider and the Gypsy." But he consented with a nod, before sniffing the air delicately. "All I can say, is that at least one of the pair of you has been bathing recently." I realized he must be talking about the packet of incense that I had been carrying, and had left a lingering smell of flowers in my breeches. Without another comment, he escorted us to the equipment box where he watched us put on our leather defenses. As we turned to walk to the center of the room, I could hear him mutter in a low whisper, loud enough only for us two to hear. "Not even any Three Kingdom blood between them!"

It made my steps falter with rage, but I noticed that Lila didn't bat an eyelid at this sort of treatment. Instead, she took a wide-legged stance, crouched, and grinned at me fiercely. "You're not going to win, Gypsy-boy," she hissed.

What has everyone got against me? I thought, thinking that maybe my father had been right. I couldn't trust anyone. It was just us Torvalds together against the world.

Even though it wasn't, was it, that treacherous part of me thought. Those bandits that had almost killed me had been Torvald soldiers, hadn't they? Someone had sent them after me because I was who I was, son of a warlord, half-Gypsy.

Slap! Greer brought the cane down, and already the girl was moving, spinning on her heel to turn in a pirouette and bring a backhanded fist straight towards my face.

Oh crap. She really is quick, I thought in alarm, stepping forward with both hands to block the blow, before lashing out with a foot at where hers should be – but she sprang back out the way, panting and grinning.

"You're quick," she congratulated me. "For a boy."

Oh no. I felt a moment's panic. *What if she does beat me?* I'd come to the monastery knowing this was likely my last chance to prove myself useful to my brothers. What good would it be if they could forever say I was only "second best Protector" after Lila? I had to be the best, I reminded myself. Not only did I have a reputation as a Son of Torvald (the smallest son, but son none-theless) but being the best Protector was my way to get the trainers and the monastery thinking favorably about me. My searches for information were going appallingly, and so the only skill that I could use to get some advantage had to be my skill at arms.

And Terrence and Archibald? Did I care what they thought? I hated everything those two seemed to stand for, and yet... I couldn't deny that I hadn't liked that nod of respect they'd given me. I wasn't ready to lose that. At that she leapt forward, one foot lashing up into the air in a maneuver I had never seen before, reaching head height and would have taken my head off had I not dived to one side, rolled, and bounced up again from the floor. She was on me already, and I managed to jab out twice at her, fighting for real, not pulling my blows like I had with Dorf. She grunted in pain as one of my punches connected.

In return, she jumped forward, delivering a knee to my chest that winded me and doubled me over, and then a kick to my backside that sprawled me onto the floor.

"Oof!" I gasped, waving a hand. "Submit?" I said weakly, and Greer gave a slow clap to Lila Lanna.

"Congratulations, Raider." He chose his words with bile. "Although just how well you do in the tests to come up against some honest Three Kingdom boys we will just have to see."

I could have growled at the man, I felt so hurt and shamed by his insults. But I bit my tongue and nodded at Lila. *I have to remember what I'm here to do. If I go picking fights with the instructors all the time, I'll never get to the bottom of the Order.*

For all of his sarcasm and sneers, the Quartermaster still allowed Lila to walk up to our victors table (me, limping behind) and I watched as she took the last cup of honey mead, and downed the lot in one gulp.

"What about us?" I heard another voice say from the girl's side of the room. It was Char, standing up and frowning, joined by none other than our ally and fellow Warden's kid, Sigrid.

"Enough." Greer clapped his hands to silence us. "Enough insubordination for one day. There are other tests to take, and there is lunch to help prepare and general to perform." There was a collected groan from us students, and the Quartermaster smacked the table with the cane with every sentence, but Char and Sigrid wouldn't sit down. I thought Greer was going to explode with fury, as he waved his little black book above our heads. "No time for any more tryouts for the Protector training – you have lunch, and *tomorrow* there will be Scribe and Mage testing. If any of you girls do so terribly at those that you cannot be anything else, then I *may* consider letting you try again to be a Protector."

"Outrageous," I heard Char say, folding her arms over her chest, and a couple of the other girls followed suit, but the Quartermaster wouldn't listen as he pointed the way to the kitchens.

"Well done," I said to Lila as we filed out of the hall. I was still bruised from her attacks.

"I don't need your congratulations or your help, Gypsy." Lila said brusquely, leaving me feeling stupid and clumsy. *What had I said?* Instead, I let the group pass me by as I sought out Dorf. I couldn't see him and the awful thought occurred to me that maybe he was avoiding me, or worse yet, resented me for winning the bout against him.

It seems that I can't do anything without getting it wrong and upsetting someone, I thought miserably, as I followed the others behind.

"Cheer up, Torvald," said a voice, and I turned to see that Char had fallen to the back of the queue ahead of me. "You're only a half-Gypsy. At least you could be a half-Wildman girl in a monastery that hates women *and* Wildman."

At that, she turned as soon as we left the hall and went the opposite way, not towards the kitchens but towards the storerooms instead, and I had the sensation that she too, had just scolded me.

Why was it every time I tried to be nice to someone, they threw it back in my face? I thought miserably. Somehow, after seeing the dragons, I had felt a glimmer of hope that here at the monastery could be different. That I could easily ace the Protector test and thus get actually closer to the dragons themselves. That maybe, after the tests all the instructors and students would regard me as one of them. And once I truly belonged, surely I could find out more about the Order, maybe even enlist others to help me, like Dorf surely could, if he became a Mage. *And that Char girl – she said she was a Scribe. She could help me get access to the Library which I was being so terrible at locating.* Now, though, it seemed there was a whole lot more to making friends than just saying the right things.

I had to find a different way to get to the Order's secrets.

CHAPTER 9
BOOKS AND DRIED APPLES

W hen I woke in the early dawn and saw Dorf pulling his robe about his shoulders and heading for the door, I was sure that Dorf was avoiding me. We hadn't spoken since the testing the day before, which was pretty difficult, given the fact that we both shared a room. I tried once again to apologize to him for yesterday. "Dorf, I didn't mean to embarrass you in the Protector tryouts—" But it was no good.

"Don't worry, Torvald. You're a Protector, you were always going to be a fighter after all," Dorf said as he pulled open the door.

"You're heading out this early?" I said, trying to hide my dismay. I had been hoping to make sure that Dorf understood that I was not his enemy. But after that first day of brawling, Dorf had made sure that he took his chores with Maxal Ganna, the monk's boy, and not with me. When it came time for dinner and bed,

Dorf stayed talking with Maxal for as long as possible, before returning to our dorm room and throwing himself into bed without a word. And now, here he was, trying to sneak out before I'd even gotten out of bed.

"Maxal has some interesting books from the Order that his father lent him. I'm going to ask to take a look before our Scribe testing," Dorf said with a sad smile. I could see that he had no intention of losing at *that* test at all, and neither was he going to share his advantage with me.

"Oh well, good luck then," I said, feeling a bit put out as Dorf left. I'd thought he was my friend. Father was right, I shouldn't trust anyone here. But maybe this was an opportunity for me to do some of my own extracurricular studies as well, and so I grabbed my cloak, my small dagger for lifting locks, and my coin purse (either for bribing a monk or hiding scraps of paper inside).

I'll find the secret of the Draconis Order and take that knowledge back for the glory of Torvald, but I couldn't shake the glum feeling as I trudged out the door.

OUT IN THE HALL, I hurried past wooden doors where I could hear the occasional yawn, laughter, and raised voice, as I went down the stairs. I didn't want anyone to see where I was headed, but as I pushed open the door leading to the central courtyard, I saw I needn't have worried. Everywhere—the courtyard, the

Great Hall, the stable and storehouses—looked deserted. I turned toward my destination-- the tower with the strange brass mirrors and dishes hanging from its open windows, already starting to burn red and pink from the first rays of the dawn.

Thuddud. A noise drew my eye away from the strange tower, however, to the door to the girl's dormitory tower, straight across the courtyard. It was open, and a figure in a heavy black robe stepped out.

Immediately I ducked back into the open doorway behind me, letting the shadows cover me. The figure hesitated, looking around as if she (for it must be a girl coming from the girl's dormitory, mustn't it?) had seen me move, and I saw a flash of platinum-white hair and pale skin. Char. What are you doing out at this time of the morning? I wondered, watching as she took a nervous step forward, peering around her, and then hurrying under the walls to the same door near the storehouses that she had used before.

She's hiding something, I thought, and, like the good son that I was, I set out to find out what it was. *It might be something that will help the clan, and she is a Scribe, after all... Perhaps she has more access to the scrolls and libraries than I do?*

I waited until her black cloak had disappeared through the small wooden door set amongst stacks of barrels and bales of hay and I followed, slipping on the ice of the stone slabs as I jogged over, panting heavily before ducking behind a bale as one of the monk Protectors above walked across the top of the wall. Once he'd passed, I slunk through the doorway, into a green world.

I was in the Kitchen Gardens. They backed onto the store-rooms, and were filled with large planter boxes overflowing with every manner of vegetable and plant, growing in unruly profusion. *But where was Char?* I was just about to give up finding her and chalk her sneaking up to the girl stealing food, when suddenly other voices filled the garden, and I had to crouch behind a tall stand of purple kale.

"Now you see that she gets two of these joints a day, you hear me?" a familiar voice said. It was Nan Barrow, the woman who had been kind to me on my first day, and mistress of the kitchens.

"I will, ma'am, and thank you, it means so much," Char whispered.

"And fruit as well, mind. Here, take some of those store apples – they're not good for much other than pie anyway," Nan said brusquely. "Normally she'd be able to forage and hunt for food, but seeing as…"

"I know," Char said, a touch of that more familiar defiance that I was used to hearing from her. "But don't worry, it won't be long now."

"Long now before what, I wonder though!" Nan sighed heavily. "Actually, I *don't* want to know. It's better that I don't. Now get away with you – I can delay breakfast by a little while perhaps, but you'll have to be back by then or the Quartermaster will know. He notices everything with that little black book of his!"

Char groaned. "That man is a tyrant."

"*Och*, shush with you, and mind who you say such things too as well," Nan scolded. "He's not the nicest man, but he's not the worst here by a long way. Now get, before I land myself into trouble as well."

I peered out from behind the fronds of purple to see Char clutching a hessian sack to her chest, and taking her leave. The Kitchen Mistress watched her go through a door that I hadn't seen before, hidden as it was under a large spray of trellised tomatoes growing up against the wall. As soon as Char was gone, the woman shook her head, muttering, "That girl will be the doom of me, I swear," before stomping back into the kitchens. I waited for a count of ten before carefully creeping out of my hiding place and towards the tomato-door.

So, Char was stealing food from the kitchens, that much was sure. Although it probably couldn't be classified as stealing if the Kitchen Mistress was also in on it. It had sounded like she was taking the food to somebody, somebody who needed fruit and meat, I mused. But just who could she be feeding? And why?

I was about to push aside the trellis and reach for the door handle myself to find out, when I heard a noise coming from behind me. *Damn! Out of time!* I turned toward the kale, only to find it was too far away.

"Ooh!" one of the serving girls said, startled from where I was lurking by the winter potatoes.

"Ah, sorry, I uh…"

"Nan!" the girl shouted, looking cross. "We got one of the students in 'ere trying to pilfer some food again!"

"No, really, I was just passing through…" I tried to explain, but Nan's large white apron was already flashing through the doorway to the bustling kitchens beyond.

"Torvald? I should have known it would be you sneaking around," she said loudly and fiercely, adding to the girl, "go back inside Elsa, I'll deal with this one." The girl flung me an annoyed look before bobbing a curtsey to the Kitchen Mistress, and heading back inside.

"I wasn't stealing food, honestly," I said emphatically to the woman, but she just tutted and pointed back the way I had come.

"I'm sure you weren't, Torvald," she said with a smirk. "But you'd still do well to mind your own business, and let others mind theirs!"

What does that mean? Does she know I was following Char?

"The monastery can be more dangerous than it looks, Torvald," she said, echoing almost exactly the same words that Jodreth the monk had said to me what seemed like ages ago. She halted at the main courtyard door as I was turned out, saying in almost the same whisper that she had used with Char. "All of you students are testing out for Mages, Scribes, and Protectors today, aren't you? Have you ever wondered how many Mages have we ended up graduating from the Order? One? Any at all?" And with that, she shut the door to the Kitchen Gardens in my face before I could ask her what she meant.

But that was what all of this was about, wasn't it? I thought, remembering what the Abbot Ansall had told us. That the Draconis Monastery trained Protectors, Scribes, and Mages. Was Nan trying to tell me that it had only succeeded once so far?

The first bells for breakfast started to chime, and I realized that I was out of time. I would have to visit the Abbot's Tower another time. I might be able to go later. Or I could find out what that Nefrette girl was up to. *All information is good information,* as my father might say – and speaking of information, and of Char – could I use the fact that I saw her sneaking around to ask her to give me access to the Library? She was a Scribe, right? So, she had to know where they kept the juiciest information.

But my stomach turned over, and I knew that it felt bad – using the Nefrette girl like that. It was something that my brothers would do without a second's thought... But she had been one of the few people (along with Dorf) who had seemed to not care that I was a half-Gypsy. With my heart in turmoil, I hurried to the breakfast hall, although I didn't feel hungry at all.

THE REST of the day was given over to the more esoteric of tests; scribing lessons. It turned out that although I could read as well as any, I was terrible at learning languages.

"Ugh." I groaned, having to prop myself up once more on my elbows to keep my head from drooping into slumber.

"Come on, Torvald," Terrence whispered with a sneer beside me. "Or do the Gypsies not bother with reading?"

I found my jaw tightening and my fists clenching as I turned, only for the table to reverberate with the sharp slap of the Quartermaster's cane.

"Concentrate, Torvald!" he shouted, making me flinch.

"Yes, sir." I ducked my head back to the book, trying to translate and transcribe one set of words written in the Old Delian Age tongue to the different languages of North Wildman, Southern Raider Tongue, March Dialect.... It made my head whirl.

What made it all worse was that I was forced to sit at the same table as the other 'victors' of the Protector match at the front of the class (why, I had no idea, because being good at fighting was nothing to do with being good at scribing). But it was something that the Quartermaster insisted, and so I found myself squeezed at the end of a table that housed Terrence, Archibald, Lila and a few other of the boys. Lila frowned at the word list herself, and ignored all of us boys as she worked.

I wish I had the same dedication, I thought glumly, as I heard a stool scraping further behind us.

"Sir?" It was Dorf's voice, and I turned with a broad grin to see him standing up from his seat, holding his pen in the air. "I've finished, sir," he said.

"What? Already, Lesser? Are you sure that you did the second exercises as well?" The Quartermaster marched to where Dorf sat, while Dorf, to his credit, said nothing as Quartermaster picked up his collection of papers and worked through them one at a time.

"Simple verbs." Greer nodded. "Double-clauses, tenses..."

"And I've included the Western Islander dialect variants, sir, at the back," Dorf pointed.

The Quartermaster flinched as if poked, before raising his eyebrows. "Well, master Lesser, it seems that we have found something that you are finally good at after all. Here, to the

Scribe's table." He pointed to a bare table with a flagon of honey mead and a number of glasses.

The second to join him was, *not* surprisingly, Sigrid Fenn, and I managed to give her a grin and a thumb's up as she took her place at the table. She smiled momentarily, as if pleased that her skills had been recognized at least. *Good for you,* I thought, having to admit that not only was I glad that I had more friends with access to the Library, but also that I was glad for her as well. The Quartermaster seemed so intent on putting the women down, that it was good to see them succeeding. Greer had forced both Sigrid and Char to go through the testing procedure again, as 'there were so many other students here now.' I took it as another pointless cruelty on the part of Greer against the girls of the class.

Maybe I could ask Char and Sigrid about the secrets they might be uncovering about the Order, if I can't ask Dorf. Then came Maxal Ganna, after which Greer clapped his hands that we were done, and the rest would be decided on how many we had gotten right, and how many mistakes that we might have made. Char did well, as did Terrence, but both of them had a few blotches on their copybooks and words which they had spelled or translated wrong. Lila did surprisingly better, which actually made her look alarmed, I assumed because she feared she was closer to being chosen for the Scribe's table rather than staying with us Protectors.

"And you, Torvald? What is this mess on a page – it looks like a drunk spider has crawled across it and had a heart attack," the Quartermaster berated me in front of the whole class. I felt small and ashamed of my work. There were other students here who had more wrong answers than me, but my copy work and penmanship was truly awful, even to my own eyes. Dorf's, on the other hand, was clear and even had flowing curlicues and swirls to emphasize the capitals and the pauses. The ink didn't seem to want to obey my quill the way that it had with the others, and I couldn't stop the end of the feather from making me sneeze as I leaned too close to the page. Of course, father had raised his sons to be fighters, after all – even if that meant I only knew my way around a brawl. He made sure that we could read and write battle reports, but not much else.

So I was not to be a Scribe, and my friend Dorf was. I was glad for him, and told him so.

"You did well, congratulations." I gave him a pat on the back.

"Yes, I did, didn't I?" Dorf grinned, as the dinner gong rang and I gratefully slid from my seat. It seemed that his success had eased the feelings of hurt between us a little as it had boosted his confidence.

"Well, all I can say is thank the stones that is over." I laughed to myself, but the laugh died in my throat when the Quarter-master barked, "Light dinners tonight, students!"

It seemed that our trials were very far from over indeed, I thought as he continued, "Because your lessons will not be ending so soon today. Tonight, his holiness the Abbot himself will be taking you out to the mountain for your first exercise and selection for magic." He caused an excited whisper to spread through the room. "If any of you are remarkable enough to show great ability at magic – despite how you have placed in other groups before – then you will be forwarded to the Mage training immediately. But I don't want you falling asleep or acting up for his holiness tonight – if I find out that any of you have failed him and me in any way, then it'll be mucking out the stables from here to midsummer," he warned, his eyes sweeping the room and alighting on me with what seemed a particular zeal.

CHAPTER 10
CANDLES, ROCKS AND STONES

The Abbot came for us just after dinner, drifting into the Banqueting Hall as quiet as a ghost, and making the hairs stand up on the back of my neck. There was something that I didn't like about the man, but it was an instinct that I couldn't put my finger on. Was I just spooked by this place, and that man? The few times that my brother Rubin was ever cordial to me, he would talk about 'the warrior's sense' of being able to know when someone was tracking you in the wilds, or when an opponent tipped over from sizing you up to getting ready to strike. At the time, I dismissed it as my brother pretending to be wiser, smarter, and tougher than he really was. But now I wasn't so sure. *My nerves are a jangle, that must be it,* I told myself as I put down the cup of clear mountain water I had been drinking and looked around, over the heads of the other arguing and laughing students. To my surprise I found both Char and Maxal doing the same. Our eyes connected briefly, but I could not read what the other two were thinking, before the Abbot cleared his throat.

"Students," he said gently, in a tone that nonetheless sent chills through my chest. For some reason, I found myself wondering if he knew what I was up to, why I was here. I suddenly felt like an imposter. "Tonight," he continued and he didn't have to tell us to be still or be quiet, the imperative filled us up of its own accord. We *all* stopped eating, drinking, and making merry, and turned to see the black-clad, austere man standing in the corner of the room, with his finely made black cane. "I will begin teaching you magic—magic no one else in all of the Three Kingdoms can do. Dragon-magic."

And I would take that secret back to Father, I thought. At that instant, I felt a flush of cold as the Abbot's eyes sought me out, and both Char and Maxal flinched as they too, were noticed by his holiness. Or maybe I was just imagining it. It felt like the time when my father had taken me to stand on the edge of a hill to look down on a battle of clan troops against our foes. It was terrible and too large to all take in at once. But why would the Abbot seek me out? I wondered. Could it be that the prickling feeling I got whenever he looked at me meant something greater, meant that the Abbot recognized—not that I might be a traitor— but something else? Could it be that I, Neill Torvald, really did have a touch of magic in me after all? The sudden hope filled my heart, but it wasn't because of what learning magic might mean for the mission my father had sent me on. It was because of what possessing magic might mean for me. What would it be like to have something which was my own, that brought me closer to the dragons and called upon the strength of the Gypsy blood that coursed my veins? What would I give to have a power that had nothing to do with wars or politics or anyone else? But then the likelihood of it came crashing down on me. Of course, I didn't have dragon magic. Why should I? There had been no sign of me possessing magical tendencies even once in my life.

"Come with me," the Abbot said simply, turning to walk out of the room. I could see fear and apprehension in the faces of my peers as they looked at the retreating back of the Abbot's thin form, moving as silent as a ghost. It felt solemn, like a funeral, but followed him we did.

OUR FEET CLATTERED on the stones of the Great House, as he led us deeper into the building than we had been before, via a route that I had not seen. We walked past tapestries of the queen and of dragons, threaded in many different styles. I tried to keep my eyes peeled for signs of the source of the Order's magic. Was it woven through the stories the tapestries told? Were the secrets kept in these back corridors? Was it in these rooms that they kept their magical documents, the ones that allowed them to supposedly manipulate mountains and summon storms?

"Here, take one of each," the Abbot said to the leading student, handing the boy a black cloak and white candle. "Light it and walk through the door." He pointed to the sconce set over a small wooden door with black iron bands, and the boy, pale and shivering, did as he was told. The Abbot stood to hand the black cloak and a white candle to every student that passed by, watching us as we filed through the door one by one. I had no idea what was on the other side, and half-expected there to be another Great Hall like the other one. When it came to my turn, I once again felt that wash of cold that seemingly came from nowhere as his eyes bored into mine, and the Abbot pressed the black cloak into one of my hands, the white candle into the other.

"They say that the Gypsies of distant Shaar have magic running through their blood," the Abbot said to me, as if he'd been reading my mind. "I wonder if it is true." The Abbot gave a half-smile that I sensed wasn't entirely generous or kind. I shivered again, my heart filled with that trembling feeling that could be hope or fear. I knew what the people said in the marketplaces at home, that Gypsies could read palms and tea leaves, and that we could put curses on people with one eye closed. Maybe I could too, with someone to teach me.

It would be nice, wouldn't it...to be magical? Maybe then I would be something special. Something worthy of my father's respect, and my brothers' too, once Father was gone. Maybe then there would be a purpose for all the hours I'd spent daydreaming about dragons. My fingers fumbled as I slipped on the cloak, lighting the candle and following the others outside.

It was not as bad as I had thought, to find myself on the bare escarpment of Mount Hammal, with a line of candles weaving up ahead of me, as if they were climbing into the very skies above, I had imagined the training to be like the Protector training somehow. Fighting, shoving, having to think on my feet – or otherwise like the Scribe training, long, boring and tedious. Even though it was eerie being out here on the mountain, I also found it oddly nourishing to be outside and under the stars.

I fell into line with the others, the night so dark that I could barely see my feet below me, though the cold permeated through my legs and through the thin fabric of my cloak. The circle of candlelight extended to my colleague's jet-black cloak ahead of me, and to the sides of the rocky path that we trod upwards and upwards. For a moment, I experienced a sudden feeling of dizziness and vertigo, as I tried to make sense of the lights and sounds all around us.

Somewhere to our left and below us the ground shook with heavy, almost rhythmic vibrations and I wondered if I was listening to the sound of one of the dragons clawing its way out of the crater. I was glad for a moment that I couldn't see the edge of the crater that had to be very near to us, as we could hear the heavy roars and breathy whistles of snoring dragons somewhere very close.

I stumbled over rocks and my legs started to ache with the constant climbing, but after a while the sounds of the sleeping dragons nearby faded, to be replaced with the low but insistent *whoosh* of the mountain wind. Our candles spluttered and threatened to go out, but not one of them did. *Maybe this is our first taste of a bit of magic.*

"Students," the Abbot's sonorous voice called through the murk. He had somehow managed to get ahead of us, although the path had not been any wider than from one corner tip of my cloak to the other. I heard Lila gasp and say something under her breath in her own native tongue, but I was not so easily impressed.

"There might be other paths up the mountain," I whispered to Lila Lanna, who nodded, her eyes still wide and round.

"You all will have heard about the strange powers of our sacred Order, and that is probably why, in the end, your parents sent you here to learn from us," Abbot Ansall said. His blunt and simple honesty made the situation even more eerie, somehow.

"Your fathers and mothers will have thought that you can be trained up in magic, and then you will be sent home to further whatever petty feud or rivalry they have," the Abbot sounded weary, "and they would be wrong."

What? I thought in alarm. But that is precisely what I had to do—return home to help my father and our lands, using the magic if I could to protect Torvald from all threats. What did the Abbot want us to do? What if we weren't here to study magic at all? Or what if I couldn't learn it?

I heard a gasp from someone in the crowd, which I guessed had to be Terrence. His father was a prince, after all, and, aside from Char, he had the most reason to use the Draconis Order to further his father Prince Griffith's claim to the throne of the entire Three Kingdoms. It was exactly as my father had always said— *Many rivers can come together to break a bridge, but further down, they'll just be streams* - even those we allied with had their own ends to pursue, and at some point, our interests, even with our closest friends, would diverge.

But if alliance-making or breaking was on the Abbot's mind, he showed no sign of concern as he glossed over the interruption.

"Not all of you will be able to learn magic. In fact, hardly *any* of you will be able to learn it," he said sadly. "And of those who do, even fewer might be able to truly master it in the way the rest of the Mages of the Draconis Order have."

'How many Mages have been trained?' I remembered Nan Barrow's rhetorical question from earlier.

"But *some* of you will, and those will be the ones who will be able to usher in the new Dragon Age with us," the Abbot said gloriously, as a figure stepped forward from the darkness to his side.

It was not someone that I recognized at all, nor had I seen this person before, but I heard a few muttered gasps from the assembled crowd of students. Some people recognized the tall, thin young man with the midnight hair, save for one lock of silver from brow to braid. He also wore a black cloak, but beneath it was a deep plum-colored jerkin and trousers with deep umbral blue edging. He was no Draconis Monk, that much was clear, for his clothes were of a fine craftsmanship which far outshone anything that even Abbot Ansall was wearing.

He also had a thin silver circlet around his forehead, with a single red gem contained within.

"On your knees before your ruler, students; Prince Vincent of the Three Kingdoms!" The Abbot ducked his head, and swept a hand to all of us assembled students who, like a wave, knelt down at his command. My knees hurt as the hard and cold stones of the mountain bit into them, and I saw other students wincing similarly. We were in the presence of one of the three princes, this one the ruler of the Middle Kingdom itself. It was no secret that his ambition, like each of his brothers', was to unite all Three Kingdoms under just one ruler--himself. I looked over to where Terrence was kneeling near the front, and saw his jaw clench in anger. He was the son of Prince Griffith—making Vincent his uncle—and there was clearly no love lost in that family.

"What nerve!" whispered a voice at my side, and I turned to see that the black-cloaked student next to me, and peering out from her own hood was none other than Char, daughter of Prince Lander. "The Draconis Order is supposed to be about equality and peace for all of our realms, not just the Middle Kingdom!" she hissed to me, but I did not know what to say in response. I felt torn in my loyalties.

Father always said that Vincent was a self-righteous fool, but so were all of the princes – but aren't we Torvalds sworn to the Middle Kingdom? Don't we owe this man our fealty?

Maybe this meant that the Middle Kingdom was now safe, and that I could send word to my father that all was well, that the Draconis Order was supporting the prince, and so Father didn't have to worry so much about the Order's loyalties?

But Father had never trusted the dragon monks, and certainly never trusted the prince either! My mind kept returning to that point. My father had always told me that the prince would not keep the kingdom safe, and that it was our job to do so. But safe from what? From who? It could only mean one thing—my father didn't want Vincent on the throne. He wanted the secret of the Draconis Order to keep the realm safe *from* Prince Vincent.

I reeled at the revelation, panic making my heart race. I felt truly that I was now in hostile territory, and that Prince Vincent was my – or at least my father's – enemy. But I was not the only one who might consider Prince Vincent a foe. I looked over to the others whom I knew might find it similarly excruciating to bow before a man who they did *not* want to see rule over them, and indeed Char and Terrence – even Lila– all wore expressions of horror.

"Thank you for inviting me here to your demonstration, your holiness." Prince Vincent's words swam and eddied over us. "I trust that these new recruits have been applying themselves well and bravely in the service of the great Order?" He had the same sort of Middle regions accent as Dorf, although far more cultured and posh. The warrior-gypsy in me bridled at staying on one knee before him (or anyone).

"Of course, your highness," the Abbot said. "Now, students, look to the East!"

We all did so, our heads moving the way a flock of birds turn in mid-flight, back the way we had come, back towards the Draconis Monastery, and what we saw almost stopped the heart in my chest.

OUT OF THE darkness there flew a boulder, a rough granite block that was larger than any of us standing, and about the size of a cart. It swung across our view from the east further up the mountain of its own accord, and we heard no rumbling or crashing or grinding as the slab disappeared into the gloom.

What? But how? I had heard of the powers of the Draconis Order of course – everyone had! But I had never believed those stories until now. There were tales that the monks had helped build Queen Delia's old castle – that they had 'summoned the stones of the earth' (or so the old tales said) to create it. Or there were the everyday folktales told in every town square – that a Draconis Monk could tell if you were lying just by looking into your eyes, or that a monk could command you with the power of their mind, could command the heavens and summon lightning from the skies. So far, before tonight the only evidence that I had seen that the monks could do *anything* was the small ball of flame that the Abbot himself had conjured on my first day.

Until now.

"And there, students!" The Abbot pointed in the other direction, to the West, where a man appeared to walk above our heads. But it was no flesh and blood man, it was a statue of a man wearing a suit of armor, carved to appear lifelike, and even more so in the fact that we could see its knee joint opening, its legstone moving in perfect concert, its shoulder cracking, its arms swaying and moving in rhythm to the fast-paced march. If I could not see the separate sections of the statue aggregate and open apart as it marched straight over our heads (in thin air!) I would have been convinced that it was a person, not a statue. It too, strode into the darkness, and I felt a cold shiver in my heart.

I have to tell father of this. If the Draconis Order can animate the very stones, then what chance do any other warlords have against them, if they choose to side with an enemy clan??

All around me were round eyes and white faces, (although I

could see Terrence gritting his teeth and shaking his head). He must think that it was all trickery and charlatanry, I suppose, although I couldn't see how it could be.

"Well done, Abbot, very impressive," Prince Vincent clapped. "With you at my side, we will have the new fortifications and watchtowers built by magic!" He laughed in surprise.

"The Draconis Order remains in service to the Three Kingdoms," the Abbot said, which, although I knew was technically true, I noted that Vincent's brothers had not been invited to this display of magical might.

"They are showing off. Making a point," Char hissed at my side.

"Why?" I whispered back.

"Think about it, Torvald: they have all of the most important children and youths here from across the Three Kingdoms. The Abbot and the prince are telling us that they are the ones in charge from now on," Char muttered darkly, but before I could agree with her, the Abbot was talking to us again.

"Students! Now that you have seen some of what a true Mage can do, it is time to begin your first test – all of you, raise your candles," the Abbot ordered, and we did so. A forest of light appeared above our heads, and I was still amazed that none of the candles had blown out. Was it some special tallow or wax that they were made from, I wondered?

"The first step along the Draconis path is to learn how to control and center your mind. I want all of you to close your eyes, and imagine that candle flame above your head. See it clearly in your mind!" the Abbot said, and I did so, feeling stupid and cold, but able to visualize the flickering candle flame as it had stood atop the candle that I had so recently held.

"Hold that candle flame, students. Hold it in your mind until there is nothing else at all," the Abbot said, and I tried to do so, although my body shivered and my knee ached. The moment stretched long, and after a while my breath slowed, and my mind calmed until all that existed was the bright imaginary spark.

"Good, good. No fidgeting, Lesser!" I heard the Abbot say, his voice swimming towards me as if from very far away. The sudden interruption made me remember my aching knees, and the cold seeping through my clothes from the mountain below. "Now, I want you all to take that candle flame in your mind, and seek to put it out. To make it *not exist*, as if it never had done. Just darkness. Total, complete, darkness."

I tried. I really did, but the problem was that once I had started thinking about something being there, it was really hard to *not* think about it. I could imagine the candle flame puffing out suddenly, but it felt weak somehow, like I was replaying the same memory again and again: *Lit, Out; Flame, No flame.* It didn't *feel* like I was doing magic.

This is hopeless, I thought, opening my eyes just a little to try and see what was happening around me. All of us students were still kneeling on the floor, with one arm achingly in the air above us, and still all of the stubborn candles alight. Apart from Maxal's, I saw.

Whoosh! There was a sudden palpable shudder in the air that made the hair on the back of my neck shiver just like it had earlier when the Abbot had walked into the room unannounced. I turned my head a fraction as light spilled over me, and I saw that Char beside me was no longer holding a lit candle. Instead, she appeared to be holding a torch with flames that leapt upwards into the sky several feet above everyone else's.

"Sheesh!" I jumped at the sudden display of power from the girl, and my gasp caused other students to startle and open their eyes in panic. Char's flame went out as soon as she opened her eyes, leaving only me and a few others who had seen what she had unwittingly done.

"What?" Char said as I stared at her in awe. "What did I do? Did the light go out?" she asked hopefully, but before I could answer there was a feeling like a claw as a freezing cold hand seized the back of my neck.

"Torvald, I see." It was the Abbot, hauling me out of the pack of students. "You interrupted my lesson," he said simply. He wasn't angry, it wasn't an accusation, just a statement of fact as he brought me to the front of the group, with Prince Vincent looking at me with a curious half-smile on his face.

"Are you going to punish him, your holiness?" the prince said and I could see a gleam of enjoyment in his eyes.

"I, I'm, sorry, Abbot—sir." I managed to say, as I kneeled on the floor before them both. It shocked me when the prince stepped forward and addressed me personally.

"You should address the good Abbot Ansall as *his holiness,* do you understand?" He laughed. "Did I hear right when his holiness called you Torvald? You're Malos's youngest get, aren't you? The one that Malos got from his Gypsy-woman? They say she hooked him with her lucky magic charms!"

I opened and closed my mouth in shock. Even amongst the guards and the soldiers of the practice yard never had anyone been so rude to me before. For a moment, I felt that righteous anger welling up in my chest. *I am still a Son of Torvald. We are warriors. We keep the entire eastern half of your kingdom safe, you pompous idiot!* But the words died before they got to my lips as I looked at the prince's cruel eyes. He wouldn't even think twice about ordering me thrown in the jail, or of levying higher taxes against my father's land. The thought of being a failure here, and of having to be rescued by good people for my stupidity stopped me from saying anything that I might want to. Instead, I looked down at the floor, feeling shamed. "I, I guess so, your highness," I managed to say.

"He *guesses*," Prince Vincent sneered, and then whispered to the Abbot, "Well, I would have thought that any from Gypsy stock would take to magic like a fish to water, but apparently not, eh, your holiness?"

"The magic comes out in different ways for different people, your highness," the Abbot said at our side, once again in that neutral, non-judgemental way. "But it is clear who the *real* star in our midst is," the Abbot said, raising his voice and his hand as I knelt before them both.

Char. The Abbot and the prince must have seen what I had.

"Maxal Ganna!" the Abbot announced. "Come forward, boy, and aren't I pleased to see the Son of Ganna prove so useful to the Order as his father has been."

The shaved head and owlish-looking Maxal stepped out of

the crowd and started to kneel down beside me, but the Abbot stopped him.

"Do not kneel, Maxal. You are not like Torvald here, you are a victor. A Mage." The Abbot congratulated him, and he even earned a slightly inclined head from Prince Vincent himself.

"Here, Ganna." The prince took off one of the small golden rings from his own right hand, and set it on the boy's palm. It was too big for Maxal, but I could see the boy was too afraid to do anything but hold his hand there in shocked awe.

"Th- thank you, your highness, your holiness," Maxal's voice, a high-pitched, almost girl-like tone said.

"The throne remembers those who serve it well, as I am sure the Gannas have and will for generation to come," the prince purred at him.

"Yes, your highness," Maxal said, not out of apparent love or fealty but, I thought, fear.

"That is enough for tonight, students. You have shown the prince what you are made of, and you have some new tales of splendor and power to tell your loved ones," the Abbot said, this time genially. "You may return to the monastery, where you will return to your normal duties tomorrow morning." Behind me the students started to shuffle and stand up from their protesting and aching knees. I was about to do the same but the prince interrupted me.

"Your holiness? The Torvald boy *did* disrupt your lesson, and should be punished, I feel," he said, almost as an afterthought. "Have him stay out here for the night, kneeling in that spot so he has time to think about the perils of disobeying his superiors."

Really? What? I felt a surge of Torvald anger, and would have stood up there and then and denounced him, did I not remember what father had advised me: Trust no one. Keep to yourself. Keep yourself unseen. I couldn't pick a fight with the Prince of the Middle Kingdom, and launch my clan into war. I had already let them down too much this night. I had failed to make the torchlight move. I had failed to become a Mage of the Order, and privy to the innermost secrets of the Order's magic.

I hung my head in shame – not at disrupting the Abbot's lesson, but at not being a better son to my father, and worthy Torvald heir. *He had sent me here on a mission, and I am already failing at it.*

"As you wish, my prince," the Abbot said, pausing for a moment to regard me with a steady stare. He flicked his fingers like he was flicking away dust and grime, indicating that the matter of me was out of his hands now, and that there was nothing that he could do about it. A piece of my heart hardened against him. *What was that you told me about unwanted children having to be strong?* I thought insolently. He had never said that we had to be strong *together* though, in the way that Dorf, Sigrid, and Char had.

I tried to ignore my creaking knees and shivering body as the rest of them returned to the life and light of the Draconis Monastery, leaving me alone in the cold, dragon-haunted dark. I nodded, very slowly, making sure that the Abbot saw me do it. I would kneel out here on the top of Mount Hammal, all night if I had to, and afterwards I would be strong. I may have failed to become a Mage, but now I was sure that I knew what my father *really* wanted of me. He wanted me not to just *understand* the secret source of the Draconis Order, he wanted me to *steal* it, so that we Torvalds could use it to topple Prince Vincent.

Even though the prospect of such an undertaking was huge – both stealing the source of their magic, and helping to dethrone the prince – I felt a curious sort of peace settle onto my heart. Tomorrow I would start by finally getting up into the Abbot's own tower, and seeing what I could take.

CHAPTER 11
THE WORRIES OF CHAR NEFRETTE

I t was just no use – I couldn't sleep. After everything that I had seen on the mountaintop, there was no way that my brain was going to settle down enough to catch the sleep I needed. I felt like a lightning bolt, buzzing and flashing.

"Char?" Sigrid murmured, rubbing her eyes blearily from where she sat up in her bed. It was still dark, hours and hours before dawn, but I had been unable to sleep ever since we had made our way back from the Abbot's first lesson in 'dragon magic.'

Dragon magic? Huh! I thought in annoyance. Just what did anything that we were shown have to do with dragons? Not that it wasn't impressive, of course, in its own way. But when I thought of the natural grace, speed, and strength of the growing Paxala, then *that*, to me, seemed the real magic. Not an old man's conjuring tricks in the night.

"Char? What's got into you? Are you getting up to talk to

snow or whatever?" Sigrid was grumbling, reaching for her flint and tinder to light a candle.

"Shhh!" I said quickly. "Please, don't light a candle." *It will only draw attention to the fact that we're awake up here,* I didn't add. I was feeling anxious and nervous about everything I'd seen this night, especially the way the prince had singled out Torvald just because of a mistake. It made me realize that what I'd thought was my high degree of caution here at the monastery had actually been far too simple and childish. Really, I should be worried for drawing *any* attention, even for the slightest infraction. I couldn't risk anyone finding out the real reason I was waking so early!

"Well, I don't see why not – as I'm awake anyway, but all right." Sigrid groaned, thumping her head back on the pillow.

"I'm sorry, Sig," I said to her. "I just can't sleep after, you know, last night on the mountain." I was also worried about what I had seen must mean for my father. If the Abbot Ansall was so friendly with my uncle, then that meant he would use the monastery's magic against my father, didn't it?

"Yeah, I know," Sigrid said, "Poor Torvald, huh?"

Torvald. I remembered the boy, getting in trouble just because of me, it seemed. "Yeah. It seems like they *really* don't like him at all," I said glumly. At least I wasn't so alone in being regarded with so little respect here, I thought. Not that I was really ever alone at all. I had Sigrid here, and of course I had the beautiful, noble, and inspiring Paxala. *But none of them had the childhood I had,* my mind stubbornly pointed out. I had been caught between the courtly world of my father, the watchful scowls of his official wife, and the world of my mother's people. One side wanted me raised as a lady – but never expected me to become one, and the other thought that I was wasting my time 'with all this Three Kingdom politics.'

Maybe the Torvald boy went through similar. A tool on someone else's chess board. Maybe I've finally found someone who can understand—I resolved to be a better friend to the boy in the future, we were both outsiders here, really. Hated in our own ways; him for being half Gypsy, and me for being half Mountain-folk, and 'wild.'

"But not only that – the suit of armor? The boulder?" Sigrid said, in awe.

"Yes, it was certainly…*spooky.*" I said, thinking about the way that the objects had floated past our eyes. *And then came the torch-flare.* I remembered feeling *something*, a flare of energy rising through me like the call of the dragons at first light – but, no. Surely not. They would have signaled me out like Ganna if I had. "Well, I didn't make the torch flame move," I said out loud.

"Me neither," Sigrid commiserated, her voice drowsy. "It's a shame though – how great would that be, huh? To have all of those magic powers like the Abbot does?"

"That is, if they would let us use them," I muttered sulkily, thinking about the way that we girls had so far been treated up here. At least, *I thought* all this aggression and disregard towards us was because of our sex. In a way, it was easier to think of it as just Greer and the Abbot and the prince being ignorant and arrogant towards us rather than the idea that they might resent us for other reasons.

Because my father is a prince. Or because I'm from the north. Or because they see me as a bastard child.

"What? Why wouldn't they… Oh." Sigrid caught on.

"I don't know, I'm just tired," I said. "Maybe they would train us as Dragon Mages if we had the talent for it, but I keep thinking about how the Quartermaster wasn't even going to let Lila, probably the best skirmisher of all of us, the chance to train as a warrior. Do the dragon monks just hate girls, then? Would we even be here if it weren't our fathers forcing us to come?" I grumbled.

"Well, *I* wouldn't, for sure." Sigrid said, and her voice in the darkness sounded amused. "If it weren't for my father sending me here, then there is *no* way I would be here! I would much rather be out riding my father's horses."

"Yeah," I agreed, although there was something about this that left me feeling a little put out and insulted. Why couldn't I be a dragon monk if I wanted to be? I mean, I wasn't sure I even wanted to be one, but I at least wanted the same chance as anyone else.

What I really want is the chance to learn about Paxala, I thought, with sudden clarity. She was fascinating and strong, and funny, and good company too. If that meant I had to stay here and train to be a dragon monk (or would that be Dragon Nun, I wondered?) then I was prepared to do it even though, I realized with another flash of insight, I would rather leave here with Paxala. That would be the best of all possibilities.

Sigrid yawned loudly from across the room and turned in her blankets. "If you're going to get up anyway to talk to the frost or whatever it is that you weird mountain people do," her muffled voice said, "could you at least rekindle the embers in the fire before you go?"

"Southerner," I chided her, but did as she asked anyway. There were still a few embers left glowing, and it didn't take much kindling and dried leaves to get a small fire burning again. I waited until the fire had taken, added a couple of the heavier seasoned logs and then the metal grate over the opening, knowing that the fire would smolder and burn through the logs, releasing heat into the room until we had a chance to get up and go down to breakfast.

We, I thought, as I stretched and walked to the window. There wasn't going to be a chance to get out onto the mountaintop and to the lake and Paxala this morning, not after last night.

"No Char? No ham?" The reptilian words appeared in my mind as if I had dreamed them, and I shook on my feet, breathing through my nose. Had I dreamed them? Or was that Paxala sharing her thoughts with me? *From this far away!?*

"No ham." The words returned (a little sulkily) and I could feel the dragon's annoyance flowing towards me, as did another person's as well.

"What's that? You're huffing and puffing like a dragon." Sigrid groaned. "Some of us have to sleep, we're not all part-mountain, you know?"

"Yeah, sorry. It's just... the floor is cold," I said, grabbing my things to get changed and rush towards the door.

"Oh, you *do* get cold then? Have you tried being quiet and sleeping in a warm bed like the rest of us?" Sigrid said in tired annoyance, and I heard a whump as she rolled over to bury herself even deeper into her blankets.

After getting dressed and grabbing my things, I stood on the cold landing outside our dormitory room and tried to think this new thing through. So, the dragon could share her mind with me, and she could do it from even a very great distance away. *'Pax-ala?'* I tried, thinking *towards* her.

No reply.

It's just too risky to go, I thought to myself. What if there are other dragon monks out there, cleaning up, or keeping an eye on Torvald? After our night-time lesson, my morning escapes to the distant lake suddenly seemed very dangerous indeed. Was it usual for the Abbot to go out at night? Had he ever seen me out in the dawn? Had he ever followed me? I had thought that I was alone up there, and the only person who was crazy enough to walk out onto Dragon Mountain alone, even with native dragons roaming around!

No, I couldn't go to Paxala this morning, but there might be something else I could try. *Paxala...?* I thought, not even knowing if I could get a response or not.

There was silence inside my own head. Maybe I was doing it wrong. I had never initiated contact with her yet, anyway. Not all by myself. Was there something that a human had to do? A magic word? How did Paxala do it? Could she think a spell, even if she couldn't speak one?

'Char.' I felt suddenly enfolded by invisible reptilian warmth, as if she were here right next to me. I had to bite my lip to stop

from laughing at the sheer joy of it. I had done it! I had managed to talk to the dragon just using my mind!

'Char can always talk to me, here. Here is us,' Paxala said. What did she mean by that? But I didn't want to waste time worrying, when poor Neill could be out there starving to death.

'Paxala, there's a boy, stuck on the mountain. Can you keep an eye on him, somehow? Fly over him? Near him? But... You will have to be quiet. As silent as a mouse.' My heart thumped in my chest. *'Don't go near if you smell or hear any other creature, you hear? You cannot get caught by Zaxx or the Abbot.'*

'Yes, Paxala can fly nearby, quieter than a mouse, more silent than the wind itself. Even if friend-Char won't bring ham.' The dragon twittered in my mind, before withdrawing just as suddenly and just as easily.

'I promise that I will bring extra when I can!' I tried to thank her. *'But don't let him know that you are there. No one can know that you exist...'*

No reply in my mind, but I could *feel* her agreement somehow, like a nudge or a gentle shove in the back of my mind.

"Thank you," I whispered, knowing that I would have to pay her, when I could. If there was one thing I had learned about dragons during my time with Paxala, it was that a dragon never felt indebted to anyone or anything. That seemed to be one of the reasons why it was so difficult for a large enclave like the crater to exist. Zaxx demanded that the other dragons obey him; but none of the others felt indebted to him, making fights and even dragon killings much more likely. I knew that if I asked for some service from Paxala, I would have to pay in kind at some later date, no matter how much food I'd brought her over the past year. She had never asked it of me—I had done it freely. But for now – I had to think about what all of this meant; Paxala, our sharing of minds, Lord Vincent, dragon magic... What did it mean for my father? Could he use it to his advantage?

But I couldn't risk leaving the Dragon Monastery until tomorrow, until I'd planned and deliberated a way to see Paxala. For all I knew there were Dragon Mages out on patrol, keeping watch over Torvald, or not. Instead, my footsteps took me to the Library, where Greer had me working most of my free time. He thought it was a punishment, but he didn't realize that it was also one of the few places in the monastery where I could think, in peace, and without being disturbed. I would go to the Library to learn as much as I could about dragons and speaking to dragons with your mind. There had to be old stories somewhere, right? It must have happened to others before me, hadn't it? *And if anyone catches me and asks me what I am doing, I will just say that I am studying.* Which was true, in a way. The perfect disguise!

CHAPTER 12
STRANGE VISITORS

'*Y*ou will never be a true Torvald.' Rik was laughing, shoving me so hard that I fell backwards, straight out of my father's halls and to the muddy, churned up floor of a battle-field. It was cold, and every muscle in me hurt. The clan room where I had been standing was gone, and instead all around me there was mud, bodies, and broken weapons.*

'How are you going to be fit enough to rule when I am gone?' came the gruff voice of my father, as he appeared, looming over me, his russet-blond hair contrasting with my dark Gypsy color-ing. He moved back out of my sight, leaving me in the deep mud. Above me floated grey clouds, interspersed with clear blue sky. It was peaceful in a way, just to concentrate on that sky and not the mud and death and war all around me.

'Skreayar!' A sudden sound split the air, as a shadow cut across my vision. It was gone almost as fast as it had arrived, but

in my heart, I saw what it had to be. A dragon. A mighty, crimson-red dragon.

Instead of scared I felt excited, and opened my mouth to call to it but for some reason I couldn't. When I brought my hand up, intending to touch my face to find out what was wrong with my mouth instead all I saw was a stone fist where my hand should be. I had been turned to stone. I was never to fly or to meet a real dragon. I had failed my father, and my blood was not good enough for my brother either. I was just another stone puppet, ready to be used and directed by the Abbot and the prince...

'Skreayar!' The same call once again, and this time the dragon swooped lower and faster, growing larger and larger in my sight. It was not gold, nor white or blue, but a red dragon and it seemed to be flying straight for me. Its mouth was a nest of sharp fangs, and it opened them to swallow me whole...

"TORVALD?" Voices on the mountaintop. *"Neill?"*

I was not lying on a distant battlefield, and neither was I being stalked by a dragon. Instead I was frozen, kneeling on the unforgiving rocks, my body long past the point of shivering and now slowing down into the gentle caress of sleep.

"By all the sacred roads and stars!" someone cursed, and I found that I knew the voice. *That cannot be. I must still be asleep.*

Hands grabbed me by the shoulders, lifting me up and as

soon as they did, pain exploded down and around my thighs and legs as blood surged again. I cried out, before biting my mouth down against the pain. I would not show weakness. I could not, I would not. "I will be a worthy leader of my clan. I will show the Abbot how strong I am…" I said, my teeth chattering as I forced the words out.

"What madness is this? He's raving! What have you done to my nephew?" It sounded for all the world like Lett Shaar Anar, the brother of my long-dead mother. *You are a dream, uncle.* I tried to laugh, but the pain coming from the lower half of my body was too real.

"Not me, friend, but the ones down there in the monastery. Here, we must rub the blood back into him, and get him warm," said another dark shape in the predawn light. It too, I recognized. *Jodreth?* I opened my mouth to confirm, but my teeth only chattered. I could not stop the shivering now, even though as I had knelt through the long night I had gone past shivering. Now it was uncontrollable and threatened to shake me to pieces.

"I was right to visit this strange place," my could-not-be-there uncle said, as I was laid gently on my back atop bundles of cloaks and blankets, and hands started massaging the life back into me. "When I tell him how they have treated his son, he will descend on the mountain like a storm, and the family Anar of Shaar will help him."

It sure sounds like my hot-blooded Uncle Lett, I thought, trying to blink my eyes to make them see clearer, but I could make out nothing. And of course, I remembered, I was not my father's favorite son. I had never been anyone's favorite, except my mother's.

"Look, he's trying to talk," Uncle Lett said, and I felt hands ease my head and shoulders up a little and bundle cloaks and rucksacks for a pillow underneath.

"Easy, Torvald," the monk said, spilling a bit of water across my face, and allowing it to dribble into my mouth. I spluttered, coughed, and blinked, to see it was indeed the young monk Jodreth sitting at my side, as well as the large man from distant Shaar, with the same darker coloring as I, and heavy ringleted hair and a full black beard. Gold and malachite shone at his ears and his eyes, usually alive with joy and passion, were now afire with anger.

"Uncle? Jodreth? What are you doing here?" I stammered through chattering teeth.

"The family of Shaar Anar travels throughout the Three Kingdoms, you know this," Uncle Lett said. "When I passed through your father's lands to pay our respect and see how my sister's son was keeping, Malos told us that you had been sent here to the monastery – although for what reason I cannot fathom. I vowed to bring the family north anyway, and we decided to see how they are treating you, and it turns out not well at all." He glowered at the towers and walls of the monastery below.

Uncle Lett turned and looked down at me sternly, before breaking into a broad, encouraging smile. "Do not worry, little Neill, no one insults the family of Shaar and gets away with it!" Uncle thrust a fist into the air as if fighting off an invisible foe and, despite the deep ache in my bones and how tired I felt, I had to laugh. This was one of the many gifts of my mother's family it seemed. They did not turn up very often, so busy were they with their travels – but when they did they would always welcome me as one of their own. Uncle Lett had a talent for making friends, and it seemed that he had done so now as well, with Jodreth Draconis.

"You know me, Neill, I did not fancy knocking on the doors of the monastery and begging to see my sister's son so I led the caravan north and around to the far side of the mountain, where there are some wonderful fishing lakes, with silver fish as big as your forearm!" he said excitedly. My uncle, like all true-blooded Gypsies, lived life simply. He had said that he would get vengeance on the Draconis Monastery and so he would, which meant no more would need to be said about it at all. Now that was decided, he could move on to talking about all of the other things that interested him. Like wine, fishing, and the life on the road.

But how do I discourage my uncle from seeking vengeance? I thought in alarm. I had lived in that monastery. Its walls were high and strong, and if Greer was anything to go by, then the monks were fanatical. And, of course – *they have dragons!* My father's people were very few in number, and whether in a fight against the Order alone or – stars forbid – encountering a dragon as they sought to attack the monastery, then they would be easily wiped out.

"Anyway, so we were out by the lakes, meaning to come over the top the next day when we met your friend the monk here."

Uncle Lett waved a gracious hand in the direction of the younger monk, who was ignoring us as he worked to grind up some kind of ointment in a small clay bowl. "It was he who told us that he was on his way to reach you, but that we had to wait until the patrols of monks would finally lessen and go to bed. That took most of the night, it seems..." Uncle lowered his voice, casting a wary eye to Jodreth. "I think that he has strange powers, little Neill!" He whispered and nodded to me sagely. "Your grandmother had strange powers. She could sense the life in people nearby, whether they were ill or happy or evil." Lett nodded like this was the most normal thing in the world.

"And so Jodreth brought me here, to you – to find you being treated little better than a slave." My uncle's mood changed in an instant, his brows tangling and his eyes flaring with rage. "Wait until we get our hands on them! What was the man called again? Abet?"

"*Abbot,*" Jodreth said, appearing over me with the compound which was now a thick porridge. "Here, eat this." He proffered the foul-smelling mixture to me and spooned it into my mouth. At first it tasted quite nice, like honey and cinnamon, and then the fiery ginger and something floral like cardamom filled my mouth and I went to spit it out.

"Oh – no, you don't." My uncle held me as Jodreth poured more water into my mouth, forcing me to swallow the fiery mixture or choke. I swallowed, and felt the wave of warmth spread down into my chest, and then my belly, and even my arms and legs.

"Ugh! What are you trying to do, kill me?" I stammered,

sitting up and pushing them away, already feeling less achy and stiff than I had before.

"Well, it seems your potion is working, Master Monk." Uncle Lett chuckled. "He is back to his usual surly-tempered self!"

"Ha-ha, Uncle, very funny," I said sarcastically as he helped me to my wobbling feet, and laid his own heavy cloak of fantastical designs and woven reds, blues, and deep greens over my shoulders.

"Well, you are alive, and that makes me happy, and when we Gypsies of ancient and lost Shaar are happy, we tell jokes, yes?" uncle said, tapping me on the chest and getting a smirk even from the dour Jodreth. It seemed to me as though they had become fast friends in the short time that they had scoured the mountain for me. So close in fact, that the monk felt that he was able to contradict my passionate uncle.

"If you think that you or the Torvald warlord will come here to exact vengeance then all I can ask is that you wait, and think, Master Lett Shaar Anar," Jodreth said seriously, and I was relieved I didn't have to be the one to suggest the idea of forbearance. There was too much at stake, too much information I still needed to gather, for my uncle to raise the Abbot's—and Prince Vincent's—ire against me further.

"And why ever not? You saw what they did to my sister's son here! This is an insult to my people!" Uncle Lett smacked a fist into his other open palm.

In response, Jodreth just pointed out from the mountaintop, in the other direction of the monastery, over and down the ridge where the dragon crater could clearly be seen. The sun was just breaking through the heavy morning clouds, and shards of golden red light were spearing their way across the plains and up the sides of Mount Hammal. Where they touched rocks, we could see movement. Large shapes were struggling to shift their massive bulk onto them, to catch the first rays of the sun. The dragons of the Mount Hammal were rising, and with it started the chorus of chittering and calls of the dragon horde within.

"Under the stars, moon, and sun," Uncle Lett breathed in equal parts wonder and fear, as we watched the dragons wake up. Like me, I could see that he was a little afraid, but also excited by the sight. I knew, too, that the sight of them would change everything about how Uncle Lett viewed the world. Not that he hadn't seen or heard a dragon before – but I was certain that no one out there in the world had seen so many dragons all at once, and so close. There was something special about this mountain, I thought now. Something that allowed so many dragons to live here, together, under the old bull Zaxx.

One by one, the dragons positioned themselves on the prominent and up-standing rocks of the terraced crater, each pointing perfectly back towards the waking sun. It could not have been staged any better if it were a mummer's show or a sacred ceremony. Some of them were long and sinuous like snakes, their snouts coming to a direct point in the direction of the sun. Others were so large as to raise their heads over the trees around them, whilst smaller Messenger dragons crowed and flapped onto their shoulders and heads and at the elbows, each pointing exactly towards the sun.

A sound like the one in my dream came from the crater, but

fuller, deeper, and louder - like the boiling of a thousand kettles all at once, or a war between colonies of rival cats. The hissing turned into a triumphant call as Zaxx the Golden emerged, raising his head last as he settled on his vast slab of rock, dislodging a whole cloud of Messenger dragons as he did so. The dawn chorus grew as both the larger and smaller dragons around joined in, until it became a ringing cry that deafened everything else.

"SSSKREAYAAR!"

When the dragon's chorus started to fade, losing its urgency and intensity it left us all bathed in the now fully risen light of the morning sun.

"You see, Master Lett Shaar Anar, although the Draconis Order cannot control the dragons of Mount Hammal, they feed these powerful creatures every day, and sometimes even ask them to perform simple tasks for them," Jodreth said sadly. "Praise the skies that Zaxx the Golden, the largest and brood-father there hasn't given over complete control to the Abbot Ansall or else the Middle Kingdom and the world would be doomed. Do you think that Malos Torvald and the Gypsy families of Shaar can fight against such an enemy?" Jodreth asked quietly.

"I wasn't thinking of asking anyone to fight a dragon," Uncle Lett said hotly, but I could see that Jodreth's words had nonetheless hit home. He glowered and looked stubbornly at the monastery below us for a moment, before sighing heavily. "But something has to be done. This is an insult to Shaar, and an insult to my sister Feeyah."

I felt my heart twinge at the sound of my mother's name. Feeyah Shaar Anar, lover of Chief Warden Malos Torvald. She was many long years dead now, but it still hurt to remember her sometimes. But even still, I could not call down a war just for this. "Uncle, please no. It was no big slight. It was the Prince Vincent who was behind it anyway..." I said, remembering the events of last night clearly now. *Maxal had performed magic, as had Char, and the Abbot seemed to want to impress the prince.*

"Then we will have revenge against the prince, then!" Uncle Lett said heroically, again raising his fist against the sky and the whole world for all the good that it would do him. Even to me, a boy of fifteen summers, it sounded an impossible goal for the leader of a small band of wandering Gypsies.

"And revenge you shall have, Master Shaar Anar," Jodreth counselled. "But first we must understand what connection there is between the Abbot, the prince, and the dragons here. Will they go into battle for him? Or will Zaxx not care who rules the monastery? And we must let Neill here return to do his father's work." Jodreth turned to incline his head towards me, and I found myself nodding.

How did he know of my secret mission to the Draconis Monastery? I thought, looking at Uncle Lett in alarm, only to see him oblivious to whatever it was that Jodreth was talking about. Could Jodreth read my mind? Or was it obvious what I was sent here to do, to infiltrate the monastery and steal their secrets for the good of the clan?

"Yes, I see." My uncle bridled a bit, but nodded all the same. "I can also see why this one is your friend, young Neill. He is wise beyond his years. Caution before passion, for a time anyway." My uncle then turned to set both of his hands on either side of my shoulder, and looked me in the eye. "But you are certain that you are okay, young Neill? You are healthy here, in this place?" he asked.

"Yes, Uncle." I nodded. I knew what he was going to offer next.

"You can come with me now, if you like. We can travel back with our caravan along roads that few here in the Middle Kingdom remember, and I will show you the roads that your mother has walked, and danced barefoot under stars..."

Don't. As much as I wanted to, and I truly did, I had to refuse him. He could see how much I would want to throw it all away, but I had a promise to my father to fulfill as well. I could not abandon him. That would almost be like proving Rik and Rubin and Terrence and all the others right about me, that I was not fit to be a Torvald at all.

"I know, Uncle. Thank you but not yet," I said quietly. Besides, there were too many mysteries here that I wanted to unravel; where did the monks get their magic from? Was it from just learning and reading the right scrolls, like a Scribe learns? Or was it some special exercise, the way a Protector learns? Was there a magical object that the monks carried? I immediately thought of the Abbot's cane, and reminded myself that I would have to get into the Abbott's tower myself, as he was the only monk I had seen actually *performing* magic so far. Did the monks use the magic to make friends with the dragons? Where did the dragons fit into all of this? "I am fine," I said to him, wondering if it was lie or not. *I would be strong.*

Uncle Lett held my gaze for one long moment, and then he nodded. "I see. Yes. You have your mother's stubbornness, young Neill." He gave me a grin. "You may live with my sister's husband but know this, Neill Shaar-Anar Torvald - you will always be one of us. You do not need to be anything other than what you are; not a warlord, not a fighter, not even a monk. We Gypsies may travel far and wide, but we will always keep an ear to the west for news of you, and come when you have need."

"Thank you, Uncle," I said, feeling his words warm me more than any strange unguent or potion. But as comforting as it was, a sad part of me realized that it wasn't enough. I wished it was. I really, truly wished that I could believe what my uncle had said to me just now: that I was enough, just be myself... But I needed to prove myself to my father. *Just once,* I thought. *Just once, I want the great Chief Warden, Malos Torvald, to look at me with the same thunderous pride that his other sons get.*

"Take care, Torvald." Jodreth winked at me as the two men took their leave. "And try not to stand out *too* much."

"I owe you for saving my life twice now, monk!" I even managed a little bow as I folded and tucked uncle's multi-colored blanket under my own monastery-black cloak.

"Are you keeping score, soldier?" Jodreth laughed, turning as he walked beside Uncle Lett. "Because if you are, I did this punishment on the mountain top *twice!*" They both laughed.

"You did?" I asked in curiosity. I had been ordered here by the Abbot, but I thought that was only because the prince had been there as well. What could Jodreth have done? I saw that Jodreth was looking at me with a half-smile on his face, half-ironic, and half-sad as he guessed the questions on my mind.

"Remember what I said to you on the slopes below the monastery, about how stubborn dragons and princes are? Well, let's just say that the Abbot has *never* liked it when people disrespect him and question his views, and Prince Vincent likes it even less." Jodreth shrugged like it was no big deal.

"So, Prince Vincent comes here often then?" I asked. "And you went through the same thing that I did? Being tested on the mountain here for magic?" *Did you succeed?* I wanted to ask, but all of a sudden it felt rude to use the monk for information, after he had saved my life – twice – and had been nothing but kind to me.

"Yes, I was tested for magic, young Neill, and yes, I insulted the Abbot, and would not obey his every command. That is why I was punished, and why I eventually left," Jodreth said. "But enough of this, Master Torvald – there are some questions only you can answer. Not me, and not anyone else, either!"

"You almost sound like a Gypsy, master monk," Uncle laughed.

But do you have the magic? The question was burning its way up through me, but before I could ask it, my uncle and the monk were already laughing and turning to go. Dawn was upon us, after all.

I waved them off, my Uncle Lett's booming laughter echoing over the mountaintop for a long time afterwards. I decided that my punishment was now over as I turned to walk back down the mountain trail to the back door of the monastery, there to be let in by a startled monk – clearly amazed to see me grinning and alive after a night on the freezing mountaintop.

But I didn't care what he thought. I had work to do. *I will start with the Abbott's belongings – his cane and his tower and his scrolls - and I will see if any of them unlock the secrets of their magic for me.*

PART II
THE DRAGONS

CHAPTER 13
THE LIBRARY

T he next few days saw the other students looking at me with different expressions, although I couldn't quite work out what it was. Wide, dark eyes. Like they thought me bewitched, or cursed. It wasn't until I cornered Dorf as he slipped in and out of our shared dormitory room that I managed to get the answer out of him.

"I'm on my way to the Library," Dorf said, uneasily. "I agreed to meet Ganna there, and I have to study if I am ever going to be a good Scribe."

"Oh, I doubt very much you'll be anything but an excellent Scribe, whether you study or not," I said. "But I'll come with you, I could do with practicing my letters." *And I could take a look around while I am there,* I thought. *Maybe there are scrolls or lore down there that will tell me how the Draconis Order can get to manipulate rocks and suits of armor…*

Our steps took us down from our dormitory tower, out across

the freezing courtyard where a few bedraggled students had taken it upon themselves to do some training. Into the Main Hall building, where Dorf led me to one of the smaller antechambers off to one side.

"This way." He led the way to a wooden door, which led to a set of stairs that wound around and around, deep into the bones of the monastery, and hopefully to the Library beneath it.

"I've never even seen this place – how did you find it?" I asked, stunned as Dorf juggled candle stubs in front of me.

"Oh, Ganna showed me. It's where the Scribes and the Mages are going to train next year, I think he said. His father was a big shot monk, so…" Dorf said.

"So, it pays to have family." I quoted the saying from my mother's family.

"Yeah, I guess you could look at it like that," Dorf agreed, before suddenly frowning, and giving me that same look that the others gave me. Wary, and watchful.

"Okay, out with it, Dorf. Why are you and everyone else acting funny around me?" I said. "Is it because of the mountain-top?" In the two days since my punishment and our first collective lesson, I hadn't told anyone how come I had come down from the mountain alive, and seemingly full of vitality. *Let them think that I do have some magical Gypsy blood!* I thought savagely.

"The students think that you're bad luck," Dorf said, uneasily.

"What?" I almost shouted before remembering that I wasn't angry at Dorf at all, but at the monastery all around me. *Just like at home,* I couldn't stop myself from thinking, knowing that it was petulant, and feeling childish and ashamed of myself for letting myself be bothered by it. My brothers would often joke that they couldn't take me hunting or out on campaign 'because of my Gypsy blood' and that I would bring bad luck to them all. It was a common complaint across the Three Kingdoms it seemed, that Gypsies were bad luck, and that we would be bad for business, bad for any voyage by boat, that we could sour milk if we stayed under the same roof – all ridiculous, superstitious nonsense that my uncle played up and used for his advantage, but to me had only highlighted how differently everyone viewed me. *And how I would never be a true Torvald if they thought that.*

"Well," Dorf hemmed and hawed, but my stern glare made him tell me in the end.

"They saw the Abbot, and the prince himself single you out on the mountaintop, and they think that means that the monks don't like you." Dorf winced.

"They don't," I muttered sulkily. "All they can see is my hair color."

"No, that can't be true," Dorf said slowly. I could tell that he was trying to cheer me up. That he didn't feel the same about me as the others. Maybe he hadn't been avoiding me like I'd thought. "They deal with dragons every day. I'm sure they don't care where you come from…" Dorf said.

"Then why do the students think that I am unlucky?" I said, hating myself for how whiny it sounded, even to my own ears.

"Oh," Dorf hung his head. "Yes, well–there was Greer," Dorf said uneasily.

"The Quartermaster? What did he do?" Ever since that man had set eyes on me he had taken a personal disliking to me. Why? I couldn't even begin to fathom it.

"He has let it be known that treachery to the Abbot or to the Abbot's guests will not be tolerated, and Terrance has started to tell everyone that they must be talking about you disrupting the lesson, not his gasping and head shaking."

The Abbot's guests. That must mean Prince Vincent, who had now changed his reason for being here from 'official demonstration of magic' to 'royal visit,' really was trying to consolidate his power and secure his position as the sole benefactor of Draconis Order. "What?" I shook my head. "But this is madness! I'm a nobody. I'm the younger son of a warlord, not the child of one of the Princes of the Three Kingdoms. What have I done that would make anyone think that I was a traitor?"

"Terrance is the son of Prince Griffith, remember?" Dorf said. "And Char is the unrecognized daughter of Prince Lander of the North," he said slowly and clearly. "If anyone is scared of being accused a traitor, then it's those two. Terrance, and probably Char too for all I know, need to divert the suspicion away from themselves if they want to remain in the good books with the monastery and the Abbot. It doesn't matter if you actually do anything treacherous. They can always make something up."

"About me?" I shook my head, apparently in outrage, but mostly in fear. The terrible thing was – they were right. I *was* trying to get information for my father and Clan Torvald, but that was only because everything that my father had brought me up to believe was true. Lord Vincent was no true prince. It was clear from how he'd acted on the mountaintop that he didn't care for the people underneath him. If thinking that made me a traitor, then I guess that's exactly what I was. Not that I was going to go around advertising that fact.

"I know, I know – but that is just what they think." Dorf sighed. "The other students don't know you as I do."

Do you, though? I tried to grin. *Would Dorf Lesser still like me if they knew what I really came here to do?*

"Anyway, here we are: The Great Library of the Draconis Order," Dorf said as he opened a small wooden door within one of the door panels of a large, twelve-foot double door, revealing a room of light and paper beyond.

Well, I say *room*, but a more accurate term was probably a catacomb. Or perhaps cellar! We seemed to be underneath the monastery itself, as the ceiling and walls were crisscrossed with curving and vaulted stone arches, holding up the floors above it. The air was cool and dry, perfect I guess, for books (wasn't that what the monk who had been stationed with my father had once told me)? It was also – surprisingly given how far underground it was – *light*.

There were a few places where candles sat, but the light didn't limit itself to those mere instruments. There were places high up in the walls where light shone down through small apertures, inside of which must be a complex system of brass plates or polished mirrors, as they lit up these almost clear, cut crystals like lanterns. They didn't shed great beams of light, no, but they created a gentle light throughout the Library chambers. I was astonished.

"Oh, another thing that the monks know how to make." Dorf laughed when he saw my wonder. He himself appeared much more in awe of what was *inside* the room.

Shelves taller than we were, extending as far as the eye could see, and forming a maze of books, each one carefully chained into position. Interspersed with these were scroll racks which looked very much like they must have been the wine racks at some point. We heard shuffling feet, and muttered voices, and I froze.

"It's okay," Dorf whispered. "Monks use this place all the time, and we're allowed to be down here—we're studying, remember?" He gave me an encouraging smile. "You warlord families are so paranoid." He shook his head, before the approaching footsteps rounded a corner in the shelves, and the person they belonged to suddenly appeared.

"Maxal." Dorf greeted his friend warmly, and I turned to see the little, nearly bald-headed spooky boy. He looked at me with large eyes, and gave me a silent nod, before greeting Dorf.

"Dorf, pleased you both could make it, shall we get started?" Maxal spoke hesitantly and carefully, in a way that made me think that he had considered the shape of every word before saying it aloud. Despite Maxal's clear friendliness, I did feel a twinge of jealousy at how close he was with Dorf already. Was it that I really wanted Dorf to be *my* friend?

Pull yourself together, Neill! I heard my brother's voice in my ears as I followed on behind. I wasn't here to make friends, I was here to unearth secrets, and I started right away.

"Maxal? Dorf? Were you two looking to begin scribing practice?" I asked, feeling lumpen and a little stupid next to them. Dorf nodded.

"Could we, perhaps study history?" I tried.

"Of course!" Dorf looked delighted. "I know that the dragon monks have an excellent history collection, don't they?" he asked Maxal, who nodded.

"It is one of the prime functions of the Order, or so my father told me," the boy said quietly. "That and looking after the dragons."

"Well then, we could start at the History of the Raider Wars, that's always fun, bloodthirsty stuff!" Dorf mimed someone waving a saber and almost succeeded in stabbing an entire shelf to death.

"Woah there, Dorf the Deadly," I said and laughed. "Couldn't we start at something a bit more fundamental? How about the Dragon Order itself?" I tried to sound casual, feeling my heart race a bit at the ploy. This was my best chance to find the information I needed—that my father needed—if we were to protect our people from the whole kingdom being drawn into chaos and bloodshed by Prince Vincent.

"Good idea, Torvald," Maxal said, abruptly changing direction to delve deeper through the warren of shelves, turning first this way and then that. As we walked I heard a sound and looked up in surprise, expecting to see a tall and robed dragon monks, but instead saw a thin figure with platinum-gold hair, looking up at us in surprise. Char Nefrette! I blinked and looked down the aisle again, thinking to raise a hand to wave at least - but she had gone, and none of the others had apparently seen her.

Char appears to get everywhere, it seems, I thought to myself, remembering how I had seen her heading through the Kitchen Gardens just the other day. But of course, she was a Scribe, wasn't she? So it made sense she would spend her time in the Library.

"Here we are," Dorf said, pointing at a small plaza-space made of bookshelves, in the center of which was a long reading table. All of the shells forming the sort of room where stacked floor to ceiling with heavy volumes. I didn't even know where to begin.

"Uh... All of this is monastery history?" I said a little overawed.

"All of it. Isn't it wonderful?" Dorf fairly glowed with enthusiasm. I was instantly reminded of another saying of my Uncle Lett. Where is it best to hide a fish? I think that the original parable had something to do with poaching, or helping yourself to the bounties of the wilds, no matter what prince or lady of the manor says (as Uncle Lett would put it). But either way:

"Where is the best place to hide a fish?"

"Up your sleeves?"

"No, because then you will smell of fish."

"I don't know, where is the best place to hide a fish?"

"Why, in the sea of course!"

I had never really understood the Gypsy parable, but right now, looking at what must be easily a thousand books or so and not knowing which one (if any) had the answer to my questions, I think I understood what my Uncle Lett had been trying to teach me. I wondered if he was still nearby, if I could get a message for my father to him—but of course, first I needed to gather some information worthy of sending home.

EVENTUALLY, however, after two hours of back-cramping hunched over books, and my eyes starting to water with all of the peering and concentrating I was doing, Maxal and Dorf unwittingly helped me to find a clue.

Maxal had collected together what they called 'Primers' and 'Introductions' which were smaller, thinner books crammed with tiny writing that summarized the chapters of much larger books – sometimes seven whole series of grimoires. Maxal informed me that the problem with these smaller volumes was that they were often full of inaccuracies, and presented a lot of opinion instead of fact, but that they were a good place to start if I had no patience for wading through all twenty-three volumes of *Mysticism in the Rule of the Queen Delia*, even if Maxal said it was 'truly authoritative' – whatever *that* meant.

No, I did not have the patience nor the time for such an undertaking. So instead, the two boys started to teach me a short history of the Three Kingdoms, and, as Maxal asked questions and Dorf argued this way or that – I found myself even learning something.

It seemed that the Draconis Order was a relatively new invention—only a hundred or so years old. New enough in terms of the world. But its roots were in some very old traditions. There have been mystics and shamans coming up to Mount Hammal for hundreds of years, but most of them would get eaten. Only a very few would return with dreams or visions or even magical powers. They would talk of challenges and tests, of being hunted by the dragons until they could show their bravery, before being taught the ancient magical arts.

But the Draconis Order itself was founded by none other than the old Queen Delia, the mother to Prince Lander, Prince Griffith, and Prince Vincent. Or rather, the primers said that the old queen gave an awful lot of money to Abbot Ansall at the time to have it built.

"Wait." I stopped the two boys in their discussions. "I get it, the dragons are old, the monastery is old, but Queen Delia and the Abbot really got it all going…" something didn't make sense to me, and then I saw it. It was the dates. "But, that was a hundred years ago, I thought you said?"

"Yes." Both Maxal and Dorf nodded.

"Well, how old was Queen Delia when she died?" I stammered.

"Well, let me see…" Maxal started flicking through the books to find some dates.

"One hundred and forty-three." Dorf came up with the answer first. He was good with numbers like that.

"I'm sorry?" I asked again. That was impossible, it had to be.

"Queen Delia was one hundred and forty-three when she eventually died, and that must mean that Prince Vincent is in his…" Dorf tried to calculate, but shook his head. "She had her children late," he settled for.

"It says here in the chronology, very clearly, that Prince

Lander, the oldest, was only born almost sixty years ago." Maxal pointed out to the list of dates and names at the back of one of the books. "That makes Prince Griffith almost sixty, and the youngest, Prince Vincent, in his thirties, I think."

"But...." Unable to imagine it. "So, the old queen really was very old when she became a mother?" I said the obvious. "She never looked old on the tapestries."

"Some people are naturally long-lived," Dorf said. "And besides, everyone knows that tapestries and paintings are meant to portray the queen at her best."

"Well, maybe," Maxal said. "But it's also an aftereffect of becoming a Draconis Monk. They get to live like their charges, much longer than is normal."

"Really?" An idea started to form. *So, is that the secret of the Draconis Order? That they can live for much longer than normal?* "Does that mean Queen Delia was a Draconis Monk —er—nun?"

But no one answered me because Dorf started stammering. "Wow, I, uh, oh geez. Um, I think that you should look at this." He sounded creeped out by what he had found.

It was the first volume of *Mysticism in the Rule of Queen Delia,* and there were block cuts and wood-printed illustrations throughout. Volume one of the twenty-three, it appeared, was devoted to the earliest of the Draconis Order beginnings, the ancient mystics and shamans who had come up to the dragon caves through the wilds, all on their own, and seeking knowledge. Dorf was pointing at an illustration of a man sitting cross-legged in a cave, with high features, a black cap, and a sort of line across the sand in front of him.

"Okay…" I said, not following the connection.

"Here." Dorf flicked the page to a few chapters further in and another illustration, where there was now a crowd of people in a marketplace talking to a high-featured man with a black covering on top of his head, and holding some sort of staff whilst, in the air above tiny bird-like dragon shapes flew.

"And finally." Dorf flicked to the last chapter of the volume, where there were a large number of hermits being led by another with a black covering atop his head, holding a cane, and talking to a woman with a crown.

"Who has a black cane and a skullcap?" Dorf asked.

So that's what that covering was, a skullcap. Why, it almost looked like… *Abbot Ansall.* My brain, fogged and slowed by all the hours spent reading, finally caught up with what Dorf was saying. "Are you trying to suggest that Abbot Ansall is over two or even three hundred years old? Surely, it's just a family resemblance or something. I mean, Maxal here comes from a long line of Draconis Monks, right? Maybe this is just Abbot Ansall's great-great-great grandfather?"

"Look—" Maxal pointed to the caption of the illustration. Written below the figure of the man were the words *Master Ansall.*

"Maybe it's a family name, passed down through generations?" My mind refused to believe Abbot Ansall could be the same man as in the illustrations, that he could be so ancient.

Dorf opened and closed his mouth, shrugging. "All I know is that a few nights ago I saw Ansall do impossible things."

"A few nights ago?" said a new voice, breaking through our studies. We turned to see none other than Char standing there, her arms wrapped around a heavy set of books. "All *I* remember seeing was the Abbot showing off for Prince Vincent," She said haughtily, and angrily, her eyes flashing at me in particular. "Maybe you boys should be a bit more circumspect with your studies," she added.

I wondered how much she had overheard of our discussion, and considered telling her. *Doesn't she have the right to know who her father is dealing with, sending her down here?* I thought, opening my mouth before I was interrupted once more – but this time by the quiet Maxal Ganna.

"We should be going. We've spent all morning down here, and I'm sure that the Quartermaster will be about ready to have us all mucking out the stables if we miss lunch."

Compared to the hours spent peering at books and trying to work out impossible riddles, I thought I might actually prefer to muck out the stables. At least I could visit with Stamper. But even as I followed the others back out of the Library and up the stairs, my head was ringing with questions I knew I needed the answers to.

How did the Draconis Order and the Abbot get to live so old? What was the secret of their strange powers?

CHAPTER 14
CHAR'S LETTER

"D*ear Father,*"
    I instantly cursed myself for being so stupid, and crossed the words through with heavy black lines of ink. *What was it my father had said?* I bit the end of the quill that I was using where I had already stripped it of feathers.

That I had to be circumspect. That I was here to make friends, but if I found out anything that was troubling or dangerous for the Northern Kingdom, then I must rush to tell him immediately.

But maybe I shouldn't even write 'father' because then they'll know that it's me sending this message to the Northern Kingdom? I wondered, and then sighed heavily. It seemed that I was going to be useless as a spy.

It was another late afternoon between practices, and I had managed to steal a tiny bit of time to myself in the dormitory room and brought out my writing equipment. I had to tell father about what was happening here... *Or what was happening to me?* Surely, he would want to know that I had made friends with a dragon, and that I could even share minds with one?

But what if this was some secret test? I bit the end of the quill once more. *What if this was how the Dragon Monastery chose who was to be a Mage?*

No. It couldn't be, no one else had started to complain of hearing dragon voices inside their heads. And certainly no one else was raising a dragon from an egg. The Draconis Monks barely let us do anything even related to the dragons, except for watching them through the windows of the towers and reading about them. Wouldn't the Draconis Order warn us if this was something that was going to start happening all of a sudden to the students? *Was it just between me and Paxala? Or was it something that only happened to some people, like a cold?* I mused as I watched through the open window down to the main courtyard below. I could see the forms of the boys and girls sparring with their practice wooden batons and sticks. It was an unofficial training contest, organized by Lila, and a lot of those training down there were the girls who had been denied the opportunity to become the Protectors, the warrior-monks. *Just like I had been denied.* I rolled my eyes in disgust. The Raider girl had asked me to join in her impromptu training lessons, but what with Paxala, and the need to keep my father informed of everything that was going on I just didn't have the time.

"Char, you could help the rest of the girls out if you joined," Lila had said, her dark eyes steady and serious as she had cornered me after lunch. "I see that you are good with a spear, and with a bow. Your father taught you well."

"It was my mother, actually," I had said, which had only pleased the Raider girl even more.

"Excellent then. You know how important it is for us women to stick together – come be my assistant trainer." Lila had offered me her tattooed hand to grip. "We have to teach each other, if they won't teach us." But I had to refuse, as much as I had wanted to be there.

"Fine. Lay down like the rest of them." Lila had scolded me, and led her troop of would-be warriors out to the practice field. How she had managed to convince the Draconis Monks to let her raid the practice stores for weapons was beyond me.

I watched them knock and bash each other for a bit in the cold, admiring how good they were getting already, with just a bit of dedicated practice.

Anyway, back to the letter…

"Dear Sire, I have news which may interest you…" I then wrote, but how would my father know it was from me? I almost crossed out what I had written, but then I realized – of course— my father would surely recognize my handwriting. *Just write it,* I thought. Get the words out there and into the open.

I bit the end of the quill once more, trying to find the appropriate way to say 'I have started to hear dragons in my head' when I heard a shout from out of the window. The group of 'official' warrior-monks had come out of one of the storerooms, and had stopped to watch Lila's unofficial group. I heard laughing and mocking voices.

Great, I wondered, leaning forward to try and get a good look at what was going on. Lila was a Raider's daughter from the furthest south, and so that meant that her family had an on-and-off war with Terrence's father, Prince Griffith the Kind. I knew this because on occasion Prince Griffith had asked my father, Prince Lander, for aid (but never, it seemed, did he ask his other and closer brother, Prince Vincent).

Lila will kill him if he makes fun of her, I thought, tucking the note back into my things and shoving it under the bed. I needed to mull over how to best explain to my father what was happening. In a way that wouldn't make him think I'd lost my mind.

Terrence called something out to the Raider girl, and I saw her bristle, pull herself up straight and turn around, slowly advancing on the other group of boys.

"No! Wait!" Someone was breaking away from Terrence's group, it was the boy from black curly Gypsy hair, the one whom I had seen just yesterday in the Library. Torvald. What was he doing?

I saw him step between Terrence and Lila, who both looked at him in contempt. He was trying to reason with them. *Good luck with that,* I thought.

All of a sudden, the dragon pipes blew.

CHAPTER 15

THE PARADE OF DRAGONS

"**S**tand aside, Torvald." Lila was growling me, and I could see her testing the weight of the wooden baton in her hand. She had been training with her unofficial warrior group for the best part of a watch when the rest of us finished our class on strategy and tactics and went out to get some fresh air. I hated being lumped in with Terrence and the rest of his cronies, I hated even being thought of as anything like them. But luckily enough, they seemed happy to just ignore me and suffer my presence amongst their 'elite' number.

It's okay. I consoled myself. I was just playing a game, after all. I was here to find out what I could and go home – all I had to do was just ignore the looks and off-handed comments thrown my way until then.

But when we had got to the courtyard, and I had peeled off to spend time on my own, Terrence and his lot had immediately started whooping and calling at the 'girls who couldn't even hold a stick right!'

It made me feel sick. Maybe that was why Terrence's father was called the Kind Prince, as he was too lax with his own son?

"A fight would only be bad for everybody," I said to Lila, "so I can't stand aside –unless you put that weapon down."

"Why? Do you not think that I couldn't take him and the rest of you with my bare hands?" Lila growled, letting the baton fall with a heavy *whump* to the cold floor. "Now stand aside, Torvald, while I teach that Terrence a lesson in manners."

"And for what good?" I hissed at her. "So, the Draconis Order can kick you out? So that your family has to fight another war with Prince Griffith?"

"Better that then suffer his face every morning," Lila snapped back.

"You insolent *girl!*" Terrence called out. "You don't even have any royal blood in your veins…"

"Terrence, cut it out." I was tired and exasperated with him. He was a pig, but what was worse was that he really believed what he said.

"What did you say to me, Torvald?" The prince's son rounded on me too. "I should have known that a Gypsy and a Raider would team up against us Three Kingdom folk!" he said haughtily.

"That's it…" Lila grunted, balling her fists and stepping forward. An ugly smirk bloomed across Terrence's face. His remark had hit home, and he had proved to his posse of yes-men that he was right. That we were all degenerates, and not worthy of being monks or Three Kingdom folk.

"Lila, come on," I stepped in the way, dreading the punch that I knew that she was going to give me, but willing to take it if it meant that she didn't start a war.

BWAR! BWAR! BWAR! The dragon pipes blew, and Lila halted. That meant that it was time to feed the dragons, and it was one of the most important rituals of the day. Immediate compliance, seriousness, and respect were demanded of us all when we heard the pipes.

"Ugh!" Lila kicked the floor instead, sending up clods of dirt and stone chips in her frustration. "This isn't over, Terrence," she whispered at him.

"I'm sorry, Lila, but some of us have *very* important duties to perform…" He smiled, rushing to get changed, as were we all.

"HURRY! HURRY, STUDENTS." Quartermaster was standing at the rear gate with his little book and pen, ticking off our names as we emerged from the main halls, washed and wearing our plain black robes. We followed the other, fully-fledged Draconis Order monks as they wound their way out of the gate and up onto the mountain beyond. I had been expecting to feel nervous the next time I went up the mountain, thanks to the long hours I had spent slowly freezing to death, but strangely, this time I felt curiously lighter, freer as I walked. The last time I had been up here I had been met by my uncle, and by the strange Jodreth. I knew that the monastery *wasn't* such an isolated place, and that there were others that thought favorably of me nearby.

If anything, it's down in there that's more dangerous to me, I thought, casting a look back at the monastery walls.

"Torvald," the Quartermaster narrowed his eyes as I went past. "Good to see you in such *fighting* fit shape," he said with a sneer. "I do hope that you don't get into any more trouble up on that mountain."

"Ignore him," someone whispered after we had passed, and I turned to see none other than Char Nefrette in line behind me. I nodded my thanks, turning and keeping my eyes focused on the back of the student in front of me. Outside the walls we were all handed a long metal goad, with two 'tines' at one end like a cattle prod.

"Do *not* antagonize the dragons," Abbot Ansall voice called from where he was watching over us as we marched up the shingle and stone paths to the ridge. Next to him stood none other than the Prince of the Middle Kingdom, Prince Vincent dressed in all of his dark finery. I wondered if I could make out anything different about the Abbot, something that would really prove that he could be hundreds of years old. Nothing, as far as I could tell.

"You know that the Draconis Order serves the dragons, and today will be your chance to truly appreciate the glory and the might of what we strive to preserve," he called. "We shall feed the mighty dragons and demonstrate your courage to the prince here." The Abbot gestured toward Prince Vincent. "For the glory of the Three Kingdoms!" he cheered.

"For the glory of the Three Kingdoms," we all chanted, although I wondered how many were really chanting for *all Three* Kingdoms, and not just their own particular clan, chief, or kingdom.

We made our way along the single-track trail, every five students led by a Draconis Monk. My group of five, consisting of me, Char, Dorf, Sigrid, and Maxal, was led by the angry-seeming Monk Olan, who shouted every few steps, "Stand back! Back!"

After about the twentieth time, Char whispered, "All right, all right! As if any of us want to fall down there!" but we did as we were told. None of us wanted to fall into the crater with the hungry dragons.

"We're becoming a gang," I whispered conspiratorially to the others, as our group waited to be sorted and correctly spaced around the crater.

"You do know that prince's daughters aren't supposed to be in gangs," Char said with a mischievous grin, and Dorf and Sigrid sniggered. I felt stupid, as if the others – Sigrid and Dorf – were laughing at me. Why was I so worried about what they were thinking? I was here to do my fathers will, not care about the others....

But I do care about what the others think about me, I thought. Or *these* others, anyway. I'd felt that way ever since seeing Char and Sigrid and the girls get picked on and berated by Greer for no reason. It was unfair. It wasn't how things were supposed to be. Maybe it was so recently spending time with Uncle Lett – I missed his honest, simple companionship and humor. I missed having people that I could trust.

Collections of black-clad monks and students crisscrossed the skyline like strange new trees, and it seemed that every monk was on edge.

"Right, don't embarrass me, okay?" our own angry-monk hissed. "And pay attention. I'm here to make sure you learn a few things about the dragon offering and don't die in the process. Look there..." He pointed to where the two taller forms of the Abbot and the prince stood. The Abbot took a step forward, raising his hands.

"Mighty Zaxx the Golden! Accept these gifts!" he called down to the crater below.

There was the sound of rumbling from below, and a shape lifted its immense bulk from the largest of caves. A snout the size of a room, a head the size of a tower, and the golden scales of the old bull-dragon flashed in the sun. There was a rattling croak of a sound as the Gold slowly raised himself and finally stretched his long neck to regard the Abbot, face to face. The thin figure beside the Abbot – Prince Vincent – stepped back a little, and I grinned at his apparent trepidation.

Serves him right.

"Mighty Zaxx," the Abbot said as he gestured forward with his hands. The large hunks of meat resting at his feet lifted from the ground and floated in the air between them, and Zaxx opened his mouth, for the food to drop in.

"First question you lot," Monk Olan hissed at us. "Why does Zaxx the Golden have to eat first?" He kept one eye on the Abbot as he asked us our first direct dragon question. "Anyone?"

Maxal Ganna raised his hand.

"I know *you* know the answer, Maxal, or if you don't then you should by now. Dorf?" The monk quickly dismissed Maxal's offer.

"Because uh, because Zaxx is the lead dragon."

"Bull dragon it's called. He's the *bull* of all of the others down there. What does that mean, Sigrid?" the monk asked the questions fast.

"Uh, that, that he gets to eat first." She shrugged at the obviously circular logic.

"Fool," the Draconis Order monk said. "That he is *in charge* of the others. He gets mating privileges, and he is the first to hunt, the first to a kill, and all the other dragons protect him and keep him safe."

"How old is Zaxx the Golden?" I asked the monk, watching as the last of the food tumbled into the great Gold's gullet, who gave a contented grumble and sank down to the ledge, giving a strange rumbling call, that seemed to indicate the other dragons could now come and be fed. He moved slowly, in the way that I imagine a mountain would move if it had scaled legs.

"Did I tell you that this was open questions, Torvald?" Monk Olan glared at me and I decided to shut my mouth, in fear of receiving another mountaintop punishment. He kept on looking at the Abbot and the prince, as if he were waiting for the next instruction. But I noted that he still answered my question. "No one knows for sure. Five hundred years? A thousand? He's probably the oldest dragon there is. He might even be the father of every dragon in all of the realms."

"We have wild dragons. Dark, midnight blue and black, but

much smaller. Is Zaxx *their* father as well, then?" Char asked not-so-innocently.

"No more questions," the monk snapped, as the next group of dragons rose from the pit. These ones were similar in form to Zaxx the Golden, with barrel-like bodies, squat arms, and broad heads, but they were a shockingly clear white. They were also the next largest of all of the dragon sizes.

We watched as they rose to the lips of the crater, but the Abbot gestured for the next group of monks and students to feed them. *So that is what the goads are for!* I saw, as the very next group started to use the goads to spear the lumps of meat and hurl them down into the pit, where the great White dragons started to snap at them and swallow them whole.

"These are the White dragons. Can anyone name their qualities? And no, not you, Maxal," the angry monk said.

We were all quiet for a moment, until Dorf had another go. "Strong. Lots of stamina. Can fly for leagues and leagues."

"Good." The monk nodded. "They are also very good Denmothers, and often act as matriarchs to whole clutches, looking after many hatchlings for the bull at the same time." The Draconis Order monk congratulated Dorf.

Before the next group to be fed came up to the lip, there was a squabble, and a burst of fire from below. "Stand back!" the monk took up his goad in worry, peering below.

"Skreech!!" There were more calls and shouts, but the next group to climb up the terraces of rocks were the stocky green dragons. They were even smaller versions of Zaxx the Golden and the Mighty Whites, but still as large as a barn. They were

apparently fiercer, however, as they snapped and hissed at each other. We watched as the next group of students threw their food (a little more frantically, it had to be said) and the Draconis Monk lectured us on how dangerous the Vicious Greens were.

"Is that why they were fighting?" Sigrid asked, causing another scowl from the monk.

"Of course. They wanted to be the next to get the food." The monk turned back to look, keeping an eye on the nearest dragons in case they did anything unexpected.

"But I thought that they were fed in strict size dominance?" Maxal surprised everyone by saying suddenly.

"Yes." The monk nodded. "Good observation, Maxal. The Vicious Greens are the next-largest dragon, and so they are the next to eat."

"So, there are *no other* dragons that will be larger than the Greens, but smaller than the Whites and Zaxx?" Char asked, frowning deeply.

"That's what I said, wasn't it?" Monk Olan said.

"But what about the Crimson Reds?" Maxal asked. "In the Library, it talks of a larger breed than the Vicious Greens, as red as blood and fire, and not as aggressive..."

"All dead, I'm afraid, Ganna." The monk looked uncomfortable. "We did have two, but they caught a sickness and died. Sadly, one of the pair had been brooding a small clutch of eggs..."

"What sickness!?" Char looked alarmed beside me.

"Nothing catching, Nefrette, don't look so worried, now..." the monk pointed to where the Greens had finally had enough, and the next set of dragons to come where the Sinuous Blues, long-necked and long-winged, with tails that wouldn't stop twitching and thrashing as they boiled up from below. Technically, I thought that they had to be longer than the Vicious Greens, only not as broad. "So maybe that is why the Greens were fighting? Because it was usually the Crimson Red's turn to go next, and it caused conflict in the, what do you call it?" I wondered to Maxal.

"Size dominance. It's a dragon classification system by Justos the Philosopher, a Draconis Order monk of the third century," the small boy said seriously.

"Just who is doing the teaching here, Ganna, you or me?" the angry monk spat.

I don't think you're doing any teaching at all, are you? I thought as we all looked down, and this time Char was called upon to name the qualities of the Sinuous Blues: speed, cunning, agility as yet another group of students and monks fed them.

As the dragons decreased in size and the other groups of students were called forward, I began to wonder, why hadn't we been picked to feed any dragons yet? It seemed there was some method, some order to which the students were grouped. We watched as the Yellows scrambled, eager and apparently friendly compared to their larger cousins the Southern Desert Orange. Another group of students fed the Earth Dragons, a wingless breed of large lizard really that barely qualified for dragon other than their size (that of a cart horse). Their qualities were loyalty, and having large stomachs.

Thud-Thud. I jumped as behind us large hessian sacks full of the smell of meat and scraps where dumped by teams of other Draconis Order monks. Finally! It would be our turn, and wondered eagerly what sort of dragon we would get to feed, excited for my first opportunity to be near a dragon—

"Skree! Skree!" Flying and hopping up from the rocks and trees came creatures barely as big as crows, but a few reached dog or small child size. They were the smallest of all of the dragons, and they couldn't stop chirruping and whistling as they came up to us.

"Careful now, these Messenger dragons will give you a nasty nip, though they have no true fire," The Draconis Monk said, clearly irritated for having just the smallest beasts to tend. I realized now that the Abbot had intentionally given us the smallest of the dragons, that he had organized the groups by some internal definition he—or perhaps Prince Vincent—had of our families' influence or importance.

"The rest of the monastery are laughing at us." Sigrid scowled, as grumpy as the Draconis Monk was, but I could only feel delighted to be near to any of the beasts; no matter how small.

"Use the goad! The goad!" The Draconis Monk was shouting as he speared hunks of food and flung them out into the crater (where the flights of Messenger dragonets squawked and squabbled to catch them).

"Why?" Char said distantly, her eyes appearing half-closed as if she were sleepy or concentrating. Instead of using the goad, she picked up a hunk of the meat in her hands and held it up for the smaller dragonets to feast on.

She is fearless, I thought, watching as three of the Messenger dragons flashed to her arm to settle and begin pulling and nipping at the half-cooked meat, purring contentedly.

"Nefrette!" the monk was furious, batting away at the clouds of Messenger dragons that were descending all around us. One of them hover-flew right in front of my face, cocking its head first this way and then that as it whistled at me. I laughed, taking a chunk off the bone and flicking it in the air, for it to dive and catch, as fast and as easily as a gull.

"Back in the crater! Now!" the monk moved quickly, seizing what was left of the food and flinging them over the edge, sacks and all, and with it followed the flights of Messenger dragons.

"Hey? Why did you do that – they were having fun!" Char demanded.

"Why? Because of *him,* that's why, Nefrette," the Draconis Monk pointed down to where a great golden head, as large as all of the Messenger dragons put together, was regarding us solemnly from the bottom of the pit. "If Zaxx thinks that we're favoring *any* of the other dragons over him, he'll kill them. And then he might just kill *you* for insulting him."

"But that's just—" Char started to argue, her face suddenly ashen, but I stepped in quickly.

"We understand, sir," I said, interrupting her.

"You do? Good. Make sure *she* does as well," the monk muttered and cursed, aware that our group had made a spectacle of our section of the lesson. *Maybe I will match Jodreth's record of two nights on the mountain,* I found myself thinking – feeling once again that wild sort of courage in my heart as I had when I first stepped out onto the mountain this morning. It wasn't courage though, I reminded myself. It was foolishness. I couldn't depend on Jodreth or my uncle saving me a second time – and besides which, I didn't want to see Char or the others get hurt or punished as I had.

It didn't take long for the monks to start filing their charges away from the crater, and begin the trek back to the monastery. It seems as though our own personal Draconis Monk was only too happy to abandon us, and probably would have pushed us in the crater himself were it not for the scandal that it would cause in front of the prince.

"Why did you do that?" Char said, catching up to me.

"What did I do?" I asked.

"Stop me from arguing with the monk. He was in the wrong. If Zaxx feels threatened by some of the smallest and most power-less dragons having some attention, then surely that is a problem with the bull, not with us?"

"Ah…" I shrugged, unsure why dragon politics mattered so much to her, or what there was to do about it. "I guess. But, are you going to tell the Great Golden Zaxx that?" I pointed out. "Do you speak dragonese?" I had thought that Char was fearless, I now revised my earlier assumption to crazy.

"But they're in the wrong." Char insisted. "The monk, even Zaxx. You can't look after a dragon just by enforcing some weird competition on them," the prince's daughter reasoned. "It's unhealthy, they all share the same den, after all."

"Char," I whispered in alarm, aware that there were other students and fully-ordained monks around us as we hiked. "I don't *ever* think it's a good idea for us to start questioning Zaxx the Golden," I nodded towards the nearest monk and raised my eyebrows. It was clear to me that half of these monks thought of Zaxx as a cross between a monster and a god – and maybe they were right. Maybe the two were the same thing.

"Pfft." Char shook her head, not accepting what I had to say. At least it stopped her rebuke all the same, and we finished our trek down the mountain in silence.

"Ah, Miss Nefrette, Torvald," said a smooth voice from the monastery doorway as we got back to the monastery. It was the Quartermaster Greer. "Where's the others? Fenn, Lesser, Ganna?" He motioned us over, picking us out of the tide of students returning with excited, scared, and awed looks at their near-dragon encounters.

"I don't know," I lied. I had seen them go off just ahead of us, and were probably already inside the monastery by now. I didn't know what Greer wanted with our group, but I guessed that it wasn't going to be good news.

"Well, no matter, as your tutor for the day, Monk Olan has told me of how insolent and disrespectful you were of his orders up on the mountain, in front of the prince and Abbot as well!"

"Not *my* prince," Char muttered at my side.

"Enough of this backchat, Nefrette. The pair of you are on stable duty until the monastery falls down or I say so – whichever comes closer!"

"What? We were only asking questions!" Char started to argue, and I groaned. I could see how this was going to go before Greer even said anything.

"Silence! Go. Muck out the stables. Get fresh straw. Brush down the ponies. Make sure they are fed and watered, every morning, every night." He turned and marched off.

"Well, at least it's not standing around listening to the Abbot lecture at us," Char grumbled, and I had to bite back a laugh. Char was just as rebellious as I apparently was, in her way. Maybe she could make a good ally in my mission. Could I tell her what I was up to, and why?

But as we walked deeper into the monastery, its enclosing walls pressed a heavy spirit upon me. If I was going to be busy mucking out the stables – how could I sneak back down to the Library? Or up to the Abbot's Tower?

CHAPTER 16

THE SCROLL

"Torvald?" A voice broke through my morose sulk, and I turned around to see none other than the thin Greer standing at the opening to the stables, wrinkling his nose a little at the smell. It was evening, and already the bells had been rung for dinner – and we were going to be late if we didn't finish up soon.

"Yes, sire?" I tried to stand up just a little bit straighter, even though my back was aching. I heard movement from deeper in the stables to see Char warily stepping forward, pitchforking the last of the muck and straw into the wheelbarrow between us.

"I have a scroll for *Torvald*—not you, Nefrette. Either get back to work or get going to dinner," Greer said.

"A scroll, sire?" I asked, feeling embarrassed at how dirty I was. I had let Char wear the only pair of gloves we could find and my hands were filthy.

Greer offered me the scroll and I took it gingerly, not wanting to get the paper soiled. He looked pointedly at Char, still standing in the aisle. "Dinner is being eaten, if you want to get to the Main Hall." The Quartermaster sighed, turning and leaving us alone.

"Thank you," I said to his back, with a moment of real elation. *Is my father going to tell me that he's reconsidered, that he never should have sent me away—that he's pulling me out of this place?* Before instantly feeling ashamed. Of course, my father wasn't going to send for me. He had his two legitimate sons at his side. What did he need me for? I was just his muck-shoveling, stinking illegitimate son. It didn't require much imagination at all to know what the great Malos Torvald would say if he could see me now, or what my brothers would think of my situation. I held the corner of the rolled-up parchment and tried to find a way to unroll it without sullying the fragile paper.

"Here, I'll read it for you if you want," Char said. She had managed to *not* fall over several times in the stables, or have the ponies chew her robes as she worked.

"Uh…" *What if it's private?* It might contain secret information about my mission here…

As if reading my mind, Char just stripped off her gloves, revealing clean and pink hands and gestured for me to give her the scroll. "Oh, don't be so precious, Torvald, the monks have already read it, you know. I'll read it to you while you've still got dirt all over your hands."

"The monks have already read it?" I repeated in horror, looking closer at the scroll sent by my father.

"Yeah. They read all of our messages, I think," Char said. "Look at the seal. I noticed it in my first year here."

How had I not noticed that red seal of Torvald, which was supposed to be a castle (the mighty stone fort of the Chief Warden) debossed in red wax, had been sliced neatly across the middle? "What? How could they?" I was shocked. "This is a message to me, from my father. He's the Chief Warden for the Middle Kingdom—how dare they!" I said, offering the scroll up to Char to read while I washed my hands with water from one of the horse's buckets.

"Yeah, I know, and listen, my father is a prince who rules his own kingdom, and they do the same to me. It's scandalous, it really is..." Char shrugged. "But what can we do? We're here under our parents' orders, aren't we?" she said carefully, and I tried to not let her see how nervous I was. Did she know that I had a secret mission here? Had she guessed?

We had been working together in the stables for the last week now, every morning and every night. Char worked quickly and efficiently around the animals, with a skill that I admired – and, just as importantly, she was kind to them, I saw. I started to wonder if either of us were cut out to be dragon monks at all – or which part of my day I secretly preferred: the dry lessons in the Library with Dorf and Maxal about dragon lore, or the sparring with Terrence and the others, or cleaning up Stamper and the rest of the ponies, the sheep, and goat muck out here with Char!

"My beloved son," Char began (pulling a sickly-sweet face as she read that bit, and I growled at her to get on with it).

"I trust that your studies at the Dragon Monastery are going

well, and that you are applying all of your efforts to learning all that there is to know in that place. I can only press upon you how urgent and important your studies are, as we have sore need for a learned scholar and scribe back in Torvald territory.

"We have been engaged in a border skirmish with the Gull Clan, who have been encroaching upon the Northern Orchard fields. Your brother Rik has managed to get his horse shot out from underneath him by their arrows but is not in any great harm. I, however, managed to catch one in the leg. It is no discomfort, but the Healer Garrett here is treating it and says the infection will subside with rest.

"Your Uncle Lett has been asking after your welfare, and everyone here misses you. You must redouble your efforts, and come home with all of the benefits of the Dragon Monastery at your disposal! I cannot stress how much hope I have in your success, and expect great news of your successful training by the spring equinox!"

"Signed, Your Father, Malos." Char looked up, frowning at me.

Oh no, I thought, a knot of worry in my chest. My father is injured. He has been shot by the Gulls. Hot anger swept through me. What was I doing here at all, when I should be back home with my brothers, protecting our land? *And the bit about expecting great news by the spring equinox – when was that, just a few weeks away? How was I ever going to do that?*

"I'm sorry," Char said hesitantly, "about your father getting shot. If it were in the Northern Kingdom it would never have happened."

"Oh really?" I said, feeling annoyed and powerless. "I don't see how that could be true. All of the warlords are at each other's throats across the Three Kingdoms, aren't they?" I was getting nowhere with uncovering what the secret of the Draconis Order was. The only things I knew now that I hadn't before I'd come were that Abbot Ansall was potentially three hundred years old —a claim my father would never believe without real evidence— and how to feed dragons in order by size. If only I had spent more time studying as a child, then maybe I could make sense of all of these dry old names and dates that I was reading here. None of it seemed to have anything to do with magic, or being able to move mountains with your mind.

Once again, I was letting my father down.

"Not in the Northern Kingdom," Char said in a quieter tone, still holding my father's scroll, waiting for me to finish cleaning and disrobing from the heavy leather apron. "Prince Lander, my father, is trying his best to put an end to the skirmishes and squabbles that your father is having to go through. He would send aid."

"Unlike—" I started to say, before stopping my mouth. *Unlike Prince Vincent.* I looked at Char, who made an imperceptible nod.

"Look. It is what it is. For what it's worth, I'm sorry," Char said, handing me my father's scroll and reaching instead for the wheelbarrow of muck and refuse, the very last one for the night. It was technically my turn to go and deliver it to the Kitchen Gardens, so I was surprised when Char said, "Look, I'll deliver this. You go eat."

"No, it's okay," I said. "I can still do my job." *Only, you're not doing your job, are you, Neill?* I rebuked myself. *You're letting your father die, and not even learning the secrets of the monastery like he asked me to!*

"No," Char said a little more firmly, taking the wheelbarrow forcefully from my hands, and already pushing it away. "I was going to miss dinner anyway this evening."

"Miss dinner? Why?" I asked. My stomach was already starting to grumble.

"Oh, just mountain ways, you know," she said as she rounded the door.

"What mountain ways?" I asked, only to find that I was asking just the ponies, sheep, and goats. If they had an answer for me, then it didn't look like they were going to share it. I stood in the stables amongst the animals for a moment, aware of how deeply that I was failing my father, my clan – and how mysterious Char Nefrette was being. And then it hit me. She wanted to go to the Kitchen Gardens. Perhaps she was heading off to do whatever it was she was doing the last time I'd followed her there.

I might not be able to find out the secret of the Draconis Order, but maybe I can find out the secret of Char Nefrette? She was the child of a prince. That has got to impress my father, right?

I counted to ten, and then counted to ten again, before I followed the route that Char had taken before to the wall door at the back of the old storerooms, and into the Kitchen Gardens beyond.

There. Just as I thought. I hid behind a stand of long, fat-podded bean plants, peering around their leaves to see that Char had already dumped the wheelbarrow on the compost heap (as tall as a cart) and was hefting a hessian sack, like the ones that we had been using to feed the dragons just a week ago, over her shoulder. Nan must have filled it and left it there for her.

The Messenger dragons, I thought. She must be secretly feeding them. Maybe that was why they were so happy to land on her arm and eat from her hands. And that would explain why Char had been so angry about the way that the ordained Draconis Monks were treating the dragons, because she thought that she knew better, though how she'd ever decided to start feeding the dragons on her own, I couldn't fathom

I heard the gentle thump of the door as it closed, and then decided to follow the half-mountain girl, all thoughts of missing dinner evaporating from my mind.

CHAPTER 17
CHAR, INTERRUPTED

I *was going to be late. Again.* I increased my speed to a jog, crossing over the ridge in fading light. *I shouldn't have wasted time reading the boy's scroll for him,* I thought. *Why should I care whether he gets it all mucky and ends up ruining it?*

"Because Char is kind," Paxala reminded me inside my own mind.

Well, I'm not so sure about that, I answered her. *Maybe I just wanted to see if there was any juicy information in it.* I got no response, and in truth, Paxala had been right, all the same. I hated the way that the Quartermaster treated Torvald, and any of the students that he thought weren't worthy of the Draconis Order. He was always making little snide comments or put-downs on either me, Lila, or Torvald, all for no other reason than we were different.

Yeah, so that was why I had decided to try and help him out.

Poor guy, I thought, remembering what his father had written to him. His father was wounded, his older brother lucky to be alive, and from what I could read between the lines, it sounded like his family was expecting him to learn every trick and power that the Order had to offer and bring that knowledge home to help, and fast, too!

But couldn't I say the same about my father? Maybe we could help each other, I thought, before I tripped on some of the patches of scree, and had to hop to right myself.

Okay Char, never mind Torvald. Think about what you have to do! I scolded myself, making my way down the track that wound through the edges of the forests and the gullies, until I rounded the last rise to Hammal Lake.

Ah. Just seeing it lifted my spirits. In this regard, I was never lying to Sigrid or Torvald when I made the excuse that I had 'mysterious mountain things' to do out here in the wilds. It was true that I really did appreciate being under the skies and in the free and open, with the sound of the kites and eagles for company, and the fresh air in my face. The wilds made me feel free, and myself again.

"Char sounds like a dragon," Paxala said, and I heard a splash from the far corner of the lake. Is that where she was? Was she fishing?

"Paxala?" I called, my feet crunching over the stones of the beach, heading for the river and the waterfall. "Pax, I brought dinner!" I enticed her.

"What use has Pax of old pig?" Again, the voice flashed in

my mind like a fish in the depths of the lake. I laughed – she was teasing me.

"Well, I'll just take it away then…" I laughed, turning back up the beach. Just then, with a mighty plume of water, the Crimson Red burst from the lake itself, pounced onto the beach, and, with a bound, was in the air over my head. I cheered in excitement, watching as she soared low over the trees and between pillars of rocks. She didn't roar or even chirrup, moving silently as she arced back towards me.

She's learning, I thought, feeling giddy. She's showing me that she can fly quietly, and that no other dragon has to know that she's here. That she must be ready to hunt.

I ran up the beach, daring her to chase me as she descended on a killing sweep.

"Char! Down!" a voice called just before something hit me broadside, and all of a sudden, I was tumbling head over heels, spraying stones and pebbles everywhere. Pain seared up my knees and forearms, and I could barely breath under the weight of the body lying across me.

A boy.

"Torvald?" I said in stupefied anger. "What are you doing here?"

"Down! It's a dragon," he hissed, looking up into the sky frantically, but Paxala had seemingly vanished.

Good. Maybe I can pretend that this is a wild dragon… I thought, when we were both flattened to the ground by a sudden beat of wind as a dark shape rushed us.

WHOOOSH! Paxala landed behind us with a sudden flaring of wings.

"Caught you!" The youthful dragon sounded delighted, but I groaned. There was no way to explain this to Torvald, other than the truth.

CHAPTER 18
NEILL'S WAY WITH DRAGONS

"Get back!" I shouted and, having nothing but the pebbles and rocks at my feet, I hefted the biggest one I could reach and threw it at the terrifying monster.

I had been following Char, fully expecting her to take her sack of meats and scraps to the dragon crater, to attract the Messenger dragons perhaps, but instead I was surprised when she suddenly veered from the path, along a narrow scrap of a trail over the ridge and down the other side to the largest of the cold mountain lakes.

Where a dragon that should not exist started to chase her. If I hadn't pushed her out of the way, it would have seized her in its vicious claws, and torn her limb from limb. What was even *more* horrifying about the Crimson Red, was that it didn't make a sound. It wasn't like the other dragons, always croaking, hissing, twittering, or roaring at each other. No. This one was deadly silent.

We're both going to die, I thought. If only my father could see me now. The thoughts flashed through my mind in quick succession, as we were stuck in a frozen tableau – me standing over the body of the hunted Char, and the giant red creature standing tense and ready in front of me. It dwarfed both of us, was almost as large as the stable block itself (not big at all by dragon standards, but big enough to make a meal of two teenagers).

It was young, I thought, but *did that make it more dangerous, or less?* And its scales varied from red as wasteland poppies, to the scarlet of freshest blood, to the deep purple-reds of rich textiles. She had a long snout with long teeth, and thin but very sharp tines around her head and down her spine.

Now or never... I raised the heavy rock, knowing that it would just bounce harmlessly off of the things scaled hide, but maybe it would give Char enough time to run and get aid...

"Torvald, no!" To my surprise, Char's hands closed around my arm, yanking it down easily and making me drop the stone as the prince's daughter threw her cloak over my head and wrestled me to the ground.

"Ugh. What are you... It'll kill us!" I muffled through the black cloth, coughing and spluttering to tear myself away from the confinement, to see—

Char was standing directly under the beast's long neck and head, easily within striking distance. "It is not wise to make an enemy of a dragon, Torvald," she said, reaching up to pat at the beast. "There, there Pax. He didn't mean it, he's just a boy."

I watched as the dragon curled its swan-like neck and her

head swung down to bump the girl affectionately, the way a horse might do, on the girl's head.

"Wait... You *know* this dragon?" I pointed between them. I felt like I had just walked into a dream, but I couldn't tell yet if this was a good one or a nightmare.

"Hatchling and dragonet," the girl said proudly. "I was with her when she first learned to fly, and when she first discovered her taste for fish."

There was a feeling then, like a pressure in my ears, as I was sure that *something* passed between them.

"Yes, well – I'm glad you like them too," Char replied, although I wasn't sure who she was talking to. The prince's daughter turned to look at me, and for a moment they both, dragon and girl, cocked their heads to one side in the way that birds do, at exactly the same time. "Hmm. You could, but it would be messy." Char shrugged.

"Who – who are you talking to?" I asked her, still unsure why the dragon hadn't eaten her yet.

"Paxala, of course," Char said.

"And, uh, do I want to know just who Paxala is?" I said nervously.

"That depends," the girl said and narrowed her eyes, "on whether we can trust a warlord's boy from the Middle Kingdom or not."

Oh great. Shock and fear spiked through me. *Is this some Northern Kingdom trick? Does Prince Lander have dragons too? Is Char really the advance guard of an invading army?*

"Uh..." I opened and closed my mouth. What was I to say?

No? That she couldn't trust me because I was actually here on orders to unearth the secrets of the Draconis Order for my clan?

"You're lucky," Char informed me, starting to walk up the beach as the Crimson Red – *Paxala* – sat on her rear haunches and inspected me. "Pax likes you."

"Oh." I didn't feel very lucky. "What would she do if she didn't like me?"

Char shrugged, scraping out a hollow in the beach and already collecting twigs and branches and starting to stack them in a pile. The sun was fading and we could clearly see the stars starting to come out over the opposite horizon. "She would probably have eaten you." She started to strike her flint and steel together, and, using some dried moss and leaves from the woods had managed to start a fire. There was a sudden hissing snort from Paxala, which I didn't know was agreement or not, but for some reason it made me think that the dragon was laughing at me.

"Great," I said, moving to stand up.

"Grrrrr." The dragon growled at my sudden movements. I stopped them.

"Come on, you might as well let the boy get some food, Pax. No, he's not going to hurt me again." Char was sighing, unpacking the hessian sack and carefully placing some of the larger scraps and joints on the outer branches of the fire, where they started to smoke and sizzle as they released their fats.

"You've decided to trust me then I take it?" I moved very, very slowly towards the fire, keeping my eyes fixed on the dangerous beast all the while and my hands in the air, and clearly visible.

"Grrrr." The dragon growled once more, but this time not as loud or as fiercely as the first time.

"No. But there's nothing I can do about it. The cat, or dragon in our case, is out of the bag." Char prodded and poked at the fire, before looking over at me seriously. "But really, if you do tell the others, or the Draconis Order or the Abbot or Greer or anyone, I'll throw you into the dragon crater myself."

"Sure. Got it. And I won't," I said, and meant it. "I have no intention of helping the Draconis Order when they've been so horrible to me ever since my first day here." If Char heard this, she didn't indicate it.

"And besides, I think that Paxala would be in danger if the other dragons found her," Char said, a little quieter. "And you don't seem like a cruel man, Neill Torvald."

"I don't?" I asked, surprised.

"No. I saw you trying to break up the fight between Lila and Terrence, even though Terrence has never been nice to you either," Char said. "And I see how kind you are to your terrible pony in the stable."

I shrugged. "Why should we all get into trouble and risk sparking a diplomatic incident for the sake of a stupid, spoiled brat and a hot temper?"

Char laughed but there was a crunch from behind us, and I turned quickly, alarmed, to see the dragon creeping around the fire, behind Char, to sit with her paws underneath her in the way that a cat would do. The firelight flared across her scales, making them dazzle. I couldn't take my eyes off her, even after seeing Zaxx and the other truly gigantic dragons, I had never seen one this big so close before, and she appeared content to sit and watch the fire, and me.

Her eyes were a deep golden green, and they caught me in the way that a fish hook spears a fish. She wasn't looking at me in the way that an animal might do out of fear of rebuke or hope for ward – she was looking straight into my soul.

"She's beautiful," I said in awe.

"Yes, she is." Char was grinning. "I found her out here in the wilds, just hatched and mewling for her mother. I couldn't leave her, and I knew that something terrible had happened, so I brought her here to this lake and cave, always meaning to re-introduce her to the others, but..." As she talked, Char reached over to prod a piece of the meat from her fire like a spit, and chuck it in the air to the dragon. As fast as a striking snake, the dragon caught the flesh in the air and swallowed it whole, licking her lips with her forked tongue.

"But you said that she was in danger?" I asked.

"Yes. You remember what that Monk Olan said about the Crimson Reds? That the others had died?" Char looked worried, as she threw me one of the scrap steaks, which I juggled between my hands as I waited for it to cool down.

"They must have been Paxala's mother?" I hazarded a guess.

"Yeah. I think it was Zaxx," Char said, whispering the name as if just talking about the Golden would bring him roaring over the ridge, breathing fire and ruin upon us all. I shivered in the night; for all that we knew, it might.

"I thought Olan said it was a sickness?"

"Yeah, he did. But since when have the monks been honest? And Paxala remembers fragments…" she clamped her mouth shut and I saw how worried Char was. I had been right in my estimation of her in the stables. She was good with animals. "It's okay, Char, Paxala." I nodded my head towards the young Red as well, "Your secrets are safe with me," I said, feeling oddly touched to be so trusted.

Not even my own family trusted me with their secrets, I thought, a touch sadly.

"And yours are with me, Neill of Torvald," Char said formally. I had forgotten that she was a prince's daughter for a second, as I wondered just what I had got myself into here. You have to be careful what oaths you swear to anyone, but especially so to prince's daughters. The Princes of the Three Kingdoms were still royalty – even if my own father didn't have much truck with our Prince Vincent. They had power and influence that spread across the lands – and besides all of that, there was nothing worse to us Torvalds than to be an oath-breaker.

It was what my father said Prince Vincent was, I remembered. That Prince Vincent had sworn an oath to protect the people of the Middle Kingdom, and he wasn't doing it. He was having expensive parties in his palaces, and he was lavishing gifts on his favored lords and captains while the everyday people suffered.

If you were an oath breaker, then you had no honor. I nodded to myself, repeating the words passed down from Torvald to Torvald ever since we had begun. How could anyone trust the words or deeds of an oath breaker? And, I just realized: how could we ever expect to be ruled over by one?

We ate companionably for a little while, as these thoughts swirled around my head, and Char told me about Pax's upbringing, and I asking questions about the Crimson Red for as long as they could bear to answer them. I was fascinated by her in a way that I had never been intrigued by anything as much before, and it had nothing (for once) to do with my mission here at the monastery.

"Has she always been able to fly?" No. She learned a few months after hatching.

"Is she born with scales?" Of course, but she sheds old ones every now and again.

"How high can she fly?" Who knows? We have to hide from the other dragons.

"Do dragons have their own language?" Yes. Sort of.

"How strong is she?" Stronger than a bull!

"Can she breathe fire?" No, or at least not yet.

"Are you two close? Does she understand what we're saying?" Yes, and yes.

For her part, Paxala the Crimson Red seemed just as interested in me as I was in her. As the stars started to rise and true dark settled around the bowl of the lake, the dragon settled on her side, and extended her long neck to delicately snuff at my hair, and then my clothes, before pulling back sharply.

"Ha. She thinks you smell." Char laughed. "I was too polite to say anything."

The stables. "Ah. Sorry," I said, laughing. "I do stink."

There was a wittering noise, like that of a bird, but not a call, more like a muted whistle from Paxala as she half-closed her green eyes.

"Is she *laughing* at us?" I said, amazed.

"Well, she might be laughing at *you*," Char said again, throwing another hunk of meat for Paxala to catch. "Beast," she added affectionately, earning a heavy thump from the tip of the dragon's tail. "Ow!"

"Never insult a dragon during dinner," I joked, spearing the next bit of meat to throw it high in the air.

Snap. Paxala caught it just as I was sure that she would.

"Well," Char yawned. "I think that we should probably be going back."

Another tail thump from Paxala, like an insistent child, I realized. *Probably because she is young, in dragon terms.* I watched as Char made a fuss of scratching Pax's ears, causing a pleased twittering sort of purr to rattle through her chest.

"I have to go, Pax," the prince's daughter said softly. "I wish that I could stay, but you know that I can't."

Again, there was that feeling like something passing between the girl and the dragon, a pressure behind my eyes, or like hearing muffled sound from a few rooms away. Both Char and Paxala were looking at me seriously.

"What?" I asked, feeling uncomfortable.

"Paxala wants to ask you something," Char said with a frown. "But I don't know if this is even going to work. Can you, I don't know—clear your mind like with the Abbot's magic exercises?"

"Sure, I can do that. But what does she want to ask me?" I said, feeling foolish.

That was when it happened. I heard something in my mind, and felt that same feeling again, like a pressure in the air between Char and Paxala. It was muffled, and I couldn't make out the words, but I knew that it was not coming from Char, as I didn't see her lips move. It sounded like a distant twittering, as of hearing a birdcall far away.

"I hear—no, I *feel* something?" I said cautiously, seeing Char frown.

"Hmm. I wonder what that means," Char muttered to herself, before looking up at me. "But you cannot hear her?" Char said, a look of amazement and concern on her face.

"Hear, *her?*" I gestured to the Crimson Red dragon, who I could see blinking at me. "I hear her breathing and wittering in that snout of hers, if that is who you mean…?"

"Who else, numbskull?" Char sighed, before muttering to herself. "I guess that it *is* only me then." She coughed, straightened up to stare at me. "*Neill. Char. Paxala. Friends?* That is what Paxala said to you, exactly. I think that she is asking if you will be our friend, and ours, yours."

I opened and closed my mouth several times in wonder, turning to look at the Crimson Red as she blinked her eyes at me in all seriousness. The dragon was trying to talk to me. That was how Char knew her name, and that was how they were so close. Everything that Char had told me was true – the dragons do have their own language, and they do understand what you are saying. Even though *I* couldn't hear her, I knew that *she* could hear me.

I looked at the dragon direct in her eyes, and nodded. "Yes, I would be honored to be your friend, Paxala."

―――――――――

AFTER WE HAD PUT out the fire and seen the Crimson Red to her hidden cave behind the waterfall, Char and I walked up over the ridge in the starlight, and skirted around the dragon crater on the other side. We could hear the nighttime, occasional whoots and mumblings of the dragons as they dozed fitfully in their ancient home.

"I wonder how long they've lived here." I broke the silence, my head full of wonder and stories. *I was a friend to dragons. It was like one of those old fairy tales. I was a dragon-friend, me, Neill of Torvald!*

"I don't know, but I think it's a long, long time," Char said quietly beside me. She, too, had seemed lost in thought on most of our walk back. "Torvald?" she asked me, pausing before we began the final leg of our journey down to the torch-lit walls of the Dragon Monastery below.

"Yes, Nefrette?" I said.

"Thank you." She smiled hesitantly, shyly. The starlight caught her face, making it look like a dream. "Thank you for being on our side, for keeping our secret."

A flash of guilt. *Was I going to keep their secret from father? No, of course I'm not.* But I'd made an oath to Char, Prince Lander's daughter. And the dragon, Paxala, had asked me to be her friend. Friends don't betray each other's confidences.

But didn't that mean that I was betraying what my father had asked me to do? I felt torn, and resolved to not come to any decision tonight. Luckily it was dark, and Char didn't seem to notice anything of my internal turmoil as she bit her lip and carried on talking in those hushed and quiet tones.

"There's something... Not right about the Draconis Order, Neill."

"I know," I said. It was something that I, too, had been thinking for some time. "Why were they so mean to everyone? Why were the Draconis Monks seemingly terrified of the dragons inside the crater? Why was the Abbot so friendly with Prince Vincent?"

"I don't know, it just doesn't feel the same when I am with Paxala," Char said. It was somehow easier to speak our deepest fears into the dark. "She's so clever, and responds so well to being treated kindly—I don't think the Abbot has any clue about how to deal with dragons." She said it, and I felt a slight moment of fear at our heresy.

"And, Paxala..." Char hesitated. "Paxala is scared of the Draconis Order. She fears the monks, and the crater." Char looked up at me seriously in the night. "Her mother didn't live long, but she lived long enough to give her a name, and to hide her in the caves when she was still an egg—and to give her a fear of the Order. And believe me, a dragon isn't scared of *anything*."

"Okay," I nodded. "We'll get to the bottom of it, Char. Don't worry." I said, feeling awkward.

"It's just..." Char frowned as she looked at me. "I understand that you have your own loyalties to your clan, Neill... I grew up in the court of a prince, so I'm no stranger to politics and secrets..." My heart froze. What was she about to tell me? What she did next shocked me, even though it was a simple thing. She put a hand on my arm, just a light touch, like the way that friends do. "But we really do have to keep Paxala a secret, at least until we know that she can be safe. I don't trust the Order either, and neither does my father...."

I shouldn't have been shocked at hearing these words out loud – they were what I had been thinking, after all. But even though I was anxious, and worried about what it might mean – I had that same wild and brave feeling that I had on the mountain with Uncle Lett, and whenever I thought about the dragons. That this was how it was supposed to be. "I promise I'll keep your secret, Char," I said solemnly. "We're friends, right?" I reminded her.

"Yeah, friends." Char smiled.

When we got down to the kitchen gate, we returned the hessian sack, snuck through the Kitchen Gardens, and were halfway through the storeroom when suddenly torches flared, and shouting voices echoed off the walls.

"Char Nefrette! Neill Torvald! I don't care who your parents are – but anyone caught sneaking out in *this* monastery is in a lot of trouble!" It was the Quartermaster Greer, and beside him our not-so-favorite Monk Olan.

CHAPTER 19
THE ABBOT'S JUDGEMENT

"Are you okay?" I managed to whisper at Char, who just raised an eyebrow, her same old stubborn and resilient demeanor reasserting itself. I only asked because Monk Olan hadn't been too delicate in seizing our arms and tying them behind our backs, before shoving us behind the Quartermaster Greer as we were led to the tower where I had first been brought to when I had arrived. There were stairs and stairs and still more stairs, and Monk Olan was taking great delight in trying to make us bang our shins on apparently each one.

"Of course I am okay, Torvald," Char whispered with a lowering scowl. "Just wait until my father hears about how his daughter is being treated."

"His *bastard* daughter, remember," said the Quartermaster, crowing his delight at apparently catching us breaking the Draconis Order rules. "Just as you, Torvald, are also a bastard, are you not? Both illegitimate children. Sneaking around together, doing what? Creating more illegitimate children? Would never have been allowed in my day."

Ah. So that was it, was it? I had been wondering just why the Quartermaster hated us so much. For a while I had just thought it was because he was a bigot, and now I saw that it was because he was a bigot and an idiot in equal measure. But at least he'd given me an idea for an excuse we might use with the Abbot, as to why we'd been sneaking around. I just hoped Char would play along and pretend she liked me more than just friends.

"With any luck, Torvald, Nefrette, your parents will realize that your blood is too impure to truly learn such a noble art," Greer continued, his hands making that sudden, slapping noise that he liked so much as he clapped them together.

"Aha!" We came to the top, open room where no furniture adorned the walls or the floors, only the midnight air, streaming in through the open archways.

And the austere, black-clad Abbot with his black skullcap, cane, and wiry beard.

"Your holiness," Greer bowed. "I have found them, as I sent word that they had left the monastery grounds... They were sneaking around the old storerooms, it seemed, up to no good. I beg of your holiness to punish them appropriately for so flaunting the rules."

The Abbot was quiet, his gaze falling on Greer, Char, and me. "So, they did *not* leave the monastery grounds and break the direct rules of our ancient and noble Order, I take it?" the Abbot pointed out. "If you found them in the storerooms, I take it, Quartermaster Greer?"

The Quartermaster blinked, quailed. "Well, no, I mean yes, you are correct, sire. I cannot prove that they have left the monastery grounds after dark, as is prohibited – but they have certainly left their dormitory rooms after dark! They are not training, or studying, or learning – they really cannot be trusted to concentrate or apply themselves to such a noble study as that of the Draconis Order," Greer said in an almost desperate, pleading fashion that made me feel sick. "Their blood is too impure," he added as a final shot.

The Abbot just nodded, saying nothing for a long time. Instead, his eyes bored into mine, and then Char's.

"Leave us." The Abbot—the most powerful man on this mountain, more powerful, I suspected than even the three princes —spoke suddenly, making me startle. "Quartermaster, leave the children here while I *consider* their punishment."

"Yes, yes, of course, sire. Do you wish for me to wait? To fetch a cane?" I saw the Quartermaster lick his lips, as if the idea of us being punished brought him nervous joy.

"I asked you to leave us, Quartermaster," the Abbot said again in his deadpan, completely monotone way. Somehow, the fact that he had no emotion whether talking to Greer or looking at us made me worry what was coming next all the worse. I felt a tremor run down my hands as the Quartermaster made his bowing and scraping exit, and the Abbot waited until we heard two sets of footsteps disappearing down the tower beyond.

Abbot Ansall was quiet a little longer, regarding as, before turning to look out of the window. "Now. Shall we begin?" he said casually.

Begin what? I thought, sliding a look over to see Char looking apprehensive.

"*Flamos,*" the Abbot said, just as he had the first time that I had been in this tower, and sparks of light suddenly illuminated the gloom as he commanded the candles and torches to spark into life. I heard Char gasp at the power.

He's trying to frighten us, I thought.

"It is easy to see why two young people such as yourselves, the children of powerful men in the world, would prefer to play rather than study the secrets of the Draconis Order," the Abbot said.

"We weren't playing!" Char blurted out.

"Oh? Then what were you doing, skulking around the storerooms at night?" The Abbot caught her with his glittering eyes. Char bit her lip, sullenly. "No?" The head of the Order shook his head as if sad for the state that we had gotten ourselves into. I studied the man's face as he glared, seeing wrinkled, pale, paper-thin skin, but he seemed thin and ascetic rather than malnourished, or ancient. I wondered if it really was him in the etchings and woodcuts from hundreds of years ago.

"It has come to my attention, Char Nefrette, that you have been spending quite a considerable amount of time out on the mountain of late. Just what can a wild girl be doing out there if not playing, I ask myself?" The man turned to look out the nearest, cold archway at the dark mass of the mountain above us. "I would dread to think, Miss Nefrette, that you are taking yourself to the dragon crater to interfere with the dragons themselves. You know that any contact between the dragons and humans unsupervised is forbidden – and besides which is it highly dangerous, and foolhardy as well."

I felt Char tense beside me at the suggestion. She *knew* that this wasn't the case, and I silently begged her not to argue with the Abbot. Instead, she just glared at the Abbot defiantly, and I wondered if I should try telling the Abbot that we'd just wanted to be alone together, that we *cared* for each other.

Once again, the man gave one of his resigned, sad little sighs. "Such a shame, such a shame. And for two such promising pupils, as well." Next his gaze flickered to me, like a snake catching a mouse. "Despite what the Quartermaster Greer thinks, *Torvald,* I see value in having diverse and interesting students here at the monastery; even girls, even Raiders... and even Gypsies." *Was he threatening me?* I wondered. "Do you remember that little chat that we had when we first arrived, about how important it was to be your own man, and to be strong?"

I did. The Abbot had tried to tell me to ignore old family loyalties, to instead concentrate on the 'great work' of the Draconis Order. I nodded.

"Speak, Torvald!" Abbot suddenly spat, making me jump.

"Err, yes, sir, of course, sir," I said.

"Good. Well, hear me now then, *Torvald,* and *Nefrette,*" he sneered both of our names as if they were beneath him. "You have the opportunity to become something *great.* Not just strong, not just good, but remarkable." His hand suddenly snaked out, to point a thin finger directly at Char. "*You* have a touch of the dragon magic about you. It is a gift that can make you great, or can make you mad."

"What?" Char stammered.

"I can sense it, child," the Abbot said. "And it is for that reason alone that I have not expelled you, as there are so very few minds that come to me capable of holding the magic." He took a step forward, so that his outstretched, accusing finger hovered between Char's eyes. To me it looked for some reason the way my brother Rik would look when he is about to spear a fish on a hook. "You can train in magic with us, or I will have to find ways to nullify your powers. They will destroy you if you do not control them, and you will become a danger to yourself and to all of us here. You will become a danger to your father. Is that what you wish? For your father to be ousted from his kingdom because his bastard daughter is a monster?"

"I...I..." Char stammered again. I saw her flush, her eyes flicker with shame, then anger, and finally uncertainty. I felt anger seethe in my chest. *How could he say this?* But I had seen Char's magic myself, I had seen the way that her candle on the mountaintop had flared, and she was the one who had managed to befriend a dragon. What if the Abbot, no matter how cruel he also was, was telling us the truth?

"You will train, personally, with me and the other Mage students, here at this tower every evening. Do you understand?" The Abbot said.

"Y-yes, sire." Char nodded. "But... I don't understand – why didn't you make me a Mage before? Instead of a Scribe?"

The Abbot breathed through his nose at the interruption. "One day, Miss Nefrette, you will understand that every power has its checks and balances. It is true that I sensed something in you, but there are others who view the training of a *different* prince's daughter – and an illegitimate one at that – to be against the Order's principles." The Abbot made his usual dry laugh at this. "I know better, of course."

A different prince? I thought. *Checks and balances...* I was suddenly certain that he meant that Prince Vincent didn't want Char trained as a Mage, or hadn't before. That Prince Vincent (quite rightly, I suppose) didn't trust Prince Lander's daughter.

I don't know if this Mage training was meant as a punishment, but Char looked crestfallen all the same. *Paxala,* I realized. *How is she going to look after Paxala if she has to come here every evening?*

"Then leave us, Char. Go, back to your own dormitory room, and quickly girl." The Abbot waved a hand and the door to the stairs swung open of its own accord. I felt my heart clatter with surprise at the Abbot's magic.

Char paused, looking at me uncertainly, but I gave her the smallest nod. *It will be okay,* I tried to will towards her, but her eyes looked shadowed and fearful as she took to the steps.

Slam! Again, the door closed of its own accord, or the Abbot's magic. We were alone, and I wondered if he was going to expel me, or worse.

"Torvald," the Abbot said, his harsh tone lessening a little. "Char has her dragon magic, and her father is a Prince of the Three Kingdoms, so she is *very* valuable to me and to this monastery. I have a duty to try and educate her in her powers. But a warlord's son...?"

The man turned to pace to one of the arches and look out into the night. He was silent for a long while, letting me stew in my mix of fear and apprehension. I had failed. I have failed my father, and what he wanted for me. What would Malos Torvald, the great Chosen Warden of the Middle Kingdom think if I come skulking back home, my tail between my legs? My brothers would have every excuse to banish me or worse. And my father's lands might even be threatened because of it. *What sort of son am I? What sort of Torvald was I?*

"But not *any* warlord's son, are you, Neill?" the Abbot surprised me by saying suddenly. He didn't wait for my answer. "You are the bastard son of Malos Torvald, the Chosen Warden of the Middle Kingdom, with almost enough support in these lands as Prince Vincent himself. Have you ever thought of these matters, Torvald?"

Yes, I thought, but I said, "Only a little, sire." I knew that my father was powerful, here in the Middle Kingdom at least. But how powerful was he compared to all of the other princes? Given what I had already figured out about my father's wishes (that he didn't trust Prince Vincent, and that he thought Prince Vincent was unworthy of the throne) then there really was only one conclusion: that my father wanted to topple the Prince of the Middle Kingdom.

"Only a little. Well." The Abbot chuckled, but there was no humor to it. It was a mirthless sound. "Were you a Lesser, or a Fenn, then I would have already sent you home tied to the back of a mule by now. But your father is a powerful man. It is such a shame that he is dying."

"*What?*" I blurted out. "What do you mean he's dying?"

"Here. This arrived at the same time as the scroll that your father sent to you. It is from my healer stationed at Torvald Keep. Do you know the one?"

I shook my head. I did indeed know the healer: a thin, worrying sort of man who spent more time patching up my brother's horses than he did tending to people. The old man had been without family for years now, working from his small workshop to treat every flu, fever, aches and pains that the keep had to offer.

"But, but Healer Garrett is no Draconis Order monk—why would he—?" I blurted out. He did not wear the black robes, and he seemed to have no great love for dragons especially.

"No?" The Abbot gave me a cruel smile, and I felt my blood turn cold. *I had to warn my father.* "Healer Garret might not be a fully ordained Draconis Monk – he has no right to put Draconis after his name as the rest of my flock do – but he studied with us, for a time," the Abbot said. "It is one of the many benefits of this place, Master Torvald, if you will but apply yourself. We train most of the healers across all of the Three Kingdoms."

Healer Garret was working for Ansall, I thought. How could I get word back to my father?

The missive that his Holiness the Abbot offered was but a short note in the old healer's sprawling, black spidery script. He asked for some supplies of this herb and that powder, and asked after the general health of the monastery. None of that interested me, what did strike to my core was the last few lines.

"*...the Chief Warden here is ill with an infection from what seems to be a poisoned arrow. I have tried my usual creams and* *cleansers but they are not fighting the infection, which has spread from local area (ankle) to the leg. I suspect Blackroot powder was used, or perhaps Greencap. I request that appropriate remedies and restoratives are dispatched immediately, if I have any hope of halting the infection taking over his body. But the Chief Warden is strong, and should last until the spring equinox perhaps..."*

So that was why my father had urged me all speed in my mission here. Because he was dying. The Gull Clan had shot him with a poisoned arrow and he knew that if he died then my brothers would ascend to take his place. *My brothers who have no great care for me,* I thought.

"Of course, you wish to save your father, Torvald," the Abbot said. "As do I. It can be so *disruptive* to the kingdom when there is a new Chief Warden, I find. And disruption will mean that the Draconis Order here will have to take sides, and support claims, and all manner of complicated things which get in the way of our studying the great and noble beasts. Do you understand what I am telling you, Torvald?"

That you are holding my father to ransom, and in return you want the Torvald Clan to support the Draconis Order in whatever they do, I thought. "Yes. I think I do, sire."

"Good. I will dispatch the correct supplements, powders, and remedies in the morning. But it is a very long and difficult journey back to the Eastern Marches, is it not? We have to hope and pray that they will get there in time, before the spring equinox," the Abbot said, his face a picture of worry and sadness. In that moment then, I hated him with a passion that frightened me. The Abbot Ansall was no holy man. He was a politician.

Before the spring equinox. Of course, the Abbot would have read my father's letter. Which meant he might have surmised the truth about why my father had sent me here. I had no choice. I nodded. "Thank you, sire. I will do my best to concentrate on my studies."

"I am sure that you will, *Torvald,*" the Abbot said with a ghost of a smile upon his lips. "If I may, let me give you just a tiny bit of advice to help sharpen your mind: stay away from the Nefrette girl. She seems to bring out the worst in you, and I wouldn't want either of your studies here to be threatened."

I nodded, but did not say anything – but I didn't have to, as the Abbot moved a hand and the door opened of its own accord, leaving me to flee back into the night, and to my dormitory room, my head spinning with everything that had happened today.

I have until the spring equinox to save my father, in one way or another.

PART III
THEIR LOYALTIES

CHAPTER 20
PROTECTOR

It was the very next morning, and I stood with Dorf on the cold battlements of the monastery. "Is that him?" said Dorf to me. It was cold atop the walls of the monastery, and below us we could see the stone and scree of the mountain, dotted with yellow-tipped gorse, and still dusted with frost. Spring was on its way, but it was coming too soon for my liking. We were watching the small figure wearing black, on the back of a pony making his slow way down the path, his saddle bags heavy and laden with supplies.

"It's not Healer Garret, if that is what you mean," I said a little irritably. I had especially put my name forward to be on wall lookout duty this morning so I could see the healing powders and supplies leave the monastery for myself. *To see if the Abbot would keep his word,* I thought bleakly.

"Easy there, Torvald, you don't have to be quite so mean," Dorf said at my side. He looked ridiculous in the small metal hat that all of us wall lookouts were wearing. *Ridiculous but honest*, I thought. He didn't have to volunteer to join me up here, and had only done so after I had told him last night of my father being gravely ill and that the Abbot Ansall had decided to send healing remedies back to my home in the Eastern Marches.

I didn't mention anything about it being a part of a complex ransom though, as Dorf would only get upset, and probably not understand.

"I know, I'm sorry, Dorf, I'm just worried for my father," I said shame-facedly. "Please, accept my apologies."

"Already forgotten," Dorf said in a brighter tone. "For what it's worth, I'm sure that your father will be okay, Neill. Everyone knows that the Draconis Order has some of the best healers in the world."

And some of the best spies, it seems. I nodded. "Anyway, how much longer have we got up here?" I asked, looking at the low angle of the sun.

"Oh, until breakfast I think?" Dorf made a patting motion on his rounded belly. Like his warm and gentle homeland, the Lesser were known to be comfortably padded. "Not long now."

Good, I thought. "I'll just do another circuit then, and by the time I'm done we should be ready for the next watch, right?" I said.

"Oh. Shall I stay here then?" Dorf looked down at the gate underneath him, and the walls all around him. It seemed an awfully big space for just him to be watching.

"Well, we can't leave the front gate undefended, can we?" I joked, knowing that it wasn't the case anyway. There was another monk by the gate below and we were just up here as extra eyes. Not that anyone came up to the Draconis Order very often. It seemed that the place had supplies delivered every few weeks from the ramshackle village at the foot of the mountain, and the odd returning monk or messenger from all over – but they were always only solitary travelers, and nothing to worry about. I trudged along the northern fortifications that arced back towards the wilds of the mountain, and the ridgeway behind, keeping my eyes peeled– but not for intruders. What I was looking for was Char.

The problem was, that Dorf and I were only supposed to guard the front sections of the high stone wall that ringed the entire monastery, and the watch duty was split between teams of monks and students. I walked to the adjacent section of the ramparts overlooking the wilder pars of the ridge, wondering if I could catch a sight of either Char or Paxala.

I saw nothing. *If Char was studying magic with the Abbot every evening, how could she manage to get out early enough to feed Paxala this morning?* The message of the Abbot was still ringing in my ears. Char was to study every evening, and I had to be a good student if I wanted my father to live.

I reached the end of my section, and the nearest Draconis Order monk waved a hand at me to say that he had this part covered. I nodded, waved a greeting and turned, just as something bright and dazzling caught my eye and was gone.

I blinked and there it was again. A sudden flash of light, seeming to come not from down in the heavy gorse thickets near the wall.

It could be anything. A patch of sunlight catching a puddle, or perhaps some strange insect.

Flash. The light struck my eyes once again, and I blinked. I rubbed the glare from them and peered down to where it was, and saw nothing other than the overgrown wasteland behind the Kitchen Gardens. *Where Char had been sneaking out from? Is she stuck out there, on the other side of the wall?* I checked the sun, I might have just enough time to take a look before breakfast, if I were quick. I had to make sure that Paxala was being fed now – Char had made me promise, and that meant that I had an oath to keep. And not only that, I reminded myself, but I had no intention of obeying the Abbot's whims and wishes that I stay away from Char. I was oath-sworn to her and the dragon now, and I could not trust the Abbot who might at any moment order his spies and so-called 'healers' to poison my father anyway. I had to let Char know what was happening, and that *any* healer or Scribe trained here at the monastery was a danger to her father and to those that she loved. I hurried back to the front gate, just as the breakfast bell chimed. Dorf already looked anxious.

"Breakfast?" he said. It seemed important to him to make sure that he had three square meals a day.

"Let's go. Don't worry, I'll take these helmets back," I offered, hurrying to the storerooms and, beyond that, to the Kitchen Gardens. This time I kept one of the helmets on me just in case Monk Olan Draconis or Quartermaster Greer found me. I could use the excuse that I was returning it. It seemed crazy to be so eager to break the rules again, the very night after the Abbot had reprimanded me, but with the medicines safely en route, I felt certain that I could still work to find out what I could for my father. I would just have to be better at hiding how I did it. All I cared about was unearthing the secrets of the Order for my father, and my friends.

I hesitated at the door to the gardens, taking a deep breath, and heard mumbled voices.

"I know, but this is the best that I can do..." I was disappointed it wasn't Char, but instead sounded like Nan Barrow, the House Mistress and cook who ran the kitchens and the gardens. But who was she whispering to?

"She needs more. The girl has been lucky that the dragon is young, and by a lake too – but a Crimson Red of her size cannot live on leftovers and scraps. They are larger than the Blues! If the girl wants the Crimson Red to grow to her full size then she cannot be malnourished early on. The dragon hasn't even been taught how to hunt properly yet! If the girl doesn't come soon..." said a man's voice, one that sounded very much like Jodreth.

"Something bad is happening with the girl. And the Torvald boy," I heard Nan Barrow say, and I almost stepped out from my hiding place to announce myself, but I was too intrigued to hear what they had to say for themselves.

"I think we can trust the Torvald boy. He has a good heart."

Silence from the cook. "But is a good heart enough?" Nan said wearily.

"We had better hope so, for the dragon's sake," Jodreth said. "Anyway, enough of this dark talk, I will not waste my time with you - come here, my love."

I felt suddenly ashamed, as I heard the rustle of feet on the paths as the pair must have embraced. I took my ear from the door and stepped back, leaving the lovers to their secrets.

So Jodreth and Nan Barrow are lovers? I thought, the idea feeling oddly pleasing and right, were it not for the dark tidings that they gave each other. Nan was also supplying Char with the food for Paxala. So, that meant Jodreth must know about both Paxala and Char – but Char had never mentioned him. How was it that Jodreth Draconis, a fully ordained monk, knew about the student's hidden dragon but hadn't gone to the Abbot with this knowledge?

They said that they could trust us, for the dragon's sake. They knew something about what was going on, and I had to tell Char.

I SAW CHAR AT BREAKFAST, looking owlish and tired, as if she hadn't had any sleep. I didn't blame her as I had barely slept at all myself, worrying about my father all night. Breakfast at the Dragon Monastery consisted of the kitchen stay setting a long table with fruit and porridges and warmed breads, mountain water, cheeses, and leaving us to help ourselves. It was usually the most raucous of the meal times, with most of the shouting, bullying, and laughing that went along with it.

But not this morning. It was quiet at the tables as the students filed in line with their bowls, one after another to pick a selection from the feasting table.

"*One* apple, you greedy pig, Lesser!" snapped the Quarter-master, as my heart plummeted. Greer was here, and was now supervising our breakfasts, overseeing how much anyone took and directing them back to their seats in silence. But really, I had a feeling he was there for a different reason—to make sure Char and I stayed apart.

"Really, Fenn?" the Quartermaster said when he saw just how little porridge the stick-thin girl had taken, instead dolloping two extra ladles onto her plate. I knew that Sigrid was worried, it seems, about being a better fighter, and was always complaining about whether she was fit enough. To be honest, I thought that it was right that she have a square breakfast, but the way that the Quartermaster drew everyone's attention to her anxieties only made her burst into tears as she went back to her seat.

When it was my turn, the Quartermaster plonked into my bowl just one ladle of porridge and a rather small, wrinkled winter apple, and grinned. "Protectors are made of stern stuff, Master Torvald." He oozed pleasure at these small cruelties, but I ignored him. It would be enough for me.

Just as I suspected the Quartermaster or the Abbot intended, there was no time to talk to Char during breakfast at all. I tried to catch her eye as I washed up my bowl in the hot water at the end of the hall, but she ignored me, biting her lip as she did so.

Nan and Jodreth are right. *This is bad,* I thought, as we were then thrown into a grueling day of lessons. Char needs to know about the Abbot's network of spies, and she needs to know that I have her back--that I will not let either her or Paxala down.

I TRIED, I really did try hard to learn. I was aware of the monks watching us, assessing us throughout the day, calling out suggestions or rebukes and I tried to show them that I gave my all to every task. I didn't want to give them any reason to mark me down or to put my father in danger.

"Duck, Dorf, duck!" I hissed at him, as I faced off against my dormitory opponent. We were doing our mandatory Protector lessons that every student had to do, just as we had to all do a mandatory amount of scribing and meditation. The difference came when you were chosen for a particular task--as I had been chosen to be a Protector, and Dorf a Scribe. Then you were assigned to extra lessons. So I went to additional, specialized Protecting lessons, while Dorf did extra Scribing. I was using my mandatory lesson to try and sharpen up Dorf's combat skills.

Thunk-thwack! We traded blows, and Dorf looked scared of the wooden baton that he was holding.

"It's okay, Dorf," I reassured him. "Just think of it as playing."

We sparred and I won again and again, but at least now Dorf was no longer so upset when I beat him. It was better than having the sneering Terrence as his opponent. By the end of the lesson he had even managed to learn a couple new blocking maneuvers, which I hoped would help him against the others.

"Thanks, Torvald," Dorf wheezed, holding his side as the dragon pipes rang for a change in lesson. He was to go off and do extra scribing, while I was to stay here and practice with some real weapons along with the other Protectors.

"Just help me out with the history scrolls," I told him,

hoping that the nearest Draconis Monk had seen all of the good effort that I had put in. I had a few minutes to duck my head underwater and freshen up before the real lesson began, and I made my way to the buckets of water and towel racks held under the wooden galleries for especially that purpose, where a shadow detached itself from the shadows. The water troughs were busy with students – it was easy to get lost in the hubbub.

"Char?" I said. She looked troubled as she caught the edge of my sleeve.

"Our friend," she hissed, and I nodded, loudly splashing the water with my hands to try and mask what she was saying. "My schedule starts straight after dinner. I can't…"

"I'll go," I said quickly, wanting to tell her what I had over-heard in the Kitchen Gardens, but knowing that there wasn't any time.

"See, Nan," she mouthed silently and I nodded, as water suddenly splashed all over us.

"And what are these two lovebirds talking about?" It was Terrence, along with his cronies, laughing.

"Do you realize how terrible *you* are at fighting?" Char said.

"Do you want to prove that, wild-child?" Terrence growled.

Char was already braiding up her hair. "I've got to go scribe, I'm afraid, Terrence, not that I would want to spend any longer in your presence than I really have to anyway," she said haughtily.

"I'll take you up on that offer." There was a loud thump as Lila appeared from the storerooms, hefting her leather armor and buckler shield. She was also in our advanced Protector class. I saw Terrence snarl and grinned. He'd be lucky if he got out of there without being injured.

It was our first day training with edged weapons, and it appeared to be only Lila and me who had any great experience with using them. I had been training with weapons against or with my brothers ever since I could hold them. I wasn't as good as my brothers were, but I was much better than the rich nobles' children who had also made it to advanced Protector. I offered to be the first to demonstrate with Lila, who grinned savagely at me as she crouched, her shield buckler in one arm, and the sword in the other.

Needless to say, she beat me, thoroughly and completely. Where I had some knowledge of using edged weapons and even a little skill – Lila was *very* good with them. But I took comfort in the fact that we had also managed to *not* kill each other or break the skin, which I thought must count as a success.

"If you can't pull your blows, then don't practice. Only aim for the protected bits on your opponent for now!" shouted the Draconis Monk who was training us, a strong, blocky looking man with a bald head and a brown beard. I hadn't met him before, but he appeared to be not quite so sexist or bigoted as some of the others. His arms and face bore the mark of scars that ran up and down them like white rivers, and he said that his name was Feodor Draconis.

"Hmm. Good work, Neill, Lila." Feodor gave us a nod, which was more encouragement than I had heard anyone receive.

By the end of the lesson we had two students with light cuts that needed binding, but weren't serious, and many, many scrapes and bruises. Feodor gathered us all together as the afternoon bell went off, and wouldn't let us go until he had lectured us.

"Tomorrow we go back to wooden weapons, as you already have two injuries, and tomorrow you'll have more if some of you don't learn how to respect your weapons, and your opponents," Feodor said.

"Why should we respect our opponents?" Lila asked.

"Because one day you're going to come up against someone stronger, faster, tougher, and a whole lot cleverer than you, Lila – no matter *how* good you are." Feodor raised his scarred arm back to the ridgeline above us. "And just over there is a crater *full* of them, you hear me? You may think that this is all about protecting yourself from the odd desperate bandit out on the road, but it's also to protect *them*, and to protect *you* from them," he said in a loud, booming voice.

"Is that how you got your injuries? From a dragon?" Lila asked again, ever impetuous.

Feodor grinned, raising his arm high into the air so that we could all get a good look at the rivers of white scar tissue that crisscrossed it, all the way up past his shoulder, neck, and up onto the back of his head. "Yeah. This was from a dragon. I bled like a pig, and most everyone wanted to put me out of my misery, but I was too dumb to die."

"Why?" Lila asked again. "Why did the dragon attack you?"

At this, the monk Feodor lowered his arm slowly, and started to glower. It was like a chill had suddenly crossed over the courtyard. "Enough questions, Lila. Let's just say that I was stupid, and I got in the way of a dragon and its prey. Which is a good reason for you all to apply yourself to your training, otherwise you'll end up with some pretty new scars of your own." His mood had soured and darkened in an instant as he dismissed us, turning to stomp off to the washhouse.

"But I thought that the monks feed them all by hand. What do they hunt?" Lila snorted to herself, trying to act tough after being the object of the monk's wrath.

But what on earth do the crater dragons hunt? I echoed myself. Another mystery. It seemed like my life was quickly becoming full of them lately, as I went to get washed and changed myself, ready for the rest of the afternoons boring scribing lessons.

AT DINNER, we were overseen just as at breakfast and lunch, but this time the Quartermaster had none other than Olan Draconis with him, sitting at a high table and eating themselves. They watched as we ate, and they allowed us to talk as long as our conversations never got too loud or too raucous. At their table also sat Char, Maxal, and a few others, separated from the main body of the students – all of the students who were studying dragon magic, it seemed.

They all had that same tired and anxious look upon their faces as well, I saw, watching as they kept their eyes low on their food as Greer and Olan ate beside them.

There was no way that I was going to get word to Char

about what Jodreth had told Nan, about Paxala needing more food now that she was growing, or to any of the others. I cursed myself, chewing my cold meats in silent fury until it was time to wash up our dishes. The students at the 'head table,' as I was coming to think of them, filed out with Greer and Olan, leaving the rest of us visibly relieved at the sudden lack of observation. I walked to the plateglass windows there to see the small group trudge across the freezing cold courtyard and up to the tower where the Abbot presumably was going to teach them the arcane secrets of dragon magic. I waited until the top floor bloomed with a soft orange light from the torches up there. *That was where I needed to be, too*—thinking about what my father had ordered me to do. Would I be able to ask Char what the secret was?

No, not any time soon anyway. It seemed that the rest of us had been dismissed as unimportant for the evening, but we were too tired from our renewed lessons to do much of anything but return to our dormitory rooms. There was always studying and practicing to do for the next day, and plenty to keep us busy.

Of course, I had more to keep me busy than most of the others. I waited for the crowd to thin before making my escape to the old storeroom, and, beyond that, to the Kitchen Gardens.

The sun had gone down, and I was creeping past the sprays of parsnip heads when I heard a cough from one of the bowers; a collection of fruiting bushes intertwined with willow to form a protecting arc. I froze.

"I see you, Neill Torvald!" Nan Barrow called

"I, I'm sorry?" I tried, wondering just how much she knew

that I knew, or whether I had got the wrong end of the stick entirely.

"Well I'm, not. I've been waiting here for the best part of a watch, and the rest of the kitchen girls think that I've gone dotty." She reached under the small wooden bench to produce a hessian sack stuffed full of scraps of cured meat. It was larger than the sack that Char usually carried. "I've put extra in there as she didn't have the proper meal she needs this morning," Nan Barrow said, matter-of-factly. "But you *have* to get her hunting, because you can't keep her reliant on scraps. She needs a proper carcass, which she can find, hunt, and kill all of her own if she is to grow big. You understand?"

"Yes, Nan Barrow." I nodded, and then started to ask how she knew so much about dragons.

"No questions. It's better that you don't ask them and I don't answer them. Go, quickly now. I'll tell the monks that you're on an errand for me. But that will only work a few times."

"Thank you, Nan, thank you," I said, grabbing the bag and turned to go, but paused.

"But, Char–?" I wanted to ask her what was happening to her, why she looked so withdrawn and pale now, and hardly ate. What was happening to the Mage students up there in the Abbot's Tower?

"–is in trouble, but she might not see it. Yes, I know. She will need a friend."

Char was in trouble? I felt my heart lurch in my chest. I was failing her. I was failing her already. "What sort of trouble?" I asked breathlessly.

"I told you before, Torvald, just how many Mages have been successfully trained here at the monastery? One. Two, if you count the Abbot – not that he counts."

"What?" I said in alarm. But this wasn't what the Order had led everyone to believe. They claimed they had armies of mages around the kingdoms, performing their magic for the good of the realm… *But I had never seen one, nor met one.* It dawned on me that there was almost nothing that I could trust that came out of the Abbot's mouth. But what was even more pressing was Nan's suggestion that the Mage training was dangerous. "How much danger is Char in, Nan?" I asked again.

"I don't know, Torvald, I'm just a glorified cook, and for even having this conversation they could send me up the mountain to freeze. Go and feed your dragon, Torvald. Go." Nan hushed me with a flick of her hand, and I did as I was told, rushing into the night on the mountain, breaking the monastery rules, and running to feed Paxala. My heart was in turmoil by what I had just heard, and even though it seemed that I now had the opportunity to actually get to know a dragon for myself, and to take that knowledge back with me to my father – I felt that right now the more important duty was to try and keep Char safe.

———

"PAXALA?" I whispered, as my feet crunched on the stones of the beach. How did Char call her again? Was there a special technique, a signal that she used? Despite the fact that I had met the Crimson Red and knew that we were friends, I still felt that shiver of apprehension at the idea that I was here, just a small human invading an almost feral dragon's territory. I hoped Paxala would remember me.

"Skreep-pip?" A chirruping croak from the dark of the trees. Was it the dragon? Or another dragon? Or an owl, or night hawk?

"Err… hello?" I tried again, looking into the darkness.

"Ssss…" A rumbling, hissing sound came from the dark, as two great lambent gold-green eyes opened, and seemed to glow. The red dragon pushed her snout forward out of the trees and into the moonlight, sniffing suspiciously towards me.

"I, I'm sorry – but Char couldn't make it," I said.

"Skreych!" The great dragon issued a sharp croak of rebuke.

"But she will be here as soon as she can get away." I wondered just how much the dragon could even understand what I was saying without Char here, but the great beast seemed to be following every action of my body avidly. "She – Char is having to do extra lessons…"

"Skrich?" A confused sort of whistling chirrup from the Crimson Red.

"Uh, like how she teaches you, I guess? Chores. Work. Exercise…" I tried.

The Crimson hissed a little, and lashed her tail against the ferns in the undergrowth, sniffing contemptuously at the ridge above us, and the Dragon Monastery beyond.

"Yeah, I know – I wish that you could just fly over there and save her too," I guessed at what the gesture must have meant, before opening the sack of food from the kitchens. "But we can't. It's too dangerous. Look – I brought food,"

The dragon gave a final snort to the unseen captors of her closest friend, and turned her head back to me and what I had brought. I could tell that she was worried and sad, and so I knelt down, keeping my movements slow as I threw first one hunk of food towards her, and then the next, slowly drawing her closer to me. This was how I fed some of the guard dogs in the dog kennels when I was younger, befriending them so they wouldn't look at every human with worry and alarm. Dragons are not like puppies, of course I knew that, but it worked a little. Paxala crept forward until her immense red and scaled snout was just inches away from my hands and I could feel the warmth radiating out from her body, as if somewhere deep inside there was a constant fire burning. She had a long, strong neck, with two lines of muscle on either side of her throat that looked to me like they would become the long fire-muscles that the dragons used. I hadn't seen Paxala make her fire yet, and wondered when it would start.

I was also amazed at how precise she was with her teeth, delicately seizing each piece of meat very daintily, careful not to drop any or pick up any grass or pebbles that lay around. I put out my hand, and found that I could touch the side of her head quite easily.

"*Skrip-pip?*" Again, Paxala made that chirruping sound as she very slowly and very carefully raised her head away from my touch to regard me warily with one eye, head cocked like a bird.

Oh crap. Had I gone too far in touching her while she ate? What was good etiquette for a dragon, anyway?

She huffed hot, sooty sort of air at me and nudged me in the chest with her snout, like one of the Shire horses in my father's stables did. She was much stronger than even a Shire though, and pushed me back onto my bum, to a crunch of beach pebbles.

"Ow!" I laughed, and the Crimson Red turned to eat the rest of the meal that I had brought. I took it as a sign that she was happy to be in my presence, but not to be touched while eating, thank you very much.

"Okay, then. I can obey that." I laughed, standing up again. "But I have to go now too, Paxala. I wish I could stay, I really do," I said, feeling real remorse. "I have exercise and lessons like Char too, but I will try to get out here as soon as I can, either tomorrow morning, or tomorrow evening." If she understood me, she made no indication of it at all. I wondered if she even knew how to hunt for herself. What was it that I had overheard Nan and Jodreth say? That the dragon couldn't live on scraps?

Paxala was immersed in sniffing the ground for the last traces of food, ignoring me completely. "Okay Paxala, I'll be going then?" I said again, a little louder.

She lashed her tail as if to say 'well, get on with it' and I shook my head. Although making friends with a dragon was an amazing thing, it did not mean that I understood our friendship at all. I left her to her food, and trudged back up the lake, my legs already aching from all of the walking and training that I had done over the last few days alone, and it was only going to get worse, I thought, as I had to keep up appearances with the Quartermaster and the Abbot that I was doing nothing unexpected. And I had to ensure that no one caught me coming and going, because I didn't want to find out what punishment the Abbot might have in store for me next.

I sighed at the weight of all of the troubles that were stacking themselves against me. Char's lessons, the Quartermaster's hatred, my father's injury, my mission at the monastery. Somehow, I had to (do what??), when all I wanted to do right now was to spend time out here, in the wilds, with a dragon.

CHAPTER 21
CHAR'S LESSONS

I stood in the freezing cold tower-top room, about an arm's length apart from the other Mage trainees, whilst the Abbot Ansall lectured at us, asked us to perform various physical and mental exercises, and peppered us with questions, all the time refusing to let us sit down or have quills, paper, or even desks. It felt infuriatingly pointless, when all I wanted was to be with Paxala.

"And what would you call this type of power?" the Abbot asked at the front of the class. "Ganna, again?" The Abbot pointed one long finger at the shortest trainee in front of me.

The tower room had shutters, but the Abbot wanted them open. For warmth, I suppose, he allowed us each a candle and told us all to concentrate upon it, while shouting above the wind, "To feel the cold is weakness! To feel anything that distracts from the magic is weakness."

"Dark power?" Maxal hazarded, and a couple of the other students beside me nodded in agreement. I had completely lost the thread of what they were saying, or why these different types of energy could be called different things.

The Abbot's lecture was long and tedious and complicated— amounting to there being many different invisible energies, like the currents of air that flew through the skies. Some of these 'energies' were attracted to heat, light, and fire, others to war and suffering, others to the growing things, and the secret urge that made a seed sprout. Now the Abbot was quizzing us about it all.

The Abbot frowned at Maxal's answer. "I suppose that you could call this family of powers dark, if strength, stamina, and might are also to be considered dark. Explain your thesis, Ganna!"

The boy swallowed nervously. "We-we were talking about the sort of energy that might exist in a battle, or a fight between people. Anger and fear, and how a magician has to know how to tap into it to power their own magic..." The boy looked fearful himself. "Well, that, that seems to be dark to me. Like, ill-fated. Unlucky..." Ganna tried.

"Bah!" The Abbot made a loud, croaking sort of cough that I realized was his laugh. I shuddered at the sound of it. "You, Ganna, really! Always thinking the world only needs a drop of honey to make it better." The Abbot wiped his eyes in mirth. "But I understand what you are saying, and perhaps you are right – but do not great heroes also do great deeds in battle? Isn't our very own Three Kingdoms founded on the conquests and victories of great people? Cannot people be brave, and strong, and powerful in righteous anger?"

We all nodded. The Abbot might appear to be asking questions, but he didn't really want to hear our opinions.

"So, you see, the powers of strength, of might, even of anger are not always dark. We can harness these energies like a farmer harnesses great steeds to his cart," the Abbot said. "Try not to think of it as being angry or being happy or sad." The man glowered at us. "I do not want you to feel happy or angry or sad."

I was confused. How were we supposed to use or feel these energies then?

"Be like the cart horse." The Abbot illustrated by raising one fist, and then adding another behind it. "It does not know or care what it pulls. It could be a cart load of weapons, or a cart load of remedies. The cart is the energies that I tell you to channel, and you pull them, you fill yourself with them, and you direct them as I tell you. Understand?"

No, I thought. To me, it sounded like he was asking us not to care about what we felt, or what we did. But that couldn't be the secret of magic, could it?

"Nefrette!" the Abbot suddenly barked at me. "You are scowling. What don't you understand? Or do you presume to disagree?"

"No – I do not disagree, sire…" I lied sullenly. Despite the apparent 'mountain blood' in my veins, I was getting cold from the open windows letting in the freezing midnight air, and my legs were starting to shake with effort of standing in one place.

"Then let us see how well you understand. Close your eyes.

Remember the breathing techniques, try to pour your anger into that candle in the middle of the room, but try not to get angry yourself!"

"I don't... I don't know how..." I shook my head. This sounded impossible.

"Do it!" the Abbot suddenly snapped, and it was easy for me to find my anger then. I closed my eyes and took the deep breaths that followed by the shorter breaths that he had taught us, in a quick, repetitious cycle until I started to feel a little dizzy and lightheaded, and the concerns of my body started to melt away.

My anger, however, was easy to find. I was angry at the Abbot. I was angry at the Quartermaster Greer, I was angry at having to be here and not out there with Paxala. *I hope Neill got to her,* I thought in worry and alarm.

"Woah..." someone said, and I opened my eyes to see the candle was now a puddle of wax on the floor, its wick drowning with a guttering spurt of flame. Just a second ago, the candle had been fat and tall, and would have taken many hours to burn through so steadily. Maxal Ganna was looking at me in horror, but the Abbot was looking at me with an appraising smile.

"Well done, very well done. Maybe there is some truth to what they say about the famous mountain temper of your people," he said, his smile slowly vanishing. "But you didn't control it, did you? You were not the cart horse pulling the anger behind you, or the bottle containing the wine, you were furious at something, weren't you?"

"I, uh, no," I lied.

"Liar!" the Abbot said, and something hit me in the chest with a *thump,* pushing me back like a hard shove, although there was nothing touching me. My legs, already aching, wobbled as I staggered backwards and stumbled against his desk of books and papers.

Silence fell through the room, pierced only by a long, mournful sound of a dragon call from somewhere up on the mountain. *No, Paxala, don't let it be you...* I thought in terror. My face must have blanched pale, because the Abbot nodded to himself, and I prayed he took my expression as a sign of his mastery over me and not what it truly was—my fear for Paxala.

"Yes, I know when you are lying, girl," he said in disgust. "I have many years' practice at telling a lie from the truth. But also – if you had managed to perform the deed as I had told you, then you would not have burned through the candle so quickly, and so suddenly. You would have been able to hold that emotion and the flame instead. *That* is why I am trying to teach you all this, because otherwise you might become like *her* – a slave to your emotions, and good for nothing!" The Abbot ranted, stalking between the students.

"That is why you can have no heat, and you must endure the cold. Because you cannot give in to weakness! You cannot hanker for warmth! That is why I ask you to practice here, every night, and under my personal supervision. If you were to allow yourself to become slaves to your emotions then you would become dangerous. You might take out your thwarted dreams of power, or your petty rivalries, or your idiocies on others." The

Abbot rounded on me, as if he had been talking about me all along.

"You must feel nothing. You must think nothing. You must only do as I tell you. You must become a receptacle for the dragon magic. Do you understand?" He shouted again.

"Yes, Abbot-sire," we all muttered.

"Good. Now–physical endurance." And with that he ordered us to spend the next few hours doing the most painful and grueling exercises until, one by one, we all collapsed into shivering heaps. When we had all succumbed, the Abbot finally nodded.

"The flesh is so weak, so very weak my students. That is why you come here, and that is why I try to make your spirits strong. The lesson is over for tonight, and I will expect you all ready to learn and on time tomorrow evening after dinner. You are dismissed!"

I left the tower room trudging behind the others, none of us having the energy or strength to talk, but just feeling pummeled and exhausted. It was little Maxal Ganna that I feared for the most, as he appeared to be taking the physical side of the Abbot's lessons much worse than the rest of us. I reached out to touch him on the shoulder as we crossed the courtyard and he flinched, but nodded as he acknowledged me silently.

The Abbot's going to end up killing us, I thought in alarm, wishing that I had energy to do anything other than collapse into bed. Every other student here had been in the beds for hours by the time that we crept into our respective dormitories. With less sleep and what felt like insane tortures, I wondered which of us

Mage trainees would be the first to stumble or mishap. But I was too tired to even think anymore. As I pulled the scratchy woolen blankets up to my chin and felt the darkness of deep, dreamless sleep rise to take me, one last question hovered, *and what does any of this have to do with dragons? And how will any of these cruel exercises help me keep Paxala safe?*

CHAPTER 22
NEILL, THE FEAST, & THE
DRAGON'S BARGAIN

My life turned into a whirlwind of activity. The next few days blurred, and I saw even less of Char, apart from her ghostly, pale appearances at dinner with the other Mage trainees. I couldn't tell her about Paxala needing more food, and needing to learn how to hunt.

My mornings started by getting up as early as I could – still in the middle of the night, really, unless I was on watch with Dorf before dawn (we were all seemingly being given more responsibilities now that we had been selected for our different paths; we had to take turns guarding the monastery, sorting the grains, cleaning, running errands, feeding the dragons with the others – all of which was supervised, of course). If I managed to get up before Dorf, then I would have to calculate if I had enough time to get dressed, sneak down to the Kitchen Gardens, pick up whatever scraps Nan Barrow would have left for me by the back door, and run across the mountaintop to feed Paxala, before racing back for the dragon call at the break of dawn, and to get washed and breakfasted. I hadn't had time at all to continue my own investigations of the monastery for the source of the Order's magic – but now, since what Nan had told me about the scarcity of actual Dragon Mages, I was more and more certain that the information that my father so desperately desired would be up there in the tower, with Char and the Abbot. He was the only monk who had magic here, so I would instead find out the secret of *his* power.

And that meant getting access to Char, which again, I couldn't do. *If I could just get to her to ask her questions about her practices, about what incenses or magic rocks or whatever it is they use up there…*

Yesterday, in the late afternoon I had managed to accompany Dorf down to the Library where the Scribes could now freely spend more time, saying that I still needed to practice my penmanship skills. I had tried to ask him about the components of dragon magic, and all that he had come up with were a few dusty compendiums of folk tales.

"No magic stones? Crystals? Magic rings?" I had said bewilderingly, looking at the list of strange and unusual words and names of things that didn't make any sense to me.

"Magic stones? There's *loads* of stories about magic stones," Dorf almost laughed. "But they're all just folk stories. Not the true teaching that we get here."

What teaching? So far, the only people actually getting taught seemed to be Char and Maxal and the others. Not the rest of us!

"Look here, at Fibinola's Tales: here's a woman who has to steal a piece of dragon eggshell that she uses to heal her baby. Here's a story of a talking ax..." Dorf carried on. "But it is just rumor and superstition. We're told in Scribe class..."

My ears had pricked up especially at this point.

"...that most of this is mistaken or forgotten herbalism. So, the dragon mystic with the eggshell probably crushed up the eggshell with a lot of Meadowsweet, or Nettles or something and it worked because of the healing properties of the plants. But we still collect all of that lore anyway, as it has to do with dragons, you see?"

Well, no, I hadn't seen. My father's mission was becoming ever more frustrating, like chasing my own tail. It seemed as if most stories of the Draconis Order's magic were false, and no one would talk about it. But I had seen the magic with my own eyes, I kept reminding myself. I had *seen* that boulder fly through the night. I had *seen* that suit of armor.

And still the spring equinox was drawing closer, and I was no closer to any of my goals. A few mornings I missed breakfast and claimed I felt unwell, just so I had more time to feed Paxala and then to run down to the Library and again look at old fairy tales and superstitions - but this only made me even *more* tired during the long days ahead.

There were other times when I couldn't even get away before Dorf woke up, and Paxala had to wait until after dinner. I would announce to any nearby student or monk that I was going to study, or to the bathhouse, when in fact I would be running to the Kitchen Gardens, and then to the hungry dragon hidden on the other side of the mountain. Otherwise, my days were spent mostly on the practice ground, either during advanced Protector's class, or through the day-on, day-off regular Protector classes and physical exercise with all of the other students. I was getting leaner, and taller, and the aches and knocks and pains started to fade from my body, to be replaced by new ones. My off-lessons were spent either in the Library or, through the next few days, in the Great Hall, where the Abbot himself would lead us in his obscure and strange 'meditation classes.' These would be held in near complete silence, after a short lecture by the Abbot at how important it was to clear the mind and to think only of one image at a time, which he would supply, such as a candleflame, a sword, a crown, and a dragon's fang. We were to concentrate on that image alone until all other cares faded away from our mind. Always, his especial Mages-in-training would be separated and taken to the front of the class as they did their meditation exercises, and so I got a chance to at least observe how Char appeared to be doing, if not actually talk to her. She was growing paler and thinner if that was possible. She wouldn't even catch my eye when I tried to get her attention. *What were they doing up there, in that tower? How long could I go on feeding Paxala like this, in the off times between my many other duties?*

I never managed to achieve the same states of blank serenity that the others did, however. Always, I had worries gnawing away at me, destroying any carefully cultivated image the Abbot had us construct in our minds. Images of my injured and stricken father would replace those of the candleflame, or the sword, the dragon fang, or the crown. Or else I would think about Paxala and the strong curve of her back, or the sinuous tail that could already knock down young trees.

My muscles started to ache and it wasn't long before I managed to strain my ankle, and had to have it wrapped up and physicked. Luckily it for me, it wasn't Monk Olan or the Quartermaster Greer who ordered me to show them the state of my swollen and bruised feet, but Monk Feodor, who took the Protector advanced classes.

"What are you doing, boy, running up and down the tower stairs all night?" Feodor asked me when he saw me limping during practice. I sweated, knowing that was precisely what I had been doing.

"Boots," he demanded in the cold practice ground, as he marched over to me and ordered Lila instead to take the class in advanced blocking techniques (diving, rolling, and turning the body). Lila the Raider was getting good at fighting, *really* good, and it wasn't a surprise that Monk Feodor was giving her more responsibilities, even talking about the possibilities of studying strategy and group tactics with her.

I shucked off my boots and he tutted at my feet. "Warmth, air, and support," he berated me. "Those are all that you need to keep you on your toes, and you seem to be spending too long in the cold, and putting way too many leagues under your feet." He called for a healer to get him some bandages and a poultice, and proceeded to treat me himself. The poultice eased the muscle pain almost immediately, leaving my skin feeling warm, and then wrapped the poultice up tight with multiple layers of clean gauze. "Take it off every night to let your feet dry out, and re-apply every morning." He plonked a tub of unguent and bandages at my side. It wasn't such an unusual sight after the short while that we had devoted to advanced Protector's class – each one of us had been wrapped up or bandaged from some knock or fall or another, but this injury was different as it seemed to not result from any fight that I had.

"How do you know all this stuff?" I asked Feodor as he worked.

"Used to be a soldier. A captain even, in the Old Queen's Army before Vincent took to the throne," he said brusquely.

"But didn't everyone try out to be a Draconis Monk at an early age, like we are?" I asked.

"Huh. In those days, no," Feodor said with a frown. "I came from a poor background. No son of a prince or a warlord like some," he said, and I thought he was angry until I noticed his bushy eyebrows creasing. He was teasing me. "I would have spent my life as a damn good soldier too, if it wasn't for the Abbot himself, seeing the way that I had with the cavalry horses, and testing me for aptitude. It turns out I was good at handling dragons and scribing too."

There was an uncomfortable silence between us as the large monk looked worried – the first time I had ever seen Feodor worried about anything. Was he supposed to tell me that? I wondered as I looked at the mass of white lines, some as thick as a finger were clearly visible stretched from hand to top of his head. He broke the tension with a laugh. "I know what you're thinking lad, not *that* good to earn these, huh? Well, – *I'm* still alive." He grinned. "I survived a bull dragon attack, so the Abbot reckoned that I *did* know a thing or two after all." I saw a flicker of something behind his usually calm-as-stone eyes. *What was it – indecision? Wariness?* I wondered how he had even been allowed into the dragon crater to train with the dragons, when we students were expressly forbidden to. *He didn't trust me yet,* I realized. Which was something that I had to work on. As Feodor seemed to know the most of any other monk about the dragons, then surely dragon information was just the sort of information that my father would want, wasn't it?

And, more importantly, were there any records of those encounters? More hands-on information about how the monks approached and worked with the dragons other than just throwing bits of half-rotten meat down to them might help my father—might help me know what else I could do with Paxala, or expect from her. And had the Abbot been present at these encounters? *Did he use his magic?*

"It's sounds awful," I tried, clearing my throat as I felt vaguely disloyal to this man who had so far been nice to me. *But asking a few little questions didn't hurt, did it?*

"It was," Feodor agreed.

"You must have been very brave to approach a bull dragon – was it the one before Zaxx?" I tried to ask in an innocent voice. "Was it just you on your own, or was the Abbot with you? Couldn't he use his magic to save you?"

"You're done," he said suddenly, throwing me my boots to catch, before standing up to bark at the others. I was left feeling like I had hit a brick wall with Feodor. The advanced Protector tutor was far more cunning than I was, it seemed.

My time with the Crimson Red proved to be the few scant moments that I looked forward to in my hectic routine. She was growing fast, and would now greet me just under the ridge with a chirrup as I brought her food. If I had missed a feed for more than a day, then she would greet me by bowling me over and leaving me with a nip from her long fangs – always so delicate as to just bruise, and never break the skin. It was obvious she missed Char, and would often raise her head to the night skies, in the direction of the so-close Dragon Monastery, and let her haunting, whooping call echo through the ravine. I didn't know how to stop her from doing it, and didn't know whether I should even. It reminded me of the bond I had seen between the kennel dogs and the dog handler of Torvald– but more so. Paxala and Char had bonded together, the way young animals do to their guardian.

Running through it all, of course, was the worry that my father might die, and I had to find something out to give to him by the spring equinox. Even if Healer Garrett saved his life, I had to warn my father of Healer Garrett's affiliation to the Draconis Order. I felt torn between my need to look after the dragon for Char (and for myself) as well as fulfill my father's wishes. There was no way that I could do both of these things without someone getting hurt – either a young dragon starving, or my father being at the mercy of the Draconis Order.

How could I choose between them?

And so, it was with a terrified urgency that I decided to do something to break the deadlock in my heart, as soon as the first opportunity arose. I would concentrate my efforts on the Abbot's

Tower. Perhaps it would yield information that would benefit my father and help me understand what was happening to Char.

My chance came in the form of the First Day Feast. The First Day Feast was a way to mark the first day of spring, which was different from the spring equinox by only a matter of days. I knew that during the actual spring equinox, everyone would be expected to be in the fields or their gardens or at home, as the spring equinox was a Three Kingdoms-wide celebration to announce the end of spring and the start of summer proper —and prosperity— to the land. From now the days would be getting noticeably warmer and longer, and all of the crops that the land grew would start coming up in earnest. It was customary for rulers, warlords, and captains to celebrate spring a few days early, so their servants could then prepare for their own festivities. In our case, it was announced that would come in the form of none other than Prince Vincent visiting the monastery for a grand feast.

"We here at the Draconis Order are honored to welcome the Good Prince Vincent back again, to feast with us on the first day," the Abbot announced after a particularly frustrating meditation class. "Leading up to it, you will all have extra duties, but the day of the feast itself will be considered a holiday."

There was a ragged cheer from some of the more naïve of the students around me. *Poor fools,* I thought a little piously. They hadn't heard what the Abbot had said to me privately in his tower (obviously), they didn't quite know yet what sort of man was running this place, and how nothing could be taken for granted here. If the Abbot was 'giving' us a holiday, then I was sure it was for his own ends, not for our benefit at all. Even so, I could have joined in – but for entirely different reasons. If it was a holiday, then the free time was also my opportunity to try and sneak into the Abbot's Tower.

MY PLAN WAS SIMPLE. To sneak up to the Abbot's Tower – the same one that Char and the others took their classes in–and take whatever I could: scrolls or lesson plans or whatever material they used, and somehow get them to my father. *And especially that cane that he walked around with, if it was there, and the little silver chain he sometimes wore.* One of these things had to be the source of the Abbot's power, surely! If what I found wasn't good enough, then maybe he would be happy with just a primer or a grimoire.

Maybe, I thought with a grimace as I re-adjusted the scratchy and uncomfortable cream-white tunic we had all been given to wear for the feast.

"After all that sweeping that we've done for the celebration, my back is breaking!" Dorf Lesser moaned from beside me.

"Well, you can thank Prince Vincent for all of this effort," I muttered. It was no surprise to Dorf that I had a very low opinion of our prince, especially after the 'example' he had made of me on the mountaintop.

"Well, I hope that Prince Vincent appreciates all the hard work we put in here this morning…" Dorf agreed with a moan.

"It's not like you to criticize your prince," I muttered under my breath, my mind on other things.

"Our prince, surely?" Dorf corrected (ever the keen observer of words and grammar).

Oh yeah. I wondered why I had said that, and realized that I no longer thought of Prince Vincent, ever after that night on the mountaintop as 'my' prince at all. *He was just some bully.*

The monastery fairly shone from our efforts. Every tile, mosaic, flagstone, brick, slab, and block had been brushed, scrubbed, and mopped. Every piece of martial equipment tidied away, and from somewhere large crimson and black tapestries had been produced, to flow down the walls, with pictures of dragons whirling, fighting, and swooping. Gold candelabras stood by every door, their beeswax candles burning steadily and slowly. Fresh herbs scented the air with lavender and citrus.

"At least you can say the *monastery* is clean," I muttered, taking note of Dorf's already stained white tunic. Of course, my comments, however fleeting, was not appreciated as we walked to the feast and caused an angry snap from the Quartermaster as he led us.

"Is *this* how the Good Prince wants to see his money spent? On two squabbling brats?" The Quartermaster called out in the echoing chamber.

So, he's funding this place, then is he? I thought. *No wonder the Abbot wants us to swear our allegiance to him.*

We kept our heads lowered and then were hurried down the hallway toward the feast.

"I am so hungry!" Dorf said under his breath after we'd gone a bit further.

"You're always hungry, Lesser!" said a voice, and I turned around to see that it was Faris, one of Terrence's cohort. The kid had given way to let Terrence become a Protector instead of him, even though he was clearly the better fighter. He was like a string-bean with dark hair, from some rich merchant's family from the south, and hated Lila with a passion. Faris and Terrence had seemed to know each other before coming here, and it hadn't taken long for Terrence to convince Feodor to allow Faris to become a Protector too, meaning that me and Lila were evenly matched versus those who supported Terrence in our class.

"Haven't you got something better to do, Faris?" I snapped at him. He was a good fighter, but I thought that I might be able to beat him. I still didn't particularly want to brawl in the hallway, right before the feast.

"Yeah, I do. *I'm* going to be at the head table, along with Terrence and the prince," he said with a smarmy smile, jogging ahead, to be early to the festivities, I supposed.

"Wow, he's just going to love that, isn't he?" Dorf said. "As son of the Southern Prince, Terrence hates Vincent with a passion, and the Abbot's going to be spending all night stopping Terrence and his lot from saying something awful!"

"Yeah." I shook my head wearily. I didn't care about the internal politics. I had my father to worry about. But... Does that mean that Nefrette will be at the head table too? I wondered. As daughter of the Northern Prince Lander?

I learned the answer just a little while later.

Monks in heavy black robes with gilt red edges started to appear and take their places, and there were monks here that I had never seen before. Almost all of them were men between the ages of about twenty and forty. Some wore beards, while others were clean-shaven, and a very small faction were like Maxal, with shaven tonsure. I wondered if there were factions even within the Draconis Order, and whether that was something that I should tell my father.

No sign of Char though, I noticed, wondering if she had managed to sneak off to visit Paxala on this one evening in the same way that I had to. I hoped for her sake that she had – because she didn't appear to be here, and I saw Terrence dressed in his own cream tunic and black robe, with also a small silver circlet at his brow, to indicate his noble status. If Terrence, a prince's child was here in his finery – then why wouldn't Char be? Some may consider her to be illegitimate – but she was still Prince Lander's daughter.

"They must have come from all over the Middle Kingdom," Dorf whispered in awe.

"All over the *Three* Kingdoms, lad," said a finely cultured voice that I recognized, one with a touch of the Northern kingdom about it. I turned around to see that there was one Draconis Order new arrival here who still wore his heavy black cloak and looked far shabbier than anyone else. His attire was not the finery that most of the other monks had turned up in. He wore a gray-colored wrap around his hair, an eye-patch, and his face was blotched with the scurf of some kind of skin condition. He looked like an old man, even though I knew that he wasn't.

"Jodreth?" I said, "Is that you?" I was sure it was, under the disguise.

"What did you say, novitiate?" the one-eyed older monk said in a high pitched and querulous voice. "I am Monk Jocana, *Jo-caaa-na*. Now be off with you and get out from under my feet, boy. Some of us *real* monks have work to do!"

It was him, I knew it was under all of that make up and I nodded and tried to hide my grin as I watched him perform an excellent impersonation of a slightly batty, slightly diseased older man, hobbling through the thickest of the monastic gabbles.

The dragon pipes were sounded and the two double doors at the back were thrown open. The retinue of Middle Kingdom knights in full plate armor appeared, and between them strode His Grace the Abbot Ansall, and His Majesty Prince Vincent himself.

"Make way! Make way for the Good Prince!" the knights chanted, driving a wedge through the gatherings.

"The Dark Prince more like!" someone shouted from the crowd, causing a ripple of consternation from the assembled, and beetle-like looks from the Quartermaster, but the heckler could not be isolated.

The Abbot wore his usual minimal finery: that is to say, black robes with a black cloak of a deep, velvety sheen. He wore his simple gold chain of office with the black gemstone, I saw. If *that* was the source of his magic power, then he definitely had it on him. *But no staff.* He didn't have the thin cane with the stylized silver dragon adornment. I remembered seeing it when he had his private audience with me and Char in his tower, leaning against the wall. He didn't look infirm enough to need a walking cane – and the newly arrived monks around me all carried staffs – but they were much sturdier, heavier things – not the fine walking cane of the Abbot.

Was that it? Was the secret of the monk's magic really as simple as a magic staff? I wondered. I looked to the grand doors behind me, eager to get away right now – but there were just too many knights and monks in the way just yet.

It took seemingly ages for the Prince and the Abbot to make their way to the head table, as they looked to be spending a long time in emphatic conversation with each other. I wished that I could sneak over to find out what they were talking about – but every time I tried to slip away, it seemed that Dorf was there, moaning about food or about the other monks. I liked Dorf, really, I did – but right now I wish that I had told him about my mission and made him understand what I was doing was important – for my father's sake, for all our sakes.

Once the prince was finally seated, the Abbot accepted the cheers and claps with a short address. "The Order thanks the *Good* Prince Vincent for his most gracious visit to our humble halls, may we extend to him every courtesy, and assure him that out there," the Abbot pointed out beyond the main doors and the front gate of the monastery, "out there his duties may be heavy, but in here, he is with allies – and his worries can be light!"

Someone made a puking noise from the assembled crowd,

but the Abbot ignored it. *I bet that was Jodreth--* I concealed my smile behind my hand--or Jo-caaa-na or whatever he was calling himself in here.

"Let the First Day Feast begin!" The Abbot clapped his hands, and the dragon pipes roared again.

Now was my chance, while the monks and the important of the Order took their seats at the head of the room, and the younger students milled about and chattered as they looked for seats. I waited for Dorf to start talking excitedly to Sigrid before I slipped to the back of the crowd, ducked into the corridor – and ran.

IT WAS EVEN EASIER than I'd thought to sneak about tonight of all nights, but I still hurried toward where the Abbot's Tower stood alone.

One monk, or maybe two, have actually become ordained Mages. I remembered Nan Barrow's words once again. That was what all of this training that Char was being put through was about, wasn't it? When would *she* get to go into the Astrographer's Tower – and should it be *there* that I needed to be searching?

Tympani-like music drifted across the darkened courtyard from further inside the building. The Abbot had hired minstrels for the evening, and there was a low murmur in the air from the feast. I wondered how long it had been already – was the first course over? I didn't have time to dither—I had to be decisive. The Abbot's Tower then.

I edged across the courtyard, wrapping my cloak around my shoulders from the sudden cold, and trying to avoid the pools of light from the many torches that uncharacteristically burned in their sconces. Absolutely no expense had been spared, it seemed, for the arrival of the 'Good' Prince.

Up the stone stairs to the wall, my feet made a slapping noise on the stone – loud in my ears, but no one raised an alarm. Maybe if any guards were watching they would think that I was just another lost student. This unexpected holiday season made us all relax our usual strict regimes and routines a bit, and I hoped that extended to the guards—and to the Abbot.

There. The doorway to the Abbot's Tower – a stone arch with a wooden door I had been taken through just a few months ago as a fresh-faced new arrival. *What if it was locked?* I thought in alarm. How could I be so stupid? I got to the edge of the simple wooden door, and breathed carefully, remembering my father's lessons before battle. 'Breathe. Focus. Strike!' he had told me and my brothers, which had helped me so far in my Protector's lessons. I waited, couldn't hear anything from the other side, reached out—

And the door swung open on oiled hinges. It wasn't even locked. Why? The thought flashed through my mind, but I ignored it, eager to believe that perhaps I was just being lucky. It was about time that things went my way, after all!

It was the Abbot's desk I wanted. Surely there I would find what I was looking for, but as I headed to the spiraling stairs that led to the top, a strange open room with the Abbot's desk in the center, a voice called out.

"Halt!" the voice said, breaking my moment of reverie. I looked up the stairs to the final window and landing, to see a figure standing in the shadows, blocking the door.

It was Char.

"CHAR?" I said in relief. "Thank the stars I found you – I was so worried," I greeted her as I walked up the final steps.

"Halt," she said again, this time raising one slender hand to hold in front of me in warning. Her voice sounded curiously flat, devoid of her usual sparkling wit and sarcasm.

"Char?" I said again, daring to take a few more steps. "It's me, Neill," I repeated.

"Halt," she repeated, and this time, her other hand went to the handle of her short sword. There was something wrong here, something seriously wrong. Her voice was different, her eyes were glassy and she looked at me like I was just another piece of furniture, not a friend. There was an air of aggression and anger to her voice, not the warmth that I was used to. What had happened? Had she changed her mind about what we were doing, about Paxala?

A long, drawn out dragon's shriek came through the open, empty windows, and although it could have been any dragon's cry from their home, I knew it was Paxala. She must sense the change in her companion somehow.

"Char – why are you acting like this?" I hissed at her. "Let me past – lives are at stake." I thought of my father, lying on his sick bed many leagues away, being tended—or poisoned—by Healer Garret. "Think of Paxala..." I said desperately. *Maybe Char doesn't want me to learn about magic, maybe she thinks that she can uncover the secrets all by herself.* No, my heart rebelled, thinking about how she had touched my arm and asked for my help, asked me to keep her secret with her. She wouldn't be so selfish all of a sudden. We were friends, I had to believe that. So, what is wrong with her then? I looked at the glassy sort of stare in her eyes, the way she didn't move, how her attention on me didn't waiver for a second. *Has she been bewitched by the Abbot?* I thought in horror.

There was another anguished dragon cry from somewhere outside, this one even louder than the first.

"Pax...?" Char murmured and something flickered in her eyes; an uncertainty – a moment of hesitation.

"Yes, Paxala," I said. "She needs you. She is pining for you." I gritted my teeth, feeling a hot ball of doubt and frustration rising in my throat. How could the Abbot do this to her? I didn't want to have to lie to my friend Char, or fight her, but seeing her stationed as a guard there made me even more certain that the Abbot had concealed information there that I needed. I had to have the secrets of the magic that lay in that room. For my father's sake. "Char?" I swallowed my doubts. "I need to get into that room behind you. It is important."

The instant the words left my mouth, all doubt that she might snap out of whatever spell she was under, any thought that she might recognize me vanished. A door slammed on the light in

Char's eyes, as she braced her back foot against the door and drew the steel of her short sword.

"Halt!" she barked.

"Char, don't do this…" I begged her. How could I fight her? How could I attack a sworn ally? My heart was torn – but how could I let my father down?

The steel of her blade rang as she drew it, and now she stood a step or two above me in a classic fighting stance, sword held low and back, her free hand out front. I could try to disarm her. I could try to get her to lunge at me, and then grab the weapon, I could try to kick at her knees to get her to stumble-

My mouth went dry, and my heart thumped in panic as I raised my hands. *No. Char is* my friend. I let my hands fall uselessly to my side. I couldn't do it. I couldn't attack her just for the sake of what my family wanted. *She was my partner, she had shared the secret of Paxala with me, and she needed me right now.*

Another loud dragon screech echoed from the mountain. This one was even angrier than the previous ones.

"I, I can't fight you," I whispered to Char. *I'm sorry, father.*

CHAPTER 23
THE WAY THINGS WERE MEANT TO BE

Char's body tensed. She was going to strike me. She wouldn't let me seek the secrets of her magic.

"I can't fight you," I repeated, as if that might stop her. As if there were any reasoning with her in whatever state she was in.

"*Domus!*" A voice hissed behind me, and hands shoved me out of the way. "*Reve, Reve!*" Jodreth in his shabby black cloak stood there, still in his camouflage as Jocana the monk, holding a hand up between me and Char. My ears buzzed, like they did with the pressure before a thunderstorm. "*Reve,* child. Sssh now, *Domus-Reve,*" he repeated the strange words, and Char's eyes fluttered as her knees buckled. Her sword clattered to the floor and slid down the steps, where I stamped on it to avoid it clattering any further.

Char slumped against the wall, but Jodreth swept forward to steady her, and lower her gently to the doorway.

"Jodreth?" I gasped, "How did you—"

"Because that young Red dragon of yours is caterwauling and waking half of the crater!" Jodreth said, checking Char's sleeping eyes and the pulse at her throat. "She will be fine, I think. When she wakes up this will all be a bad dream, but she will be herself again."

"Herself?" I asked.

"Good lord, Torvald – catch up!" Jodreth sounded annoyed. "The Abbot has been hypnotizing you all. Or trying to, anyway. He tried the same thing with me when I was here, and with the other monks. All of those strange meditation sessions? They don't mean much on their own, or if you only do the classes once a week or so – but if you are like Char here, and unlucky enough to be doing those exercises every day, then you'll end up just another fanatic like the rest of them."

"A fanatic…" I said, my mind racing. "The Abbot is trying to create fanatics?" I thought about the strange symbols he wanted us to memorize and repeat in our heads – the very same ones I could never accurately create because I was so worried about my father and Char and Paxala. The dragon, the sword, the crown… I thought about how tired I felt after the classes, rundown and sluggish as if I were slowly being intoxicated. *This is what the Abbot had intended all along.* I knew it. That was why he was always telling us about 'if we were good enough' or studied hard enough then we could become elites, make the grade, master the ways of the Draconis Order…. No wonder Greer was like he was, with an almost pathological hatred for any of us that he didn't think was 'pure' enough for his Order. The Abbot was trying to make an army of blind followers…

"A religious army." Jodreth scowled. "But his techniques are so dangerous that I'm the only one to survive the Mage training with my mind intact. If Char kept on being fed all of that mind control stuff then she'd probably flip and go insane before midsummer, and the Abbot would just blame it on her mountain blood."

I stuttered, my mouth opening as I searched for the word to describe the horror. "But that's monstrous."

"Yes, but it's not exactly as if I can go around broadcasting what's happening and keep my head," Jodreth said, looking out of the window. "Now, we haven't got long. I'm sure I wasn't the only one to notice the dragon noises and we have to get out of here, now."

But the secret of the dragon magic! I looked at the door.

Thud! There was a noise from downstairs, as the door was slammed. It could have been the wind, but the sudden and steady slap of feet on stone heading up towards us wasn't. I looked at Jodreth, who was scowling at our terrible bad luck.

"Can we fight?" I mouthed, but Jodreth nodded to the unconscious Char at our feet.

"We cannot," the monk whispered back. "There are too many monks out there loyal to the Abbot, and Char will get hurt."

The sound of footsteps grew louder, as if there were more than one or even two people running up the stairs. Maybe it was just an echo? I could only hope.

"Stay calm, Torvald," Jodreth said, turning to hold me by the shoulders. "You have to trust me," he whispered, and I nodded, feeling terrified. "We climb out of the window."

"What?" I said in alarm. We were fifty or more feet straight up from the ground! "What about Char?"

The footsteps were closer. And it was clear now they weren't just echoes.

"Please, Torvald, it's the only way to stay alive," Jodreth said. "There's a ledge on each floor under the windows. This isn't the first time that I have had to do this. Go, now, and I will keep us safe."

With my heart in my mouth and the approaching footsteps thundering in my ears, I crept to the open, narrow and tall window. I had to turn sideways, but I could manage to squeeze through. I gripped onto the masonry and eased my shoulder and one foot out. I made the mistake of looking down, and saw the walls of the monastery below, far away and very, very solid. I felt my stomach lurch.

"Go!" Jodreth hissed at me, and I turned my head to the stone of the window, feeling for the narrow ledge with my foot. I found I could easily stand on the four or five-inch-wide outcropping on tiptoes, as long as my fingers were gripping between the stones above. Easy if it was three feet from the ground, not fifty. I swung myself out, and started to sidle along the edge to the right of the window, my fingers clinging to the stone mantle of the window's arch for as long as possible, until I absolutely had to reach out to jam my fingers between stone blocks.

What the hell am I doing? What am I doing? The words went around and around in my head as I inched along the tower wall. I felt as if I was going so slowly, that it would be morning by the time I made it to safety, but nonetheless there were no sudden shouts of discovery. I clung to the side of the Abbot's Tower, my legs and my back clenched in agony, my cloak whipping in the winds. A moment later and Jodreth was also climbing out, pushing next to me on the ledge. He was much more confident than me, but I could tell from the grimace and the silent snarl on his face that he was in just as much pain as I was.

Thud, thud, thud... The steps reached the landing not a moment later.

"What's this?" We clearly heard from inside. It was the voice of the Abbot himself, apparently talking to someone. Several people in fact, as we heard voices answer him.

"I knew that you couldn't trust her, your grace – just look, she is sleeping on guard duty!" It was Quartermaster Greer.

"We have no time for this nonsense from her. I told you that what you heard was probably this girl talking in her sleep. The prince is feasting downstairs. You've accounted for all the other students, haven't you?"

"Of course," the Quartermaster said. "Counted them all myself." For a brief moment, I wondered how it was he hadn't missed me, but then I thought of Jodreth. Somehow the Quartermaster must have counted him in my stead.

"Take her to the feeding chamber, then," the Abbot said. "No one will miss her for hours. If at all."

"Well, you heard his grace!" sneered the Quartermaster.

"Yes, of course, sire," Monk Olan said.

There was scuffling and grunting as I presumed Monk Olan picked Char up. My heart raced, and my hands went clammy and damp. What are they doing to her? The feeding chamber? What was that?

From the wilds, Paxala howled in fury and outrage. If only I could understand her, the way Char could. Perhaps then I could get some insight into what was truly happening.

One pair of feet thumped down the stairs. Were they all going? I was desperate to move, my arms shaking and my back in spasms. I had to get off this ledge. I had to save Char.

Paxala shrieked again, louder this time, as if she were flying closer.

"Hmm. The dragons are noisy tonight," the Quartermaster murmured.

"Yes, they are. Strange," said the Abbot, his voice coming from the window. All he had to do was lean out and he would see Jodreth and me hiding there. "But Zaxx the Golden will soon put a stop to that."

Zaxx, I thought in horror. If he attacks Paxala—I had to find some way to stop her. But how?

The Quartermaster's and Abbot's steps joined Monk Olan's, all of them retreating back down the tower. I wanted to scream in agony—from my clenched and aching muscles, from my anguish over what might happen to Char and to Paxala, but I bit my lips instead until the pain from them was sharper than all the rest. Jodreth was panting, unwilling to move. He must have wanted to be sure the others were truly gone.

We waited, my arms shaking even harder, my shoulders burning. We waited some more, until my hands started to slip from the rock.

Thump. From far below, a door slammed, and from the corner of my eye, I caught the movement of a small group of people, carrying a smaller. I craned my neck to see—was it Char? Was she awake? Could she somehow call off Paxala? And suddenly my hands gave way. I hissed—some ridiculous sense of self-preservation keeping me from calling out, as I fell backward.

Jodreth's hand seized mine, gripped my wrist hard, but I was too heavy, and he too peeled from the window ledge.

"Avianis sanctis, sanctis zephyrus!" Jodreth Draconis hissed, and suddenly our falling slowed. We were still tumbling to the ground, spiraling as if we were feathers or leaves, falling only slightly slower than we would have without Jodreth's spell or whatever it was. Jodreth mumbled the arcane words under his breath, over and over and over, the strain of the effort costing him mightily as he clutched my wrist and wrought his magic.

"...sanctis zephyr, sanctis zephyr..." Jodreth was almost pleading with his powers as we fell, and I stuck out my arms and curled my legs as we plummeted through the gorse bushes outside the monastery walls, Jodreth's hold on me breaking as we tumbled body over body.

When we finally came to stop, I could not help the groan that came to my lips. Every bit of my body felt bruised and battered, but I wasn't broken, not yet. A few feet away, Jodreth lay on the rocks, a nasty gash under his hairline. His eyes were open though, and he blinked at me, looking as battered as I felt.

"It looks like you saved me again." I gasped for air, and in a flash, it came to me that it had not been pure fighting skills that had allowed Jodreth to save me all those months ago, but magic. How had I not realized?

"And now we have to save Char." Jodreth pushed himself up, hobbling a bit toward me. "The feeding chamber – it's a tunnel that they use from below the monastery, that leads out to a water-fall near the crater. It's a secret place—one of the many tunnels this mountain is riddled with. Only Zaxx knows them all." He braced himself against the monastery walls, clearly in pain. "But I know where the waterfall is. Come."

I joined him, hurrying overland over the sides of the moun-tain, while Paxala hooted and shrieked from somewhere above us, coming for her companion Char just as we were.

We had avoided a confrontation up in the tower, but how would we ever save Char without one now?

As soon as we had fought our way through the gorse bushes and staggered along the narrow gully, to plunge headlong down the sides of Dragon Mountain, Paxala shrieking all the time from the overcast skies above, Jodreth turned to me. "Can you tell her to be quiet?" he asked seriously.

"Who, the dragon?" I said in alarm somehow feeling as if I could not share her name without her permission.

"Yes, the dragon – who else? She will bring down Zaxx on our heads!" Jodreth said in alarm.

"No, how could I?" I shook my head. *Char could do it.* "I can't control her," I said.

"Oh," Jodreth looked at me for a long moment, as if something didn't make sense. "I was sure that it was *you* who had the ability..." he shook his head once, abruptly, before indicating that we were to push on, and to be quiet.

What ability? I wanted to ask, but before I could do anything there came the sound of splashing water. The waterfall.

We stood on the rocky edges of one sharper side of the mountain, looking down into the dragon crater. Scraggy trees and bushes dotted the cliffside like giant spiders and waterfalls tumbled from several tunnels. *How would we know which waterfall was the one they were taking Char too?* At least the dull roar of water hid the sound of our movements easily, as Jodreth pointed below us, and crept forward. He had spotted something.

To our right, and below the rocky cliffs we were clambering across, there was a large opening, like a giant had scooped out a hole with his hand. A warm, flickering light spilled from it— torches, I thought—shining through the waterfall that coursed over the far side of the cave's opening.

Raised voices echoed from inside the cave–whoever it was in there must have had to shout to be heard over the roar of the water. Jodreth raised up a hand, and we both stopped to listen.

"No, leave us!" the Abbot shouted, and though I could not see anyone, I guessed it must be the Quartermaster and Olan. "Leave the girl and me here."

There was a reply, from too far inside the cave for us to make out the words.

"Tell the prince I've been momentarily detained. This will not take long," the Abbot scolded and silence fell once more.

Jodreth looked at me, and the meaning was clear. The Abbot Ansall was down there on his own, and that meant that now was the best chance to rescue Char. I nodded that I was ready, although all I had on me was my belt knife. Could Jodreth's magic be a match for the Abbot's? I wondered. I had seen the Abbot break through boulders the sizes of carts, but then, Jodreth had managed to save us both from splattering over the mountainside. They were both powerful, I knew – but who would win?

We inched closer, right to the lip of the cavern, until we could see inside. The Abbot stood alone in the center of a large, dry space, Char's unconscious form to one side.

"ABBOT," a terrible voice broke into my mind, and into my ears, a voice that seemed made of clashing swords and grating bones. Even stranger, I knew it wasn't human, and I could hear it in strange double-exposure, both physically and mentally. I looked over at Jodreth, who had pressed himself against the back of the wall of the cliff. He had heard it too.

There was another creature with Ansall.

"Your most gracious servant," we heard Abbot Ansall say.

"What is this? A gift?" The voice like cracking teeth said once more, making my head buzz with headache. What could be causing such a reaction? It was a vaguely familiar sensation— and then I remembered. *When Char and Paxala were talking to each other, in their minds* there had been that same kind of buzzing. Only that had been more pleasant, perhaps because they were my friends...? Now I could *hear* the bull dragon right here, in my head as well. It must be because he was so powerful.

"Of course—a mighty gift for a mighty lord of his people," the Abbot purred.

"And what do you want in return? Have I not given you much already? Allowing you to clamber all over my mountain, infesting my caves like rats?" The voice was scolding, and it made me want to shut my eyes. "Can one girl really make amends for that?"

"Ah, but she has magic. Strong magic in her veins," Abbot Ansall said. "Just smell her and see…"

There was a sudden movement from the side of the cave walls, and the roar of the waterfall changed as a shape pushed its enormous snout through the waterfall and into the feeding chamber below. It was the gigantic, horned head of Zaxx the Golden. I bit my lips in horror as the creature squirmed and shoved its fat neck through the tunnel, water playing all over it and running down the sides of its mantle like a flaring scarf. His head was almost the size of the entire feeding cavern I guessed, almost the size of the entire Main Hall. The bull dragon's scales were the color of burnished bronze, a ruddy gold and not flashing or shining as some of the younger dragons. Instead there were scales as thick and as encrusted as shields, cracked and faded, and from the creature's mouth came the stink of rotting meat. Without bringing its forefeet or its wings forward, it reminded me of some kind of serpent, or a worm as it undulated towards Abbot and the prone body of Char below.

I watched with utter disgust as the dragon reached forward to sniff at Char.

"Hmmm. Natural dragon magic in this one? What a surprise

that must be for you, Abbot," the dragon boomed. Every time that Zaxx the Golden said Ansall's title it was with a sneer, like the dragon was mocking him.

"But first, we need more," the Abbot said sharply, daring to defy the lord of the crater. "There is a Vicious Green dragon with one foot injured. It is weak, and the crater will not miss it I am sure."

"Erlok? No. She is still a good fighter. There is Dumaston, an Earth Dragon that can be culled."

"A flightless brown Earth Dragon?" The Abbot sounded appalled. "Are you insulting what we do here, mighty Zaxx? This child has natural, wild dragon magic in her veins! Dumaston is little better than a lizard and no equal trade. If you wish us to continue to protect your brood, then you know we need to be brave in our choices. I want Erlok, or one of the Sinuous Blues."

The mighty golden dragon was silent for a long moment, and I could sense him fuming, his anger as clearly visible in my mind as strong as if it were the heat that steamed the waters falling on his shoulders. *I... I can feel this dragon,* I thought with something like awe, and something like horror as well. As soon as I recognized it, I knew that it was something that had been there all along, lying beneath my perceptions the way one might not notice the color of a rug or a blanket under your feet – but there all the same. I could *feel* a little of this dragon's thoughts and feelings – and unlike Paxala's quick and birdlike mind, this beast's thoughts were dark, ancient, and full of bones.

"Hugaia, then. You may have Hugaia," Zaxx finally agreed, and moved.

A sound like rattling swords and shrieking eagle cries split the night sky from above us, and we heard distant calls and shouts of alarm, as the dragon pipes sounded.

In response, Zaxx flinched as if struck, and every time that they were blasted, Zaxx appeared to shake his head as if the sound hurt his ears. *"Ach!"* I winced, as some bleed-over of the great monster's thought tumbled into my head too.

"STOP THIS!" Zaxx roared, and my chest vibrated with the force of the sound.

Still the dragon pipes continued.

"It is not me – the monastery must be attacked!" the Abbot cried in fury. "One of your kind has broken free from the crater perhaps. I thought I heard dragon call in the skies this very night."

Paxala! The realization shot me through with dread. She had not followed us here. She must have circled back to the monastery—but why? Was she trying to create a distraction to help us? But how long could she keep it up, if the dragon pipes affected her the way they affected Zaxx?

I didn't have a chance to wonder any further though, because the dragon pipes sounded again and Zaxx roared once more.

"None of my brood!" Zaxx thrashed his head as the dragon pipes played again. "Stop your infernal pipes, Abbot, and you can have Hugaia. Get me a proper feast and you may have Erlok too!"

It occurred to me that maybe the pipes were a trick, designed to force Zaxx to give up more of his brood than he would have otherwise offered, but Zaxx the Mighty, unable to stand the piercing sound of the dragon pipes withdrew back into the water-fall. As he went the awful feeling of the bull dragon's presence retreated from my mind as well, as Zaxx sought out peace in his deep subterranean burrows under Dragon Mountain.

Paxala, tormented by what was happening to Char, continued to hoot and call as she circled above the monastery somewhere far above us, above the cover of the clouds.

"Enough of this nonsense. What a shame to do this, but at least it will bring me great pleasure..." the Abbot snarled at the form of Char below, and I gasped, rising from my hiding place.

But Jodreth was quicker. "In the name of the Draconis Order, I accuse you of heresy!" he shouted, pushing me back and out of sight as he leapt over the ledge, landing with a heavy thump in the feeding chamber below.

"What is the meaning of this? Jodreth?" the Abbot took a step back from Char. "Is this all your doing, you meddling pup?"

"Of course. Who else, Your Grace?" Jodreth said sarcastically.

"You should have had the good decency to die the last time we met," the Abbot said, starting to raise his hands into the air.

"Probably. I know you're killing dragons, Ansall. That is not the way things were meant to be..." Jodreth stepped forward, his limp obvious. "The Draconis Order should be protecting the young dragons, not bartering for their deaths..."

"You know nothing of what I am doing here. You were always stubborn, never willing to learn what I had to teach you," the Abbot said as he drew himself to his full height. In a sudden forceful gesture, he threw his hands forward and roared "Flamos!"

I watched as a jet of fire plumed from the Abbot's fingers, growing larger and stronger until it engulfed the place where Jodreth had been standing.

"No!" I gasped.

But there was something happening in the center of the flame, a dark shape that was becoming clearer and clearer. It was a hunched form of Jodreth, holding one forearm up as if he were holding a shield of blue and white ice. The Abbot's magical flames burst around it in a wave, and the shield protected Jodreth, even as its surface hissed and dissolved, only to be constantly renewed by his own magic.

The Abbot roared in frustrated exhaustion, and the flame winked out. Jodreth staggered backward from the onslaught, the ice-energy shield shimmering on his arm as he threw it like a discus at the Abbot.

With a terrible crunching sound, it burst apart into a thousand scintillating fragments, sending the Abbot tumbling against the far wall.

"Torvald! Get Char out of here. Quickly now," Jodreth shouted as he limped towards the Abbot. Using the magic was having a terrible toll on Jodreth, making his body shake with fatigue, and I would have done almost anything to help. I scrambled down the ledge to Char who was still sound asleep and slumped by the side of the wall, keeping my eye on the Abbot, who was thankfully still sprawled on the ground, not even moving. I'm not proud to say I felt a surge of relief and pleasure at the sight.

"Jodreth, come with me," I hissed at him as I hefted Char on my shoulders like I would lift a stack of spear poles for my father. "You can come to Torvald, we can look after you."

"No, Neill, I have to finish this. The Abbot Ansall has been killing dragons," and with that, Jodreth turned back to the groaning form of the older man in the black robes, and I ran – well, I stumbled.

I reached the edge of the feeding chamber when I heard a snarl of anger from behind me. The air smelled burnt and singed and light bloomed through the night sky.

"Neill?" murmured Char. "My head hurts, what is happening?"

"We are getting you to safety," I said, hoping and praying that Jodreth would be strong enough to deal with the Abbot as I staggered out onto the mountainside, while the magical battle raged on again behind us.

"Okay, okay – put me down." Char whispered after a while, and I did so. Soon we were both stumbling over the rocks and around the end of the cliffs and gullies until we were at the edge of a deeply forested part of the mountain. I'd never been there before. The flashes of the confrontation between Jodreth and the Abbot had dulled behind us, and now there was only the occasional boom as we collapsed to the ground, gasping for air.

There was a screech and something very large hit the edge of the mountain. We're going to die, was my first thought, but when that didn't happen, I opened my eyes to see Paxala was here, standing over us, sniffing Char's body.

"It's me, my heart, it's me," the mountain girl was saying, reaching a hand to touch the Crimson Red's nose. "I don't know what happened," Char told both of us. "One minute I was so tired all the time, and going to the Mage classes, and then it all became like a waking dream. Never-ending lessons with the Abbot, candles, swords, and so tired…" Char shook her head in horror.

"Jodreth said that you were hypnotized," I explained. "That the Abbot was doing something to all of you Mages up there in that tower, turning you into his personal fanatics or something."

"Jodreth?" Char collapsed against Paxala's neck, who hunched over us warily, her nostrils flaring at the sounds of the disturbed night around us. "Who's Jodreth?"

"He's a monk. Or was a monk. He's a rebel of the Order, and a Mage like you," I explained, telling Char the brief bits of history that I knew and how Jodreth had saved my life several times already and helped take care of Paxala too.

"And now we know," Char said, her face pale and appalled. "They kill dragons. The Abbot and Zaxx. It's not a sacred order, it's, it's more like a *farm.*" She sounded revolted. "It must be what happened to your parents." Char looked up to Paxala, who purred and crooned mournfully at Char below.

"Paxala came to your rescue," I explained. "When you were hypnotized, she started circling the monastery looking for you, and that set off the alarms," I said proudly.

But just then there was another blast from the dragon pipes, and the magical battle went completely silent. As I looked at Char's owlish, worried eyes, it was clear we both knew that the feared magical battle between Jodreth and the Abbot was over, and that the Abbot could have won. Someone must have won. The dragon pipes called again.

"We should find Jodreth, in case…" I hazarded.

"You're right, and get Paxala hidden away, before they send out search parties for her…" Char agreed.

She was interrupted by a new sound rolling through the night from somewhere below us.

"What is that?" Char said in alarm, while Paxala called a trumpeting alarm down the mountain, across the forests, and towards the foothills of what was coming towards us.

As the sound grew louder from the darkness down there, it was a sound that I knew very well indeed. It was the sound of an army marching to its band. And I recognized its song.

"I thought that the dragon pipes were blowing because they were warning the Abbot about Paxala," I said. "But now I see—they were blowing because they were warning the prince about what is coming for him." I looked out into the night, my legs still shaking. Beyond the wilds, off in the distance, I could see the stone road that led past Dragon Mountain. It was clogged and glittering with torches and lanterns.

"Who are they?" Char stood up to look at the snaking river of torches marching towards Mount Hammal. Paxala started to growl in the back of her throat.

"Those are the war drums of the Sons of Torvald," I said.

CHAPTER 24
THE DEMAND

"Everyone to their guard stations!" The Quartermaster was shouting by the time we stumbled through the Kitchen Garden gate and the old storehouses. Although Char appeared almost fine, she was pale and thin after the weeks of not eating nor sleeping enough. *I* on the other hand, felt like my entire body had been pummeled and bruised – which I guess that it had, after falling from the Abbot's tower like that. With Paxala swooping and attacking the towers of the Dragon Monastery, we had sought to get to her first, knowing as we did that if Jodreth failed, we were no match for the Abbot and needed to get to Paxala first, and if Jodreth had succeeded he would either follow hard behind us, or send us on our way to convince Paxala to come to safety. By the time we reached the monastery itself, we found it in turmoil.

With the Abbot and Jodreth locked in some sort of mystical battle that neither I nor Char knew how to break – and with all my brothers' armies approaching–we had decided it best to try and get everyone that we could to safety. To hide Paxala. To encourage our friends Dorf and Sigrid and Maxal to flee…

The monastery was a den of calamity and activity. The visiting monks raced this way and that, batting students out of their way as they buckled on leather jerkins and seized bows. A phalanx of the Dark Prince's knights, his honor guard at the feast, formed up by the main gate.

"Will Paxala be okay?" I hissed to Char, who nodded, her eyes darting here and there.

"Better than us. I told her to stay on the other side of the ridge until we had a chance to find out what had happened to Jodreth, and help the others."

We had to check if our friends at the monastery were okay. There were Dorf and Sigrid, and even Lila, whom we couldn't leave here to be captured by my brothers. I dreaded to think what Rik and the others might do to the monks here – or what even they might do to me, as they had been searching for an excuse to get rid of me for a long time. *My brothers,* I kept thinking – but somehow, I couldn't feel the same companionship to them that I did to Char or Paxala. I knew exactly what my brothers were capable of – I had once seen Rik drag a soldier through the marketplace by his feet for daring to be insolent. Rik had been drunk at the time – which had made the punishment worse but it still unsettled me. My brothers reveled in war. They were born for it in a way I was not. They were merciless, and savage in their campaigns against any Torvald enemy.

But these students – at least some of them – are my friends, I

278

reminded myself. They were not enemies of Torvald. Finding a way to communicate that to my brothers though? It seemed impossible. Let alone convincing them some of the monastery's inhabitants were our allies...

It was easy to sneak our way back into the monastery during all of this confusion, and I thought we might even get all the way to the Main Hall, where I had last seen Dorf and Sigrid and Maxal, when a voice caught us.

"Torvald! Nefrette!" It was the Quartermaster Greer, standing in the center of the main practice yard with a little leather crop. Every time he barked an order he gave it a swish, as if he wanted it to taste flesh rather than air. "There you are! Get over here!" he barked.

"Char?" I whispered to her in confusion, and hoped she understood my question from the look on my face. Should we run now, or...?

Char shook her head. She was right—there were too many people around – knights and monks and the scowling eyes of the Quartermaster himself. We turned slowly, and found the Quartermaster striding towards us, as well as two others. One was a woman with long blonde hair and full armor (one of the Prince Vincent's knights, it appeared) and the other was Monk Feodor, now wearing a leather cuirass and leather arm greaves. As my gaze went from one to the other, I found myself wishing that I had a weapon at my belt.

"Here, Torvald," Feodor said as he thrust a large dagger with a sheaf into my hands. "Strap this to the small of your back, so you can reach for it under your cloak when you need to." I noticed Feodor didn't say "if", and his face was serious and grim as he instructed me how to use it.

"Monk? What are you doing?" hissed the blonde knight. "You should be taking him in for questioning – he's the son of the traitor!"

"He's my student," Feodor growled back.

"This is ridiculous. The prince will want the Torvald boy's head. Along with the rest of his kin. Unless…we could ransom it for the treacherous Warden's surrender…" The blonde woman huffed and shook her hair. "Do I need to get an order from the prince himself?"

"This is still *my* province, Madame Knight…" coughed a fourth voice, and we turned to see hobbling towards us, leaning heavily was none other than the Abbot Ansall himself. As soon as Char and I saw him, my blood froze. He hadn't died. Jodreth hadn't beaten him.

"Neill," Char whispered at me, and I nodded that I understood. *Jodreth must have died down there. He had been too weak compared to the centuries-old Abbot in his magic.*

Does this mean that Jodreth, my friend, lay dead at the bottom of the feeding chamber somewhere below us? The very idea sickened me.

Converging on us, the Abbot looked haggard and his skin was blotchy and discolored. I wondered if he was holding a leg strangely as he hobbled – was he wounded? Did Jodreth at least manage to get close to stopping his vile plans?

"My" province," the Abbot repeated, his eyes flickering at the captain, and then me and Char. "Torvald, Nefrette. What a

surprise to see you here, at the heart of things… As usual." He looked calculatingly at Char in particular.

My throat closed up, unable to speak in terror and anger. *He has just killed my friend. He has killed my friend, and now he wants to kill my brothers and warriors and scouts that I had grown up with.* I opened my mouth to accuse him, but Char stood on my foot as she stepped forward, saying, "Abbot – I am sorry for neglecting my duty." She looked confused, wiping a hand over her brow. "I remember you asking me to guard your study rooms, but then I don't remember anything else…." She was play-acting I knew, but would it fool Ansall?

"And I woke up, sire, I cannot explain it, but—I was on the hillside. Do you think that I sleepwalked?" Char said.

"Really, you remember nothing of how you got there?" The Abbot hobbled closer, and I felt my skin crawl. He now stood over the girl, peering at her with coal-dark eyes.

"No, nothing, sire. What was I doing down there?" Char asked innocently, causing the Abbot to scowl and mutter to himself. It was clear the Abbot didn't entirely buy Char's story – and I rather suspected from the sharp looks that he sent her way that he thought that it was all a lie – but he must know as well as we did that he had a lot of other more pressing problems right now than a teenaged girl. *Like my brothers about to burn this place to the ground.*

"Well, no matter. Probably just as you say; you were sleep walking," the Abbot said sharply, turning back to the others. "Madame Knight, tell the prince that I will handle this situation – and that the prince can be assured of his safety. We do, after all,

281

live next door to a crater full of dragons! Who would be fool enough to actually launch an attack on us? This is nothing but bluster on the Torvalds part. They'll never get up the mountainside unscathed."

"Quite, your excellency!" the Quartermaster Greer crowed.

"Torvald. I am going to send *you* to negotiate with your brothers, on behalf of the monastery. I do not need to remind you just how serious the ramifications of your failure would be." He looked at me. *You mean the Healer Garret poisoning my father, don't you?* I thought, but nodded.

"Monk Feodor, see to the boy's equipment, and then take charge of the defenses of the gate," Ansall barked.

"Yes, your grace." Feodor bowed his head, giving me and Char a serious look, before the Abbot beckoned me closer to him.

"I want their full and complete withdrawal by dawn, you understand me, Torvald?" Ansall said.

"Yes, sire," I nodded.

"But *even that* will not save them from my lord's wrath," added the blonde knight. "Tell them to expect punishment for this outrage."

The Abbot winced at the knight-marshal's apparent lack of diplomacy, but I knew that was to be the case anyway. When my brothers went to war, they did so with just one intention: to not leave until they had fought, and had either won or been defeated. I do not remember my brothers or my father accepting a parley at all in my lifetime. The Abbot and the knight must surely have known this – so were they merely hoping for me to get killed in the crossfire when the monastery refused to surrender?

"Never mind, boy, come with me. Follow my advice – and you might just live." Feodor was mumbling as he turned me around and led me away.

Char? I turned to look worriedly at her, as Ansall laid a bony hand on her shoulder.

"Now, Char, you and the other Mage students will come with me. It is time to put all of your training into practice, to save the Draconis Order."

Char face was full of alarm and disgust, but as she turned toward the Abbot, her expression became mild and blank, and she muttered, "Yes, sire."

"WEAR THIS, UNDER YOUR TUNIC." Feodor threw a small leather cuirass at me, which I caught awkwardly, and started stripping clothes to strap it on. We were in the area of storehouses known as the Arms Locker, and monks were coming and going all around us, seizing armor, weapons, and getting themselves ready.

"Seven Hells, lad," Feodor swore when he saw my body, festooned with old scars as well as recent scrapes and bruises. "Is that all from training? Because if it is, you are doing it wrong."

"No, sir." I shook my head, pulling the leather sort of padded jerkin tight, and allowing the monk to cinch it tight at shoulder, ribs, and across the chest. Even though it constricted my movement a little, it actually made my many recent injuries a little easier to carry. "No, I fell down the stairs," I lied.

"Huh." Feodor was regarding me unhappily, clearly not buying a word of it. "And the scars? The white lines on your shoulders, arms, side?"

"Oh," they were much easier to explain. "They are from my childhood, sir. Growing up in the Torvald Clan had always been a fierce business. My father encouraged his sons to train and fight each other." I shrugged. To me it was normal – it was only since hearing about soft Midlander Dorf Lesser's life that I came to understand that not all children lived like that, with every day of their life designing them for war.

"Well, that fills me with confidence," Feodor muttered doubtfully, nodding towards the constant thud and rattle of my brother's war drums. It didn't bother me so much because I knew the special unit of Drummer's Guard who played them. Those men were all as wide as an ox and with arms as thick as tree trunks, daubed in blue war paint. They hammered their war drums in complicated rhythms, designed to terrify and scare the opponent before battle and rally our own troops. Looking around the other monks here, the approach seemed to be working.

But not on Feodor though, as he said, "Well, we'll show them yet." He knelt down on one knee before me. "Now, lad, I know your brothers are out there, and I know what the Abbot himself has told you, but I want you to forget all of that."

"I'm sorry, sir?" I said, confused as to what the Protector thought he was doing, giving me orders.

"I'm the one in charge of the defense of this place, so I think

I have a right to say this," Feodor nodded. "I want you to ask for parley. I want you to tell your brothers that we have the Good Prince Vincent himself up here, and that I am sure that we can come to some arrangement, you understand?" Feodor hissed the words so that only my ears could hear them. "You also tell them that we have children of the Northern and the Southern Princes here as well... That will mean that, by morning a Messenger dragon will be arriving at castles and forts up and down the Three Kingdoms with word of what the Sons of Torvald are up to.

"Your brothers like a scrap – but do they want a Three Kingdom War? A civil war again, like the old one? What if north and south united to move against them? Do you understand what I am saying, lad?" Feodor said.

I nodded. "I do, sir." I had spent a lot of my childhood playing in my father's war room, underneath his table of maps and overhearing his strategists and captains discussing this or that campaign. "It's a battle that no one can win, sir."

"There we go. Now you go and ask them for parley. We have the prince here, so we have a mighty big bargaining chip," Feodor said, a little uneasily.

"They won't do it," I said to him, as I slipped on my tunic and cloak, and added arm greaves. I carried no weapons save for the hidden blade under the crook of my back.

"They will if they have sense, lad," Feodor growled and reached for the very last item I was to take. It was stowed in its very own wooden carved trunk, longer than Feodor was tall. The monk set it on the ground between us and unlocked it, to reveal long wooden shafts of banner poled, with a variety of rolled up cloth banners in different colors.

"A long time since we used these, lad," he said with a roll of his eye, flicking through reds, purples and blacks. "The Monastery at War," he pointed to one of a red dragon rampant. "The Monastery in Mourning," a pure sable black bolt of cloth. "Quarantine," a green cloth. "Now, here we have it. Parley." Feodor took out a white banner, with a red dragon standing in the center. He took out the pole, and then affixed the white cloth banner to it, before handing it to me. "Here, carry this high, so no one can claim that they misread your intention."

I told him that I understood, and Feodor escorted me to the front gates, which had been closed with a heavy bang, and metal stanchions had been placed to brace them – save for one small wooden door that was cut into the larger wooden gates, which was opened especially for me.

I craned my neck to see where the Abbot and Char had got to, but I couldn't see them. Instead, there was an eerie silence. The dragon pipes stopped, and so did my brothers' war drums. More than one hundred eyes were on me as the monks and the prince's knights all watched me with a mixture of pity and hatred. The knights had formed up in two ranks inside the gates, and the monks stood along the walls and clustered the towers, bows in their hands and arrows filling the iron brackets on the walls. In the torchlight, I could see large metal cauldrons had been brought up to the gates, some of which steamed, others of which appeared filled with rocks. There was no way that people weren't going to die tonight if my brothers attacked, I knew.

Maybe I could parley with them, as Feodor suggested, I thought, despairingly. I could offer them Vincent for the lives of the students here. Surely, even my brothers had to recognize the value of that? When had my brothers ever seen sense? But I had to try, otherwise a lot of innocent students were going to die here.

"Go on now, lad, get it over and done with and keep your head straight," Monk Feodor said to me, not altogether unkindly.

"Thank you," I said a little awkwardly to him, but he shook his head.

"Don't thank me yet, boy," he said, and I stepped through the smaller door and out onto the mountainside in the dark hours of the morning, and heard the slam of wood and metal bars behind me.

I COULD JUST RUN AWAY. The thought flew through my mind as I trudged down road from the slope of the upper mountain, past rocks and gorse and heather, towards the lower slopes where my brothers must be. I knew that I wouldn't run, of course – there were too many things holding me here; Char, Paxala, and Jodreth first of all, but also Dorf and the others who had been kind to me in my time here; Nan, Feodor, Sigrid…

Why are they doing this? *Why now?* I thought angrily. It must be because of my father and his illness. But did he know they were here? Did he approve of their task? Would I be able to contain my anger when I saw Rik and the others? I had been so close to my goal – if my brothers had just stayed out of it, then I would have been able to tell my father about how the Abbot was one of the only Mages here at the monastery, and that the alliance with the dragons of the crater was fragile to say the least. There might have been another way to do this, I kept thinking. Char's father, the Northern Prince. Could we have joined with him before now? I held the banner high so that it's white cloth flapped in the gentle breeze, and kept on walking until my legs ached.

The stone roadway was wide, but the trees were taller as I descended from the mountain and walked towards the army. I could no longer see the light of a thousand glittering torches spread out around the base of the mountain, I could only hear a distant murmur on the breeze, and the occasional sharp jangle of horses' tack.

I was almost to where I thought the troops should be when something hissed from the trees to break apart on the road near my feet. A war arrow. I paused, raising my banner high. They must not have seen the flag clearly.

But then another arrow speared into the ground on the other side of me. I was a sitting duck here on the open road, and for a brief instant it occurred to me that perhaps Feodor had tricked me—perhaps the flag I carried did not signal that I wanted to parley. I had only just thought this when slowly, shadows emerged from the trees. I recognized them immediately as my father's scouts. They were rangy, thin sorts of men and women, armed with bows and short blades, wearing muted browns and forest greens, their hair and beards long and braided. Most of them were hunters for my father, who also employed them to range ahead of his armies and bring back information.

"Halt!" shouted the first, a man with an explosion of ruddy hair.

"Parley," I called out. "Parley from the Draconis Order."

"I'll believe it if the monks all walk out of there and beg for forgiveness," the man hissed, keeping his bow taut as he crept towards me, before suddenly looking at me as if I had sprouted wings. "Neill? Is that the chief's youngest?" His expression changed to consternation, but he eased his grip on his bow.

"Aye. Rudie, isn't it?" I said, acknowledging the head scout. "It's Neill of Torvald, son of Malos Torvald, and sent to learn at the Draconis Order."

Rudie, the chief scout, shook his head that this was past his authority, but put his weapon down. "Well, follow me, little master. Seeing as it's you, I won't tell the lads to tie you up."

"Wow, cheers then, and well met," I offered, but Rudie apparently wasn't open to humor tonight. He appeared wary and nervous, and I guessed it was because of the occasional dragon cries and shrieks—no longer Paxala's, but the residents of the crater—that could be heard way up behind us, as the wyrms sensed so many humans nearby.

We walked in silence, me still holding the white banner of parley as I was escorted off the road towards the army encampment surrounding the village. We were challenged by my father's guards as we crossed the hastily-dug ditches, but Rudie waved them off.

My father and brothers had wasted nothing, apparently. They

had brought nearly every trained soldier and fighter that we had. We Torvalds were good at warring, and I had been to a few army encampments in my time, and was used to seeing the many smaller campfires, which small squadrons of men and women organized themselves, encircled with tepees or bivouac dirt-scrape tents. Not many tell you this about war, but there was an unexpected loudness to the camp, as there were also a few minstrels dotted here and there, and people loudly arguing, shouting, or declaring how many monks they were going to kill.

My stomach churned. I didn't care too much about Olan and his ilk – but some of the people up there, Nan Barrow, monks like Feodor—there were a few good souls who might get caught up in the slaughter.

It wasn't a festive noise though, as tension rippled between the camps as people kept on raising their eyes heavenwards, to see if that shadow scudding the predawn skies was an errant cloud, or a dragon.

"Is it true they have dragons?" Rudie asked once we got close to the giant yurt with double smoke holes that would house my father and brothers. I hoped that my father was there, I could tell him what I knew. I could parley for the lives of my friends.

And I could parley to be left here, at the monastery. I bit my lip. It was something that I could see I might have to ask of him. How was Paxala going to survive without me and Char there looking after her? Could the dragon be moved to some other location? But where? Where else could Char and I both work with Paxala—teach her what she needed to know? To learn from her the secrets of the dragons?

"Yes," I said simply, and neither of us said anything after that. It seemed enough for both of our worries. I did not want the dragons harmed. Well, not Paxala and the other younger dragons, at least. Zaxx, on the other hand…

Two of my father's largest guards made to challenge me, but, upon seeing who it was and inspecting the parley banner to make sure it wasn't secretly a spear or a blow dart, nodded that I was to go through. I could hear muttered curses and amazed whispers around me as the assembled fighters of Torvald wondered if I was a traitor or if I had truly been a spy for my father.

Both, I thought sadly, ever since that evening when Char had shown me Paxala, had I felt conflicted in my loyalties, and now I knew that I would rather see Paxala and Char safe than help my brothers to ransack the monastery. My uncle had been right all along, I may be a warlord's son, but I was still me, Neill Torvald. I didn't have to act like a warrior just to please my father, but in keeping my oaths, I was my father's son even if I didn't act like my brothers. I ducked under the tent flap to find myself almost knocked back by the smell of roasting meat and laughing people. The command yurt was a large round space, with two fires on metal brackets in the center like a double-yoked egg. Around half of the tent were wide benches at which sat the captains, head-men-and-women, chosen fighters, and trusted advisers. It was customary for the Torvalds to feast before a battle as well as after it. As my father would put it, "At least have one belly full of food in this world before you meet the next!" He would end in a roar of laughter, but I had never quite seen the humor of it.

At the far end of the yurt there was a raised area built out of wood, and three chairs draped with skins and hides. The central one—my father's—was empty, but at one dozed the form of my brother Rubin, while standing on the decking with a wine cup in his hand exhorted Rik, his whole leg splinted and bandaged from the last skirmish. He was cheering and shouting at a wrestling match being held between two drunk fighters, which gradually came to a thudding standstill as everyone in the tent saw me standing there, dressed in Draconis Order robes, and carrying the Draconis Order flag.

"Little brother? What is the meaning of this?" hailed Rik, greeting me with a raised wine cup and a cruel grin. "You carry the flag of *that* place up there?"

"I carry the offer of parley for the Draconis Order, yes, Rik," I said wearily as I set it against the nearest table. I knew that my brothers would be hostile and aggressive to me, and I was sick of it. I am no oath breaker, I reminded myself. I have tried to do my father's bidding, and in so doing I have found that there are more important things than kingdoms and crowns and swords. There is friendship. There is trust. I walked forward to warm my hands before the nearest fire bracket. I was tired of this arguing and bickering, and tired of the hatred and condescension from my brothers. "Is father here?" I said irritably. "I have important matters to discuss with him."

"Father?" Rik sneered at me. "You come here, bearing that flag, and beg to speak to my father?"

"*Our* father, Rik – and I didn't beg," I said, turning around to face him. "This is important, Rik. We haven't got time for your squabbles."

Rik glowered at me, throwing the wine cup at the nearest wrestler. "How dare you, you little worm!" he shouted. "You're not even a full-blooded Torvald. You're nothing but a treacherous bastard." He made to leap off of the platform, but his injury only allowed him to stumble and snarl as he got to the floor opposite me. "Why don't you crawl back up to the monastery there and beg *them* to take you in—we don't want you!" he spat. "Father isn't here, because father is gravely ill– because Healer Garret was filling him full of Ghoul's Cap!"

His words caused a ripple of alarm from those around us. Ghoul's Cap was a nasty little green mushroom that could make you sick in small doses, and weak and feeble in larger amounts.

"Healer Garret?" I said in alarm. *Thank the stars, they stopped him.*

"Oh yes, we found out your little friend Garret when we caught him writing scrolls for a Messenger dragon. Thought you could poison my father, did you?" Rik thundered. "All so that your new friends could appoint *you* be the Chief Warden, is that it?"

"No!" I said, outraged. How could he think that?

Because it's true, my heart knew. Wasn't it just what the Abbot had told me, up in that tower? That he would rather there wasn't the hassle of a new Warden, but that he would seek to have a new Warden that he had personally chosen. *Was that why he had invited me here in the first place?* The realization bloomed in me, as I saw how almost all of this year's students were from important families in one way or another. I mean, I had known that the Draconis Order wanted to influence us, wanted all of the royal scions, the sons and daughters of the clans to think favorably of them – but then had come the strange meditations. Maybe the Abbot wanted to use all of us to install his own fanatics in every high seat of power throughout the Three Kingdoms.

"That was nothing – nothing to do with me! Father sent me to the monastery, remember?" *Although, I had to admit that my brother was right in the fact that seemed to be precisely the plan that the Abbot Ansall appeared to have for me.*

"All I know is, brother, is that my father is gravely ill at home, and the true sons of Torvald will not stand for this outrage, will we?" Rik turned to where Rubin, my other brother, had woken up and was regarding us both solemnly. Rubin had always been the more steadfast and thoughtful of the two. I had to hope that would still be true now, or else there would be no hope of a peaceful resolution to all this.

"No," Rubin said heavily. "But speak your piece, Neill. What is it that the monks are offering?"

Nothing would have been the correct answer, if I had followed the Abbot's advice. However, it was clear Feodor was a much better tactician than the Abbot.

"The Draconis Order sent me down here to tell you they have the Prince of the Middle Kingdom, along with a contingent of his personal knights up there in the monastery with him. The monks seek a peaceful end to this conflict, and a reduction in hostilities by morning," I said, as loudly and as clearly as I could. The implied promise and threat was obvious. An act of aggression against the monastery would be an act of war, but also, my brothers must decide whether to honor their liege lord the prince.

"The prince?" Rik laughed out loud, clapping his hands together. "Oh, this is incredible! What do you think, brother? We could take the prince as well? Ransom him back to the palace, or to one of his brothers? Prince Lander has always seemed to be quite a sensible chap, although Prince Griffith has more money…"

"Lander and Griffith would probably pay us to kill him!" Rubin scoffed.

"Unless…" From the devious smirk that appeared on his face, it was clear a new idea had occurred to Rik. "Prince Vincent is up there. And we have the far bigger army. You know what father always said about Prince Vincent – that he wasn't good enough to lead the Middle Kingdom anyway…"

"Rik…" Rubin warned. He and I both knew the thoughts that were going through Rik's head. *This is it, isn't it? This is the moment when my brothers decide to try and topple the prince for themselves.* But the wounded Rik couldn't stop himself.

"Fancy half a kingdom, brother?" Rik said slyly. "We can send word to Lander and Griffith as well – if they want their rivalry with the Middle Kingdom ended, then now is their chance! We'll be heroes…" Rik said in awe, before adding, "We could be princes."

"Rik, please!" I begged him, thinking of Char and Dorf and the others up there. "We have to speak to father before we do this. What will he think about you plunging not just Torvald, but the Three Kingdoms into civil war?"

"Shut up, *bastard*," Rik snarled at me, turning to point a stiletto dagger I hadn't even known that he had been holding at my face. "In fact, you go and tell your priest or Abbot or whatever it is that you have up there—you go and tell him that the Sons of Torvald demand that the Prince Vincent be delivered to us by morning, or else we will march on the monastery – dragons or no."

"Hundreds will die, thousands across the Middle Kingdom and beyond," I said.

"Have you become a coward now, as well as a traitor, little brother?" Rik said. I was about to argue with him, but suddenly he nodded and hands seized me and dragged me backwards, followed by a savage kick in the back and a blow to the head.

WHEN I WOKE up again to a woozy feeling of agony spreading throughout my limbs, it was to find that I was lying on the stone roadway that led back up to the monastery, just above the tree-line, where the air was coldest. Someone had thoughtfully left the parley flag covering me, although it was muddied, ripped, and its pole broken as if it had been dragged through the mud (along with me). They didn't chuck me in chains, at least, I thought. Before realizing that of course they wouldn't – they had to deliver their 'message' back to the monastery somehow. *I had failed.* My heart thumped wildly as the sheer enormity of what was about to happen fell upon me. There was going to be a battle, and then there was going to be a war. And what would

Prince Lander or Prince Griffith do then? Why *wouldn't* they jump in to try and finally carve up the Middle Kingdom between them?

I guess that is their answer then. I pushed myself painfully to my feet, wondering when I had last had a decent night's sleep, and whether I would ever get one again, as I carried the tattered pieces of the white flag back up the slope to the black walls of the Dragon Monastery above. The light was a washed, out, mealy sort of grey. Dawn would be upon us all before long, and then the Dragon Order and the Sons of Torvald would go to war, and the Middle Kingdom would be in revolt.

"Hoi! It's the Torvald boy!" someone shouted from the gatehouse above, and there was the sound of crunching metal and thumping wood as the braces were pulled back from the smaller wooden door, through which I clambered to deliver my brothers' demand: Prince Vincent or all-out battle.

CHAPTER 25
CHAR, UNDER DARK SKIES

Once Neill was taken off by the Advanced Tutor for the Protectors, I was alone with the Abbot. The Prince's blonde knight-marshal had been sent off to organize her knights as best as she could, and the Quartermaster went to oversee more of the defenses, leaving us alone.

"Well, I don't know how you did it, Nefrette," the Abbot said with a pained hitch to his voice.

"Sire?" I asked, keeping my face as neutral as possible, wondering how I had looked when I had been hypnotized.

The Abbot gave me a hard look. He suspected I was lying. "You really don't remember anything?" he said.

"Sire?" I asked again. "Remember what?"

"Interesting. The meditation must be more powerful than I thought..." the Abbot tapped his fingers against his walking staff, before pointing towards the center of the courtyard. "There, now. Clear a space."

I did as I was told, telling the monks, students, and knights to make way for the Abbot, as Ansall sent others to collect the other Mage students like me, and gather items such as an iron fire-bracket, wood, incense, candles, and oils. During the hubbub and commotion, I had a brief moment of respite, into which I reached out to the Crimson Red, my friend.

Paxala? Pax... Can you hear me? I knelt down as if I were re-lacing my leather boots. I didn't want anyone to see what I was doing or bring even more of the Abbot's suspicions on my head.

"Paxala can always hear you," the dragon said, making me wonder just how deep this connection between us was going. *"Unless your mind becomes clouded by the old man."*

She must mean the Abbot, I thought. Maybe that was why she hadn't come to the monastery searching for me sooner, because she could sense that something strange was happening to my thoughts?

"Paxala?" I whispered under my breath, at the same time as I *thought* at her. "We cannot get away from the monastery, not if we want to keep everyone safe right now. But there is another that I need you to help. The monk in the feeding chamber, Neill's friend called Jodreth."

"The funny monk? Yes, I know him. He left fish for me at the beach before," Paxala said. *"I can smell him, you know. He still breathes, in the rocks underneath the chamber, but he is damaged."*

"Hurt?" I said out loud in alarm, but luckily the chaos of the preparations drowned out my alarm. "Please go to him. Carry him away in your claws back to your cave. Keep him safe, if you can," I whispered again. "And Pax…?" I added. "Please, please be careful. If Zaxx sees you or smells you or senses you then I won't be able to protect you."

My mind suddenly shifted, like an echo or the almost-recollection of a memory, and I realized that it was Paxala, the dragon. I was sensing how she rose from her cave and plunged through her own small waterfall to bound over the lake. I could almost feel a sort of echo of her movements and feelings, if I reached out towards her…

"Char, stay quiet. Not safe. I will keep the funny monk alive." Paxala nudged my mind with hers, and I tumbled back into my body with a feeling like waking, startled, from a deep sleep. It was *something* like the hypnotism, I realized, some entrancing connection between minds, and I wondered if that was where the Abbot himself learned the technique…

"Char? On your feet!" Ansall barked, looking at me skeptically. I had the terrible sensation that he might be able to see through my eyes and into my mind, and observe the dragon hidden there.

"Yes, sire." I nodded, "Where do you want the candles, sire?" I distracted the peering old Abbot, who waved disgruntledly that I should stand them into a circle around us.

Soon enough, all of the Mage students had joined us, as well as a very few of the returning monks. I noticed that the Abbot didn't refer to any of them as Draconis like Jodreth was, and I suspected that even these older monks might have a touch of magic, but were not full Mages either. Apart from Ansall, we had no idea what was happening or what the Abbot intended. What-ever this was about to be, I didn't like it and I didn't want any part of it – but the monks were all around me, and behind me. I tried to remember Paxala in my mind's eye, and to remember the clear and fresh mountain air... Anything to keep the Abbot out of my head.

The Abbot arranged us into a circle in two ranks, the smaller students on the inside, the taller and older monks on the outside. Next, he had the monks stretched out their right hand to lay upon the right shoulder of those in front, like we were the petals of a giant flower, or spokes on a wheel. We radiated out around the standing candles and the fire bracket, with the Abbot on the very inside.

"Now, students? Please attempt to keep your minds pure, and you minds still," the Abbot said. "This will be your very first introduction to channeling the energy of battle magic, and you will have to follow my *every* command, you understand me?"

"Yes, your grace," we all murmured or nodded, and the chanting began.

I didn't speak the words at first, only mouthing them so as not to add my will to theirs. I didn't want magic if it meant warfare and blood, but I felt myself growing heavy, and my eyes feeling sleepy once more.

No! I tried to fight it, but the hypnotic drone was too strong. The effect of the Abbot's voice was amplified by all of the monks here. I could feel my mind starting to slip...

Pax!

The monks started muttering, and then murmuring words that

my awake mind did not recognize. Words of a charm that us student shads not been taught yet.

"Evoka Bellos! Evoka Stil! Evoka Bellos, Evoka Stil!" The chanting in my ear was a low drone, and one that set the hairs on the back of my neck rising. As it continued, the Abbot waved his hands to the monks and students, as if conducting them to greater and greater efforts. Soon the chanting started to take on a constant, moaning rhythm all of its own, blocking out the sound of the alarmed dragons outside or the march and rush of the besieged knights and students.

The chanting swelled and grew around us, and I found myself swaying, my mind curiously blank and dreamlike, as the chanting swirled and rose, surrounding us all, rising, and enfolding us.

I don't know how long we were there chanting, but the entire lower half of my body went numb as the four words repeated again and again, again and again. Was it my eyes, or was the sky starting to grow darker. I wondered, as the Abbot lifted a hand with clawed-like fingers into the air. In my strange, sleepy state I couldn't tell if the Abbot was making the light change, or if it was just my imagination.

"Now, students…" he called as the chanting bombarded us. "I want you to think of the most terrible storm that you have ever been in, do you understand? A mighty, terrible storm like no other." The Abbot excitedly flung incense into the fire, only adding to my lightheadedness. I couldn't concentrate– and neither did I want to– on any storm, so instead I reached out for my dragon.

Paxala? I thought to her, as the circle groaned and shouted.

"*...*" I felt a buzzing between my eyes, like I could *almost* hear the dragon, but that she couldn't reach me through this strange storm-ritual.

PAXALA! I thought in alarm, remembering the storm of her wings as she flew...

"*Char.*" The voice of the Crimson Red sounded faint. "*The funny monk is safe...*" I could just make out her words, as suddenly from high above Mount Hammal there was a peal of thunder.

"Yes!" the Abbot shouted, cawing with laughter as around us great drops of rain started to fall. When I looked up, dark clouds were boiling down from the north and across from the west. My mother's people had a name for those types of clouds. *Dread-drear*, they called them, because whenever you saw those chalk grey and fierce black lowering clouds coming for you, then you knew that you had to seek cover quickly because they would unleash mayhem and destruction.

The Abbot was still laughing, as the sky above him flickered with lightning, and it raced towards the east, and rising sun.

"*The parley has returned!*" Someone at the gate shouted, and the storm began in earnest.

CHAPTER 26
THE SECRETS OF THE TOWER

The first hands to seize me after the gate monks let me in were those of the Quartermaster Greer, shaking me so much that I dropped the white flag.

"You have failed, haven't you?" he said. "Your brothers are still there. Did you even *try* to negotiate?"

"Yes, of course," I was saying, as the Quartermaster shook me once more. "But they won't go, not unless…"

"Maybe if we show them just exactly what will happen to a Torvald that tries to defy us," the Quartermaster raised his leather crop, before a meaty hand closed around it, squeezing the man's wrist in whit-scarred fingers.

"I'll not have my boys beaten, Quartermaster." It was Monk Feodor, glowering at the Quartermaster before releasing him. "Go back to provisioning the monastery, and leave the defenses to me, if you please."

The thin man rubbed his wrist with a sneer, but turned away

all the same, hurrying towards a circle of black-clad, chanting monks in the center of the practice ground. I caught a glimpse of Char's snow-white hair gleaming from the middle of the gaggle.

"What are they doing?" I said in alarm.

"Never mind that. Tell me what happened, and get some hot food into you." The monk shoved a clay bowl of something warm and nourishing; a type of stew with oats and grains in a thick liquor. I told him everything that had happened – including the fact that my brothers thought that the monastery had poisoned my father, which is why they were here in the first place.

"Revenge?" Feodor groaned. "If it were as simple as bargaining for the prince's life then we might have a chance, but if its revenge they are after then they won't be happy until we're really hurting," he said gloomily. "Look, child – there is no way to get out of this cleanly. I was hoping that there was, but from what you say there won't be. There is a way out, through the Kitchen Gardens. When the time comes, I want you to gather as many of the students as you can and lead them out across the mountain, can you do that?"

I nodded, thinking of Char, and Dorf, and my other friends here. *What has it come to, having to flee my own brothers?*

"But thank you as well, Torvald, for coming back to warn us," Feodor said. "I am sure that with your brothers down there you didn't have to."

I know, I thought. But there was Paxala here, and Char, and Dorf and Sigrid and Maxal. I had taken an oath to keep Paxala safe, and I couldn't just abandon them all so easily.

Oh, Rik would kill me as soon as look at me anyway, and Rubin might just let him. "What's right is right," I said with a shrug. "How can I leave my friends here to die?" *At the hands of my own brothers as well*, I thought.

There was a flash and a peal of thunder, as the dark sky boiled heavier with rain and thunder clouds. An ugly black cloud had been spreading low and fast from the north, and it brought with it a storm the like of which I had only rarely seen.

"Great," Feodor muttered. "That's all that we need." Another flash of lightning illuminated his face on the side of the white scars, making him appear half dragon himself. "Go on." He pointed me towards the nearest storerooms. "Get out of sight before the Abbot sees you."

I wanted to ask Feodor why he didn't flee now, through the gate at the back of the Kitchen Gardens – but he was already turning to bark orders at the nearest monks.

"Get that door braced! I want stands of arrows and spears up here, behind the wall!" he shouted, his mind already focused on the coming battle. "Two on guard, two off! Rotate as soon as you get too tired to fire your bow."

The rain fell in a fat, heavy cascade all around, turning the usually dry practice ground into a muddy hole in practically minutes. Students ran back and forth, some looking panicked, others looking fierce. It was only the prince's knights, sheltering by the walls and readying their weapons who didn't look worried. There must be a couple hundred knights and I had told Feodor that we were facing how many – a thousand? Two thousand? I wished I had paid more attention now to my father's lectures about troop numbers and trained fighters. Did they include the large number of villagers who acted as militia as well?

Ten to one odds, I thought, remembering my father's training. That was ridiculous. Who could beat that? *But we are in a fortified castle-like building, on top of a mountain.* I remembered my father saying something about how you had to have at least double the number of defenders if you wanted to lay siege to a place – or had it been triple? Or ten times the number?

I huddled under the eaves of the nearest storehouse, peering into the rainstorm to see if I could get to Char and the other chanters. It was hopeless. Either way, good people were going to die. Either my friends up here in the monastery, or people like the chief scout Rudie whom I had known my entire life.

The drummers of the Sons of Torvald began their steady beat, and the wall guards shouted in response. "They're coming! They're climbing the mountain!"

I HAVE TO FIND CHAR, I thought from my place in the dark of the storeroom, looking out. The war drums were deafening now, matched almost by the panicked blasting of the dragon pipes, and the shrieks of the alarmed dragons near the crater. It was getting hard to even stand in the storm that whipped across the mountaintop, but the storm benefited the monastery by the fact that my brothers' army could not hold a strong line. The Draconis Order wall guards shouted their news to those below. "The front ranks are falling!" or "They cannot move forward!" or "They are being washed downhill!"

"Archers, ready!" Feodor shouted, and I felt a moment of indecision. No! How could he shoot them? Those fighters outside were just like him, men and women raised to do their job, and doing it for their masters. But of course, should Feodor do nothing, it might be his own life that was lost, or those of people he cared for.

Lightning crackled above, bracketing across the low skies, illuminating the walls –

In that flash, I saw a group of figures standing atop the wall. The Abbot, with arms raised into the air, and surrounding him were dark-clad monks and students, apart from one with flashing white hair. *Char!* She was there with the other Mage-students and trainees. That meant Maxal Ganna must be up there too. But what were they doing? The monks and students swayed like ferns in a forest around the tall, crooked tree that was the Abbot, as he brought his hands down in front of him…

The ground rumbled, and the sky flashed once more, and the darkness from the clouds seemed to swirl *down* in front of the Abbot, as if he were summoning it. Could he do that? Was he so powerful as to control storms?

The dark vortex of cloud grew faster and faster, spinning in a tight funnel as I watched. The students swayed and chanted faster, matching the speed of the tornado, and the Abbot's shoulders shook as he sought to control it. The funnel cloud writhed in the air in front of him, twisting and jerking one way and then the other, as he pulled his hands further, and it descended past the line of the walls and where I could no longer see.

Shouts and screams rose from outside the walls and I imagined the twister wreaking havoc amongst my brothers' forces, throwing their fragile bodies this way and that like straw dollies.

Pheet. Pheeet-Pheeet! The sound of arrows being released filled my ears, so many arrows and so close I could hear them above the storm– only they weren't the arrows of Feodor's guarding monks, but those of the hundreds of Torvald archers, creeping up behind the front ranks, firing wildly into the storm. Like crows on the way of turbulent air the arrows were tossed and snapped this way and that. I saw that the hurricane was only centralized at the front gate, and surely my brothers' armies were attempting to surround the monastery. They had hundreds of archers, and as arrows began flying from behind me, I realized some had managed to find their way in.

Thock! I saw the first arrow strike at the wall of the Great Hall, sparking as its steel head hit stone. It was high and wild, but still deadly. Arrows fell like a deadly hail into the courtyard, smashing windows, piercing beams. Some were arrows loosed on purpose and well-aimed, and some were the storm-tossed arrows being flung behind the hurricane and down amongst us.

The air filled with the shrieks of the first casualty of the war, a monk who staggered across the courtyard with one of Torvald's own arrows sticking from his neck.

The dragon magic. *It was the only hope,* I thought desperately, seeing the Abbot's Tower lit up by the sudden flash of lightning. I could not wield it, but my father had sent me here to uncover its secrets. I could not offer Rik or Rubin the Dark Prince, or a kingdom, but perhaps if I offered them the secrets of the dragon magic they would relent. With that power, they could train their own monks and Mages, I could reason. Why all this death and destruction?

The dragon pipes hammered their unceasing call, and I knew that the time was now or never. I had to get to the Abbot's Tower and find a way to stop this.

———————

THE DOOR to the Abbot's study was open, knocking against its hinges and the floor dripping with rain. Someone had left one of the shutters open, or perhaps the storm had torn it from its moorings, and now rain had sleeted into the wide space, and the tornado-gales had flung the Abbot's desk to its side, and papers and scrolls scattered the floor, and candles rolled this way and that.

But where was the staff? I thought, looking around the room. Had the Abbot had it with him earlier? No, I didn't remember seeing it down in the courtyard – so maybe it was here. I pushed aside the papers with my feet, looking for anything that might appease my brothers. To stop this madness.

Thunk. In the gales of the storm that was blowing into this room, something had dislodged from behind the door, and hit the floor with a thump. I turned to see, there, rolling across the room was the Abbot's cane, the one with the silver dragon ornament atop it.

At last! I thought in a split second, before I saw the condition that it was in. Splintered and cracked. Had it been in the fight with Jodreth? Or was it some other sort of magical experiment gone awry.

No matter, I thought, seizing it up to examine it. There might still be some magic in it… but no sooner had I thought that, then the lower half of the cane gave way to its injuries and sheered, falling with a clang on the floor below. I was holding a glorified doorknob; a silver dragon on a stud of wood.

"Are you the source of all this evil?" I asked the little ornament warily, but all that I got in return was a metallic stare. It felt just like any other walking cane. An expensive walking cane perhaps, but nothing special whatsoever.

No. I couldn't be wrong. I just couldn't be, I thought desperately, shaking it. With a sinking feeling, I realized that it didn't even matter if this simple ornament *was* magical or not, as I didn't know how to use it.

It's not magic, my heart was telling me, but I refused to listen to it. It *had* to be. Otherwise, what had all of this been for? Where *did* the source of the Draconis Order's magical powers – the Abbot's magical powers – really come from? *No,* once again my heart told me. I did not feel any of the strange sleepy feelings around it that I had in the meditations, and neither did I feel any of the buzzing pressure in my head that I felt around Paxala and Zaxx. *And either way, my brothers will never look at that little statuette and conclude that their work is done.* They would laugh at me. I needed more. I shoved the dragon ornament into my tunic and turned back to the rest of the room. Maybe there was something else in here that I could take.

"Where do I even start?" I muttered, grabbing the first few pages of notes, seeing black spidery writing starting to smudge. There were circles and lines and odd sigils drawn on them, and languages and words that I did not understand. *They'll have to do*, I thought. I stuffed them under my leather cuirass Feodor had made me wear, turning to gather other pages, and even a few crumpled scrolls.

"Torvald, I knew your treachery would be revealed soon enough," hissed a voice behind me. Ice shivered down my neck. It was the Quartermaster, striding into the Abbot's study – or attempting to anyway – with that little leather crop in his hand. I thought about once again declaring that I was on an errand for the Abbot and then, as lightning flashed and I heard more screams from outside shrugged. Why deny it now?

"Stand out of my way, Greer," I said to him, crouching to keep my balance amidst the gale.

"Treachery is in your blood, you see," Greer said, rocking from one foot to the other, the leather crop in one outstretched hand. "Your *bastard Gypsy* blood…"

I snarled, anger flashing hot through me as I moved to shove him to one side.

Crack! A line of fire hit me across the temple, and it felt like I had been stung by a gigantic wasp.

I hissed, jumping back and putting a hand to my temple, where I came back fresh with blood. The Quartermaster was using the whip. I lunged again, but the Quartermaster was much quicker than I had thought, and with his years of experience he made another flick with his wrist.

Another sharp and burning cut across my neck and warm blood seeped down into my tunic. Blood from my temple threatened to get into my eyes, and as I shook my head, another blow hit my outstretched hand, causing me to stumble backwards...

"You see you cannot even match me. You shouldn't be here, *Gypsy*, you should just accept it. You are worthless. A worm. A nothing!" Greer advanced as I took a step backwards, the gale at my back, the stones wet underfoot. I had only enough time to register that my boot was slipping and then I was down, the Quartermaster's savage grin of delight flashing as I slammed against the open window, and slid to the floor. My stomach lurched in fright as I clutched at the slick paving slabs, the Quartermaster raising the crop above me to strike me again across the face.

But there was something sticking into my back. Something heavy and angular. *Feodor's dagger!* As Greer's hand fell I dropped my guard, yanking at the handle at the small of my back and swung.

Greer shrieked in agony as blood fountained into the gale. The Quartermaster stood over me, one hand holding his other, where two fingers from his weapon-hand had been neatly severed.

"What did you do! What did you do to me?" Greer screeched as he tried to clamp his hand over the ruined one, staggering, but his feet slipped on rain and blood, and he tripped over my body, flailed once, and vanished through the broken window.

His scream was short-lived, and swallowed by the sounds of the storm and the battle outside, arrows were hailing down onto the tower, followed by more screams.

I lay there, my eyes wide, unable to truly understand what had happened. Had I just killed Greer? My eyes rested on the dagger in my hand, rain washing the Quartermaster's blood from it.

But there wasn't time to dwell on what I had done. There was more yet to do.

CHAPTER 27
A DRAGON'S WRATH

How can I get these scrolls, and this ornament to my brothers? Will they even listen to my bargain? I wondered desperately, looking from my tower vantage point for some easy way out of the monastery.

My brothers' troops now encircled the front half of the monastery and the barren slopes of the mountain. The front ranks hunkered down behind rocks and boulders to hide from the tornado, but they, along with the teams of archers hidden in the gullies, kept firing volley after volley. From the rear guard, long shapes were being brought up—iron-capped tree trunks. My brothers were going to drive a hole through the gates or the walls, wherever they could gain purchase. Even if my brothers didn't manage to break down the gates, the sheer number of their archers would bring the monastery to its knees.

There was no good way out that I could see—if I could manage to get outside the monastery unharmed, I would more than likely be shot as soon as I tried to approach my brothers' army.

"More power! Work harder!" The wind carried the enraged voice of the Abbot to me from the battlements below. He was still standing amidst his coterie, exhorting them to chant deeper, and stronger, and work whatever arcane techniques that they could. But the group surrounding him seemed to have thinned, and I saw that there were black-robed bodies lying about on the battlements. Some of them groaned and moved, others did nothing.

Have they been shot? Or are they overcome with exhaustion? From the state of Char and Maxal in the days leading up to the attack, the magic seemed to leave them tired and weak, like they had just run a marathon. Was it possible that the Abbot was using them up like steeds or cart horses, working them to collapse?

As I watched, another person buckled – a student, by the size of them—and then fell, a shock of white hair spilling from the hood of the black cloak. Char! I watched as she struggled to push herself up again.

"Char!" I shouted involuntarily, unable to silence my fear for her safety, but my voice was stolen by the wind.

No sooner had I opened my mouth to yell for Char again, but a dragon swooped down from where it must have been flying above the storm, circling us. It let loose a furious and panicked cry, and I knew it could only be Paxala, come to try and save her friend.

"Paxala!" I called out into the teeth of the storm, leaning out as far as I dared from the window ledge. I knew that the Crimson

Red had no reason to listen to me, I was just a little human after all - but I was her friend. I wanted to tell her where Char was, to ask her to seize Char up in her talons and carry her away…

There was a sudden roar as the young Crimson Red sped like an arrow towards the monastery.

No sooner had she began her dive, then the dragon pipes sounded. Paxala suddenly wheeled away from her target as the high-pitched call of the pipes speared her sensitive ears.

She cawed loudly and in pain, flapping uncontrollably around the monastery, passing the tower where I was.

"Paxala!" I hollered again, but the Crimson Red appeared distracted, worried, and confused. It was then that I understood what the dragon pipes and their whistling shrieking noise were for. I had thought that they were to call the dragons towards the monastery, but they weren't. Instead, the pipes drove the dragons away with their sharp blasts, painful to a dragons hearing.

"Pax, you must flee!" I shouted to her, but the dragon paid me no mind. She swooped low, as maneuverable as a hawk over a field, and then she was bearing straight towards me, down onto the Abbot's Tower, her talons outstretched. As I leapt back there was a horrible crash, and her claws shattered through the last of the shuttered windows, seizing the windowsill with her gigantic talons.

There were screams and shouts from the monks below, and my brothers' war drums even stuttered to a halt at the sight of the dragon hunched and huddled at the top of the tall tower, baying for blood and vengeance. Her front legs had smashed through two of the shuttered windows, clutching the room inside, while her back feet scrabbled and scored at the stone beneath.

She let out her most deafening call making the entire tower shake. Then she shoved her Crimson snout through the window, with an angry, gold-green eye gazing fiercely at mine. As I regarded her, her pupil flared and her head cocked to one side. There was a rasping sound as she scraped the stone with the young tines of her head.

"Paxala, you must flee this place, with Char," I shouted, but Paxala instead bent her head once more, this time extending her neck below the window, and leaning in. To my mind, it almost looked as though she were offering me a walkway onto her back, but that was ridiculous.

"Please, my dragon friend, flee this place," I shouted. *If there was one life I could save, then at least let it be this noble creature's,* I thought.

The dragon made a chirruping sound, lowering her shoulder and extending her neck in front of me once more. Did she want me to climb onto her back, like a horse? I'd never heard of such a thing but I had no other option if we wanted to end this battle before more damage was done – I reached out with my hands to clasp her warm scales, and slid onto her strong shoulders. At my side were the collection of scrolls and the dragon ornament, now if only I could find a way to direct her to fly me towards my brothers' forces.

Paxala made a soft chirruping call as she lifted her neck, and I found myself half-falling, half-climbing to the crook of her shoulders, just above her wings. There was a natural hollow there where her back tines wouldn't grow, and it was surprisingly comfortable, as I leaned forward and grabbed her neck scales.

Remembering my riding lessons of the fierce, little mountain ponies that my father kept, I gripped with my knees, and could feel the strong muscles and the thud of her blood under my hands.

There was a lurch, as she detached from the wall and kicked out (demolishing more of the Abbot's Tower as she did so). She made a deafening call as she flared her leathery wings, before turning to dart straight for the monastery's battlements. It was all I could do to hang on, as she swooped past the Abbot in a flash of scales and claws, seemingly on a collision course with the ground outside, before she flared her giant wings once more and threw herself upward, out over the slopes of the mountain.

Why is she rescuing me? I thought wildly—not that I wasn't thankful, or pleased! I hadn't asked her to do it – it was clearly something that she had decided herself to do.

"Friend." My head throbbed with the buzzing sensation, and I knew that the word did not come from me, or my imagination. I clutched at the warm creature, scared, and elated. She had spoken directly to my mind. Directly, to me. I was still amazed as she turned in the air and started to fly back down towards the monastery from the skies. All of a sudden, I didn't care for what my father wanted, nor my brothers, nor Prince Vincent or even the Abbot. Their magic and their politics and their games meant nothing – only this did. Saving and being saved by the people (and dragons) that you love.

"Dragon!" My brothers' soldiers shouted and screamed

below us, "Dragon!" Squadrons of fierce warriors dropped their bows and their battering rams, deserting their posts in order to flee for their lives.

Paxala's call was near deafening as she swooped back over the mountain, calling her defiance and her challenge at any who would endanger her friend, Char.

But the soldiers and the monks don't know what she is doing, I thought, watching as more of my brother's front lines collapsed, their faces pale and their eyes rolling. The Abbot Ansall on the walls above us was regarding us with a sort of horrified awe, and every time that Paxala soared near the gate house of the monastery, monks fell about themselves trying to scrabble away from her black, viciously sharp talons.

No one had ever ridden a dragon before, and it seemed that this dragon was angry.

"Paxala, please listen to me now," I leaned forward and whispered urgently as I pointed down towards my brothers' forces. "If we can drive those soldiers attacking the monastery away, then we can save everyone—Char and all of the others. We can stop all of this."

Paxala roared as if in acknowledgment of my suggestion, landing just briefly on the gate house as she turned and swooped again, straight towards my brothers' armies. I heard screams and shouts, as men leapt to the ground, or scrabbled over their fellows at the sight of such great teeth, and ferocious might.

"We're winning! They're fleeing!" I was giddied with excitement, watching my brothers' army abandon their posts in terror, and pour like a tide back down the causeway of the Dragon Mountain.

"You've done it, Paxala. You saved us all!" I called out in glee, as the dragon roared her satisfaction, and swooped low over the hills once more to make sure that the humans had got her message, before turning to fly back to the monastery. She landed with a light thump onto the walls of the gate house. Her skin was steaming with heat, and her sides were bellowing with the effort of pumping air, but Paxala didn't look fatigued or tired as she glared now at the humans inside the monastery.

Maybe I didn't need to give these scrolls and ornament to my brothers now that the battle was lost, I thought, feeling giddy with elation. Why pander to their games anymore? I felt the reassuring weight in my tunic of what I carried – not sure if anything I held was powerful at all – but I didn't have to deliver them now. I could keep hold of them until I knew what secrets they held – if any. My brothers had fled the battlefield, so I didn't need to parley with them, and I could wait until I talked to my father about what my *real* findings here were: that there were hardly any dragon Mages, and that the dragons hardly listened to the monks anyway, without Zaxx.

The monks, although more used to the dragons, appeared terrified of her this close. Most of them hadn't seen a Crimson Red since her parents had been alive, and none of them had even seen a dragon this close, out of the crater, and wild.

The dark and heavy clouds started to lift and break, allowing shafts of morning sunlight to pierce the grey air. The Abbot's magic that had created the dark storm had halted, and it seemed without him controlling it, the storm had vanished back to the elements from which it had been born. Water and air.

"Pax?" said an astonished voice, as I looked down to see that Char was walking unsteadily towards her friend, one hand on the battlement, and another on her head.

"Char, are you okay?" I called down in alarm, but she appeared to be unhurt. *How on earth was I going to get down from this thing?*

"Neill?" she said with a stunned sort of laugh. "What are you doing on Paxala?"

Paxala chirruped softly, and, in front of all of the assembled monks and knights, she slowly leant down her head to sniff at Char's raised hand, as tender as a cat with its kittens. What happened next was even more incredible – Paxala made the same motion that she had with me, lowering her neck and her shoulder, half-folding one of her wings out of the way so that Char could clamber up and onto her shoulders like me, and promptly dislodging me from my prominent position, and relegating me to a few spines back, between the wings.

"Char Nefrette, Neill Torvald, what are you doing on the back of that dragon?" the Abbot Ansall yelled, but Paxala was already extending her wings, and making a purring, joyous sort of noise.

"They saved the monastery!" I heard a voice shout, and saw, down below the weary, slumped shape of Monk Feodor. "That dragon, and those riders saved the monastery!" he called again, followed by a rising cheer from the other monks. Their previous terror and apprehension at seeing the apparently wild Crimson

Red was replaced with awe and celebration. Something impossible, incredible, and miraculous had happened here, I could see on their faces.

The Crimson Red roared one last time, in defiant joy before she leapt into the air above the monastery, carrying Char Nefrette and me with her. We would fly from all of this blood and mayhem – not because we had to, but because we could. Paxala had already saved Jodreth, and the battle had been called off. I had my tunic full of scrolls and secrets, and so perhaps we could buy ourselves a little time to ourselves, to study and to learn how to fly together. I knew that the times ahead would be difficult, and that the prince would want vengeance against the Torvald Clan, and possibly me as well, but for now, the whole game had changed. The monks and the Abbot, the prince and even my brothers had seen me ride a dragon – and that would change things.

After all, who was going to argue with you when you had a dragon for a friend?

END OF DRAGON GOD
THE FIRST DRAGON RIDER BOOK ONE

Dragon Dreams is out now! Keep reading for an exclusive extract from book two of The First Dragon Rider Trilogy.

THANK YOU!

I hope you enjoyed joining Char and Neill on their epic journey –
I certainly enjoyed writing it! If you'd like to let other readers
know this is a book they won't want to miss out on, please leave
a review :)

Receive free books, exclusive excerpts and be kept up to date on
all of my new releases, when you sign up to my mailing list at
AvaRichardsonBooks.com/mailing-list

Stay in touch! I'd also love to connect with you on:

Facebook: www.facebook.com/AvaRichardsonBooks

Goodreads:
www.goodreads.com/author/show/8167514.Ava_Richardson

THE FIRST DRAGON RIDER

DRAGON DREAMS

AVA RICHARDSON

BLURB

To unite a fractured kingdom, a reluctant hero must rise.

Neill has been charged with the impossible task of bringing the Middle Kingdom together to fight the burgeoning threat posed by the rogue sorcerer Ansall and his dragon Zaxx. Neill longs for his old life as a mere foot soldier for his father responsible only for his family's wellbeing, and is unsure about whether he is fit to lead an army. Neill's contemplative nature forces him to consider every aspect of the problems he faces, but often makes it difficult for him to take action—and failure to act could mean the deaths of many.

Now, echoing Char and their dragon Paxala, his duty beckons him to lead the Dragon Riders—and take his rightful place as king—but with doubt and new enemies creeping in, his resolve will be tested. When the mysterious Dark Prince arrives with an offer, Neill will have to make a decision that could change the course of history.

As Ansall grows in strength by harnessing black magic, Neill must choose between his own desires and the welfare of the entire kingdom. Can he rise to the challenge before it's too late?

Get your copy of **Dragons Dreams** at
AvaRichardsonBooks.com

EXCLUSIVE EXTRACT

The sweat trickled down my brow where I hung, clutching the rock walls of the cliff, and I could hear my heart thudding in my ears. Just calm down, Char, you can do this, I told myself, opening my mouth to try and breathe a little quieter. It wasn't just the fall that would kill me if I got this wrong, but I knew that if I made any noise at all, then I would probably get killed as well.

We would all get killed, I corrected. I was hanging from the sides of the sheer cliff, and clinging to the rocks by my fingers and toes. There was the narrowest of rocky ledges under my soft shoes, but it wasn't wide enough to walk along. Beneath me the stone walls descended to the broken rocks of the dragon crater below, and I don't know why I had thought that this was a good idea.

"Pssst! Char, tell us what's happening out there," Neill's voice came from behind me, and I managed to turn my face against the rock to see he was looking worried from where he and the others sat, huddled against the outcrop of broken rock behind me. Above the heads of Neill, Dorf, and Sigrid, the grey clouds started to fragment and rise as the dawn approached. That meant that we didn't have long.

"I'm clinging to a rock, Neill. What do you think is happening?" I hissed back. From my hip, there extended a thin line of rope all the way back to the rock that my three friends were hiding beside, and then to their hands. I had shown them how I wanted the rope to be held, and how they could loop it around their bodies or around a foot in case I fell.

At least my mother's mountain family had taught me that much, anyway, I thought. I reached out with my hand for a second time, my fingers prising at the nearest stub of woody truck of the gorse-type bush that clung to the rock wall.

Almost, almost... There! I gripped the sturdy wood with one hand, then moving my foot out along the thin ledge, and sliding my other hand and foot a few feet farther along the difficult transverse.

It was slow going, and the muscles in my back and legs burned with the effort, but I was nearly there. Nearly across. We'd been at this since the dark watch before dawn, when at first even Dorf and Sigrid's eyes had glittered with excitement at the prospect of sneaking into the dragon crater. This had been my idea: a chance to sneak in and try to rescue some of the dragon eggs from Zaxx. We now knew that Zaxx was actively helping the Abbot Ansall to cull the herd, and, in the scant few months since the battle against the Sons of Torvald, I couldn't stop thinking about the dangers that those eggs – and all of the young dragons in there – were in.

"Yeah, not so excited now I bet," I grumbled to myself, as I reached out from the scrubby tree trunk to the next outcrop of rock.

Crack. There was a sudden sensation of movement beneath my foot as the rock ledge I had thought was solid slab rock was in fact layers of compressed flakes. Oh no, I had time to think as my foot disappeared, and I lurched forward along the cliff wall.

"She's falling," I heard Dorf's terrified squeak of alarm.

"Skreayar!" There was a screech of dragon call from somewhere far above us—no doubt Paxala even though I had made it clear to her to leave us alone this morning, that the dragon crater was too dangerous for her. But I had no time to let my fears about her get in the way – I pushed out with my back foot, reaching with my hand towards the nearest rock—

"Ugh!" my gloved hands caught a rocky outcrop the moment before my body slammed into it, and I hugged my arms and legs around it like I could cling to it like a spider. Please don't splinter and crack, please... I begged the rock itself, but it held.

"Char? Char!" Neill was calling, standing from his position.

"No – don't move," I called back, scrabbling with my hands until I could force my fingers between cracks and into the dirt behind my saving rock, hauling myself out to the much wider ledge I had been trying to get to. The rope I was attached to was tighter than before, but slack enough to let me flop over onto my back, groaning in exhaustion. I lay there for a moment, looking up at the lightening skies. The cold air felt chill in my lungs.

"Char is hurt? I can fly to her?" A reptilian voice said in my mind. Paxala's mind felt tense and skittish, and I could feel the concern seeping through her.

"No, don't," I murmured, knowing that the dragon would be able to hear my thought. "I told you to stay by the lake this morning." I frowned as I pushed myself up into a sitting position, pulling once on the rope for some more slack. There was an answering single tug at the rope, and then, when I pulled on it I found that there was much more give. I had told Neill how we had done such things in the mountains. One tug on the rope was 'okay, keep going' and two was 'halt!'

Get your copy of **Dragons Dreams** at
AvaRichardsonBooks.com

63543908R00194

Made in the USA
Middletown, DE
02 February 2018